CONSTRUCTING ALICE

CONSTRUCTING ALICE

Cecil Allen

First published in 2019 by
Cecil Allen
www.cecilallen.ie
email: cecilallen93seapark@gmail.com

Paperback ISBN: 9781096649571

Cover design by Brendan Bierne
Cover painting by Roseanne Mooney

ABOUT THE AUTHOR

The award winning writer Cecil Allen is the grandson of the famous actor and writer Ira Allen. Cecil is the author of the hugely popular 'The Actor – A Novel.' He is a retired college lecturer from the Dublin Institute of Technology and holds a BA from Indiana University and an MFA from the University of Minnesota. He was a broadcaster with RTE for over twenty years and represented Ireland twice at International Toastmasters Competitions.

He is the father of two sons and lives in Malahide with his wife Julie.

For Julie

As the twig is bent the tree inclines.

Virgil (70-19 b.c.)

PART 1

CHAPTER ONE

Thomas Dalton hummed happily to himself as he strolled from his hotel towards the Grand Palais. The warm sun shone on the bustling tree-lined street; the sidewalk cafés hummed with Parisians chatting over their morning coffee; the shop windows were mobbed by fashionable ladies inspecting the latest styles, and everywhere smartly-dressed men in top hats were striding importantly to work.

At the edge of the pavement, a gaggle of uniformed nannies had gathered with their baby carriages. Thomas joined them as they set off in a determined line across the boulevard. A bright new yellow Peugeot Tipo 3 was forced to stop and the driver rudely tooted his horn, but Thomas merely smiled and adjusted the flower in his buttonhole. The dapper Irish hairdresser was in an excellent mood. He was off to the *Fédération Internationale de la Coiffure* exhibition where many years ago, as a protégé of the legendary Marcel Grateau, he had scooped the most coveted award of his profession – the *Reveille Coupe d'Or.* Now, a lifetime of success later, the Dublin-based salon owner had his sights set on an even more valuable prize, the hair model Mariah Mulroney who had blushed when he'd caught her looking at him yesterday.

The boulevard cleared, the impatient driver pressed down on his accelerator and the automobile sped off. The ground vibrated as a Metro train hurtled beneath the street. Thomas strode onwards down the Champs-Elysées, his smile spreading wider with every stride. Mariah was a strikingly beautiful young woman with porcelain skin and brown sad-smiling eyes. At forty five, Thomas was twenty three years her senior, but he was still handsome with thick black wavy hair and a luxuriant moustache. He may not have been as tall as he would have liked but like many short men he had excellent posture and took pride in carrying himself like a military officer. As he continued down the boulevard Thomas decided he should acquire Mariah's services as his hair model. Currently she worked for his good friend Michael Kelly, who – like Thomas – was representing Ireland in the exhibition.

'She's impossible,' Michael Kelly had snapped, when Thomas had inquired about Mariah. 'She is beautiful, I grant you that, but she thinks that's all she has to be. She's difficult to work with, contributes nothing and she can be very demanding.'

'Then I take it, you wouldn't be put out if I ask her to come work for me?'

Michael rolled his eyes. 'Be warned, she'll drive you mad.'

Thomas Dalton had not been born into money. He had been reared on a small farm on the outskirts of Owenbeg, in County Sligo. On the day of his fourteenth birthday, his dour-faced elderly father stopped him at the cottage door.

'Son, I've something to say to you,' his father said, looking at Thomas's feet. 'You're a man now. It breaks my heart to tell you this but you must leave this place and make a life for yourself somewhere else.'

Stunned, Thomas stared at his father. 'But I don't want to leave the farm. I want to stay. I'll work harder, I'll get up earlier. I'll...'

'You know the harvest was bad this year and in the best of times this God-forsaken farm is too small to support two people, let alone four. Thomas, you are a smart boy. If anyone can survive away from this place, it's you.' The old man pulled a folded brown envelope from the pocket of his well-worn corduroy trousers and pressed it into Thomas's hand. 'In the envelope is your older brother Aiden's address as well as your train fare to Dublin and a few shillings for digs and food. Make your plans son, and don't dawdle.'

A week later, with all his possessions stuffed into a small cracked cardboard suitcase, a teary-eyed Thomas said goodbye to his family and took the train to Dublin. Arriving at Kingsbridge Station, he found his way to his brother's digs, only to find that Aiden had enlisted in the British army.

Thomas needed a job and he found one sweeping floors in Cecil Duffy's barber shop in Sycamore Street, and he quickly fell in love with the trade. For six months, he pestered his employer to take him on as an apprentice. At last, Mr Duffy relented and three years later, seventeen-year-old Thomas became a fully qualified barber.

Moiré Duffy, Cecil's wife, took an interest in the handsome lad's natural talent for cutting and shaping hair. One evening, as he was locking up the shop, she approached him.

'Have you ever cut a girl's hair?' she asked.

'No, never,' replied Thomas, surprised. 'Only men come into a barber's shop.'

'My Chloe is making her confirmation next week. Would you like to cut her hair?'

Alarmed, Thomas took a step back, Chloe was Cecil and Moiré's youngest daughter. 'What if it doesn't turn out the way you want? Will I lose my job?'

'Arrah, don't be talking rubbish. You're too good a barber, Cecil wouldn't fire you if you left the child bald.'

The following day, Thomas set to work on young Chloe's hair. First he washed it, then cut and styled it. He liked the way the girl's hair felt in his hand, the way it fell and sat, even the way it smelt. Watching the shape of the new haircut emerge intrigued and energised him but it was only when Chloe grinned and raised her eyebrows at her mother that Thomas realised he was singing to himself.

'Done!' declared Thomas half an hour later and swung the barber's chair around to face Mrs Duffy. The woman stared speechlessly at her daughter but just as Thomas was beginning to worry, her face broke into a smile and she applauded.

'Would you to cut my hair young man!' she exclaimed.

'I'll cut your hair, Mrs Duffy,' Thomas said with a burst of confidence, 'but you'll have to give me one week to prepare.'

During the next few days, Thomas spent all his free time walking Grafton Street and Stephen's Green, studying the hairstyles and haircuts of Dublin's most fashionable ladies. On Saturday he bought a pint for his friend Michael Kelly, an apprentice in Jones' Ladies Hairdressing Salon in Camden Street, and picked his brains about the new hairstyle sweeping Europe and America.

'You'll need to use "hair ratts" if you plan on giving your client the "Gibson Girl" look,' Michael replied knowledgably.

Client, thought Thomas. *I like the sound of that. My client…* He forced himself back to reality. 'What's a hair ratt?'

'Fashion-conscious ladies don't like to admit to wearing wigs,' explained Michael, lighting one of the new cork-tipped cigarettes. 'So at night, after they finish brushing their hair, they carefully remove any strands caught in their brushes and store them in glass containers. When they have enough saved, they bundle the hair into a hairnet and – lo and behold! – they have a hair ratt.'

'I don't think my client has time to gather enough hair to make a hair ratt. Her daughter's confirmation is next Saturday.'

'I'll let you into a secret. We sell hair ratts in the salon. I could pick up a couple for you, cost price. What colour is this lady's hair?'

'Mm... Light brown with a golden tint.'

As the time approached for Mrs Duffy's appointment, Thomas felt almost as excited as he was scared. On the Wednesday evening his employer's wife came into the shop after business hours and perched in the barber's chair. Thomas carefully washed and combed the light brown hair, then piled it high on the woman's head. Using a new-fangled hair-drying machine borrowed from Michael's salon, he styled it into a soft bouffant, stuffed two ratts into the back as padding, fluffed out the sides to increase volume and coaxed the locks that fell over her ears into a 'waterfall of curls'. When he brought Mrs Duffy to the mirror she shrieked with delight and rushed to show off her 'Gibson Girl' look to all her friends. Before long, Cecil Duffy's barber shop had more female customers queuing for Thomas than male customers queuing for Cecil.

Still, Thomas felt he had a long way to go. 'How can I become a real ladies' hairdresser?' he wondered aloud one evening, while enjoying another pint with his friend Michael in the Camden Bar.

'Paris,' said Michael wisely. 'All the best hairdressers learn their trade in Paris.'

And so in the boldest decision he ever made, Thomas took Michael's advice and moved to Paris. Success did not come quickly or easily. After suffering a month of doors being slammed in his face, and learning a lot of unpleasant words in French, he was granted the lowly job of assistant's assistant in a Maurice Perrin Salon. A year later, when he hadn't been promoted to full assistant, he went back to writing letters and banging on doors. After what felt like a thousand rejections, he finally gained the position of apprentice hairdresser in the Marcel Grateau Salon on the Left Bank.

Monsieur Grateau quickly recognised the young Irishman's gift for cutting and styling. He noted the ambitious nineteen-year-old excellent grasp of spoken French and the young man's extraordinary energy. He also noted that Thomas exuded a personal charm that most of his clients seemed to find enchanting.

Having spent four years as Marcel Grateau's protégée, Thomas was a much sought-after 'high stylist' who had won many national and international hairdressing awards, including the cherished *Reveille Coupe d'Or*. After his latest triumph he decided to return to Dublin and open his own salon.

Thomas thought of himself as a very lucky man, but he also knew that through sheer hard work, personal drive and a natural talent he had created his own luck.

Despite Michael Kelly's dire warnings, Mariah Mulroney didn't drive Thomas mad, instead, she charmed him, captivated him and stole his heart completely and eighteen months later when Thomas won first prize at the Earl's Court Hairdressing Exhibition in London, they became engaged. Thomas was madly in love with the most gorgeous, exotic creature he had ever encountered and he had never been happier.

Mariah was also the happiest she had ever been in her life. She loved being Thomas's model, winning countless trophies and awards, and now loved the excitement of being engaged. She adored the balls, receptions, concerts, dinner parties and the races. Still only twenty three, she delighted in being the centre of attention, and fraternising with so many important people made her feel very grown up. She charmed everyone she met; they all thought she was a wonderful conversationalist, although in truth she was an excellent listener who gave away nothing of herself.

Thomas only realised how little he knew about his adorable fiancée when his friend and fellow businessman, John Swords, asked about Mariah's family.

'She's from County Galway,' replied Thomas confidently.

'And her family are..?'

'I haven't actually met them yet.'

'What? Good God, man, the girl's a stranger to you! She could be a gold digger for all you know!'

Thomas scoffed dismissively. 'Don't be absurd. It's merely that we've been far too busy to travel to Galway. I look forward to meeting her family as soon as it's convenient.'

A few days later, while the happy couple were sitting in the Gresham Hotel waiting for John Swords and his wife Kay to join them for afternoon tea, Thomas decided to ask his fiancée about meeting her family. To his shock, Mariah's smile slipped and she looked like a frightened and terrified child.

'Why do you want to meet my family?' she asked.

He frowned. 'Dearest, as your future husband, I need to ask your father for your hand.'

Mariah placed her small hands in her lap and fidgeted with a thread on the cuff of her blouse and when Thomas next spoke her body went so tense that it quivered.

'Mariah, is there some reason you don't want me to meet your parents?'

Mariah's gaze lowered. 'Do we have to talk about this now? John and Kay will be here any moment...'

'They're not due for another quarter of an hour. Darling, look at me, you need to let me know if there is a problem. Where are your family from?'

Mariah shivered. 'I've been told they were from Boyle in Roscommon.'

Thomas sat back sharply and folded his arms over his chest. 'You've "been told"...?'

'My mother and father both died of TB when I was three years old. I have no brothers or sisters.'

'So you're an orphan!' Thomas's body went rigid. He was shaken. 'Who reared you?'

'My Aunt Molly and Uncle Vincent in Galway reared me. I always thought of them as my parents.'

'Ah...'

'They died when I was sixteen.'

'Good God, you poor thing!'

'I was devastated. But they left me a small inheritance, and a family friend arranged for me to come to Dublin and train as a shop assistant in Pim's Stores. It was there that I met your friend Michael Kelly and became his hair model.' Mariah lifted her head and met Thomas's gaze, her eyes damp and pleading. 'And then I met you.'

'Oh Mariah...' He could hardly comprehend the sadness and pain she must have endured. 'I'm glad you told me. I just wish you'd trusted me sooner.'

'I trust you.'

'Thank you and I'm glad you've told me. Let's not give it any more thought.' Thomas firmly squeezed Mariah's hand. 'Here come John and Kay. We'll say no more.'

CHAPTER TWO

As they turned into High Street, Thomas Dalton tapped twice on the roof of the Dublin cab and the horse-drawn carriage creaked to a stop in front of a vast glass shop window. Thomas jumped out, paid the driver, and helped his new bride down from the carriage.

'So, what do you think? Beautiful, isn't it?' It was one week after their Mediterranean honeymoon and he was anxious to show his wife his latest acquisition.

Mariah gazed, puzzled, at the elegant late Georgian building. 'It's an empty shop, Thomas.'

'Look closer!' He pointed his cane at a large inlaid stone above their heads. 'See? Dalton's Ladies' Hairdressing Salon!'

She was stunned. 'You're opening another salon?'

'Don't you love this shop front? Look at those glorious pilasters and that great expanse of plate glass! I'm going to have Dalton Hairdressers of Distinction etched on the window.'

'Thomas, you already have a beautiful salon!'

'Yes dear. But this will not be just another salon; it will be the finest ladies' hair salon in Ireland. It will be a magical place – one of the most luxurious and elegant places in all Dublin. It will have all the latest Parisian equipment and paraphernalia. Fashionable ladies will flock here; it will be a meeting place for the *crème de la crème* of Dublin ladies' society.'

'You're an ambitious man, Thomas Dalton,' murmured Mariah, gazing up at the stone sign.

'I have another surprise for you. I have purchased the house next door. It will be our home.'

Now she was speechless.

Thomas engaged the renowned, if somewhat flamboyant, interior designer Gerard Beirne to create his salon. Mr Beirne designed and commissioned six glass and gold cubicles, four rosewood in-laid cabinets and two Waterford crystal chandeliers.

Meanwhile, Mariah was busy decorating their home next door. She was carefully unwrapping a Tiffany lamp, when the front door bell chimed.

'Should I get that?' asked Mrs Foley, the cook.

'Please do, but remember I'm not receiving visitors today.'

Mrs Foley swung open the large front door to find herself looking down at a very short, plump, pink-faced woman with thin-ning auburn hair.

'I'd like a word with Mrs Dalton,' announced the woman in a high-pitched voice.

Mrs Foley scowled disapprovingly at the woman's heavy-knit cardigan, pleated tartan skirt and heavy brown leather shoes. 'I'm sorry, but Mrs Dalton is not receiving visitors today.' She started to close the door but the woman forced it open and almost hopped into the hall.

'I'm sure Mrs Dalton will make an exception for me. Tell her Eunice O'Donnell would like a word. I'll wait here.'

'Sorry to bother you, Mrs Dalton, but a Eunice O'Donnell is insisting on seeing you.' Mrs Foley was quivering with disapproval.

Mariah eyes flashed alarm. 'Who did you say?'

'A Miss Eunice O'Donnell. Can I send her away?'

For a moment, the younger woman hesitated. But then she said quietly, 'No… No, it's all right. I'll see her. Show her in. And please bring us tea by the fire.'

'Certainly, Mrs Dalton,' scowled Mrs Foley, clearly not at all pleased.

A few moments later, the tiny yet somehow mannish-looking woman marched into the drawing room, swinging her arms at her sides. She came to a halt in front of Mariah.

'Eunice, how are you?' asked Mariah, guardedly. 'I've asked Mrs Foley to bring us tea.'

'This is not a social call, Mrs Dalton,' announced the determined visitor.

'Eunice, please take a seat.'

'I'd prefer to stand.'

'For heaven's sake, call me Mariah and sit.'

Eunice O'Donnell perched primly on the edge of a chair. 'Mrs Dalton, as you know I…'

Mariah interrupted her. 'If you're here to discuss our past, stop right now, I never talk about the past.'

'I don't either. It's not something I'm particularly proud of.'

Mariah looked relieved. 'Then why are you here?'

Eunice opened the large brown purse she had placed on her lap and rummaged around in it. She removed two folded sheets of paper and handed them over. 'My references will tell you I am a trustworthy person who has the necessary experience to run a house of this size effectively and professionally.'

'You want to be my housekeeper?' Mariah was more than a little surprised.

'I do, and I would prefer to be referred to as Mrs O' Donnell.'

13

'Oh? You're married?'

'I never married. But it is customary to refer to housekeepers and head cooks as "Mrs" regardless of whether or not they are married.'

'But Eu... Mrs O'Donnell, why do you want to be my housekeeper?'

'I need employment. My employer recently passed away.'

Mariah hesitated. 'I have told my husband little of the circumstances of my childhood. Do you understand?'

'You can be assured of my discretion.'

Relaxing, Mariah glanced over Mrs O'Donnell references. 'It's true, I have little knowledge of how to run a house this size. Can you tell me what staff I should hire, Eu... Mrs O'Donnell?'

Mrs O'Donnell counted on her plump fingers. 'Let me see. You'll need a housekeeper, a lady's maid, a cook, a kitchen maid, and when children arrive you will need a governess or a nanny and of course your husband requires a valet.'

Mariah was astonished. 'That many people?'

'Oh yes,' said the little woman confidently. 'That would be the minimum number.'

'It seems so many. And I'm not sure I would want a stranger looking after my personal needs. Would you perhaps consider being my lady's maid, Mrs O'Donnell, as well as being my housekeeper?'

Mrs O'Donnell permitted herself a small, satisfied little smile. 'It would be my privilege, Mrs Dalton.'

The drawing room door opened and Mrs Foley marched in bearing a silver tray upon which sat a china tea pot, two cups and some pink-frosted cakes.

Mariah looked up smiling. 'Mrs Foley, Mrs O'Donnell is going to be our housekeeper! And my lady's maid! I do hope you two will get along.'

Mrs Foley scowled and Mrs O'Donnell smiled.

One week later, Mrs O'Donnell moved in as the Dalton family's housekeeper. She immediately hired a housemaid, took personal charge of the household linen, chinaware and silverware and the keys to the stores that dangled from her waist were the symbols of her authority. Yet above all, she gloried in her role as Mariah's lady's maid and considered it her most important responsibility. Whenever Mariah was out for the evening, Eunice O'Donnell would sit in her room at the top of the house, staring out the window, waiting for her mistress to return.

When the work on the salon was completed, Thomas declared himself well-pleased and he was well rewarded for having lavished so much money and luxury on his salon. From the day the salon first opened, it was patronised by Dublin's most affluent and influential ladies.

Thomas was sitting in the dining room enjoying his breakfast and reading his *Irish Times* when the fierce little housekeeper stepped into the room and asked if she could have a word.

'A word about what?' he asked not lifting his eyes from his newspaper.

Mrs O'Donnell crossed the room in six swift strides and stood in front of him, ramrod straight.

'Are you standing to attention?' Thomas asked in bewilderment, looking up from his newspaper.

'No sir,' replied the new housekeeper and allowed her shoulders to relax ever so little.

'What can I do for you?'

'Mrs Dalton has entrusted me with recruiting the necessary staff for the smooth running of the house,' said Mrs O'Donnell and paused.

'Ye-e-es?' murmured Thomas, stretching the one-syllable word to sound like three.

'I have taken the liberty of arranging a meeting with Mr Peter O'Reilly, a valet, about joining the household staff. I will also be interviewing for a new cook and a cook's maid.'

Thomas sighed, carefully folded the *Times* and placed it on the coffee table. 'You can tell Mr Kelly that his services are not required. I am perfectly capable of dressing myself. With regard to a new cook, Mrs Foley has been with me for twenty years. She is the finest cook in Ireland and I will not have her replaced. Besides, kitchen matters are not your responsibility.'

Mrs O'Donnell bristled. 'I beg to differ, Mr Dalton. The housekeeper is the most senior servant in any house, so kitchen staff do come within my remit.'

'Mrs O'Donnell, you are overstepping your so-called remit. You are an employee in this house and I will tell you what your responsibilities are.'

The housekeeper fixed her mistress's husband with a long, hard look, and clearly disappointed in him, turned and walked away.

'I haven't dismissed you yet!' called Thomas sharply.

Heaving a sigh, Mrs O'Donnell turned.

'Stop giving my wife notions. We are not gentry.'

'You are to me, sir,' said the tiny warrior reproachfully. 'Now, may I leave?'

'Yes you may.' Shaking his head, Thomas went back to reading his newspaper.

The aristocratic Dr Veale stood back and stroked his silver-grey beard, smiling knowingly.

'There's nothing amiss, Mrs Dalton. You are simply having a baby.'

The blood drained from Mariah's face. 'Are you sure?'

'Naturally! I'm very sure.' He replaced his stethoscope in his well-worn brown leather bag. 'In seven months or thereabouts, you will become a mother. Congratulations, Mrs Dalton.'

'Oh heavens…' murmured Mariah faintly.

Pregnancy was not kind to Mariah. She suffered greatly from morning sickness, she was perpetually tired and the impending birth terrified her. But towards the end of November, after ten hours of labour, Mariah gave birth to a healthy seven-pound baby boy. The new mother was exhausted, Thomas and Mrs Foley were delighted and Mrs O'Donnell had already converted one of the back bedrooms into a nursery.

In the middle of the night, Mariah's eyes blinked open. She was perspiring heavily. She'd had that dream again – the second time in the week since the child was born. She'd been walking through a barren landscape and a black creature had been following her. She'd started to run but the faster she ran, the closer the black creature got to her. Then with a frightening roar, the creature leapt onto her back and burrowed into her body. It was only when the creature moved within her, that she had struggled to wakefulness.

When it came time for the baby's christening, Thomas suggested his father's name, Jarlath, and Mariah casually agreed. She didn't care what it was called; she felt no affection for this child. She knew she was supposed to have maternal feelings, yet from the beginning she had found this squirming pink object tedious; all it produced was noise and bodily excretions too objectionable to even contemplate. To smooth Mariah's path, Mrs O'Donnell had engaged Lucy Brogan as the baby's nanny: a mature, capable woman who cared for the mewling infant in a disciplined, if somewhat detached manner.

Thomas loved the idea of being a father in theory but he played no part in raising his baby son. One night in the Hibernian Club, John Swords asked him about his views on fatherhood. Thomas said confidently, 'it is going to be simple enough. Children just need to be given rules and taught to respect them.'

John smiled. 'I prefer the old Gaelic way. *Mol an Óige agus tiochfaidh síad.* Praise the children and they will thrive.'

'Rubbish, absolute rubbish! I say, spare the rod and spoil the child.'

Twelve months after baby Jarlath's birth, Dr Veale informed a horrified Mariah that she was pregnant again. In the July of that year, baby Terrance was born. Thirteen months later, Tess arrived.

Following each birth, Mariah's nightmares returned. One night shortly after baby Tess's arrival Mariah awoke in a cold sweat. She got out of bed and walked around the house, ending up in the nursery. There, she lowered the side of the cot and took baby Tess in her arms. When the child's head touched the skin of her arm, she shuddered; the physical contact unnerved her. Quickly replacing the baby in the cot, she returned to her bed and waited for the black beast to arrive.

The following morning, when she opened her bedroom door she heard raised voices halfway down the stairs.

'What were you thinking? The baby could have rolled out onto the floor!' Mrs O'Donnell was saying sternly to Nanny Brogan.

Mariah froze, realising that she hadn't raised the side of the cot before she'd left the nursery.

'I can assure you Mrs O'Donnell, when I left the nursery the side of the cot was in the "up" position,' snapped the nanny, looming over the fierce little housekeeper. 'It must have been someone else. Maybe her mother came to see her...'

'Don't you dare accuse Mrs Dalton of maternal neglect!'

Mariah coughed lightly as she descended the stairs to the mezzanine. On seeing her, the two women parted hastily.

'Mrs Dalton, I didn't know you were coming down for breakfast. I hope we didn't disturb you,' apologised Mrs O'Donnell, practically curtseying.

'You haven't disturbed me, Mrs O'Donnell. But there is something important I should tell you.'

'Mrs Dalton, I'm attending to a very delicate matter at the moment. Could we perhaps talk later?'

Mariah dropped her eyes. 'But of course.'

As she carried on down the stairs, she heard Mrs O'Donnell announce shrilly, 'I have no option but to dismiss you and I will not be in a position to give you a reference.'

'But I'll never get another job!' pleaded the nanny, suddenly cowed. 'I did nothing wrong! I followed all procedures!'

Mariah was sitting at the breakfast table opening a newspaper when Mrs O'Donnell entered the room, looking very pleased with herself.

'Mrs Dalton, I'm sorry you had to witness that altercation. I do apologise. I'm afraid I made a mistake in engaging Lucy Brogan. She has turned out to be most unreliable and insolent. You wanted to inform me of something important?'

Mariah hesitated for a moment, then decided to let Mrs O'Donnell do as she wished. 'No, it was nothing.'

'Very well, Mrs Dalton. Would there be anything else?'

'No... Yes! Could you fetch me some Kruschen Salts? I didn't sleep very well last night.'

Mary Fields was Lucy Brogan's replacement. The eighteen-year-old nanny was a warm hearted, easy-going young country woman, who loved life.

Six months after baby Tess was born, Mariah was told she was pregnant again. When baby Róisín was born she was underweight and very pale. Dr Veale diagnosed her as suffering from pneumonia. Three days later, baby Róisín died.

'Mrs Dalton you need to rest to recover,' Dr Veale said to Mariah. 'Your body needs to build itself up. I suggest a long restful holiday. I don't mean a week by the sea in Achill. Go to Europe for a few months, get some warm invigorating sun.'

While Mariah and Thomas were away, Jarlath, Terrance and Tess remained in Dublin with Mary Fields. Terrance loved his nanny, and Jarlath liked her well enough, even though he looked down on her slightly. As young as he was, he already knew from

Mrs O'Donnell that he was "gentry" and that Mary wasn't of his class. As a precocious six-year-old, he teased her unmercifully about the odd words and expressions she used. Jarlath giggled when she used words like 'tay', 'mate', 'afeard' and 'twiced'. And when she used rude words like 'gob' and 'puss', he fell about laughing.

During the following two years, the Dalton family prospered. Thomas grew his property portfolio to fifteen houses, five shops and three hairdressing salons. Mariah recovered her nerves enough to accompany her husband to London as his hair model, representing Ireland at the Earl's Court Royal Hairdressing Competition. But on her return, she learned that she was pregnant once more and seven months later, she gave birth to her second daughter, Ann.

Two weeks after the birth, Mariah burst into tears at the breakfast table.

'What's the matter, dear?' asked Thomas, lowering his newspaper in surprise.

'I can't manage all these children. The boys are so noisy, playing ball in the hall and running up and down the stairs. It's just too much for me to cope with. Mary is too indulgent of them. They need the discipline of a boarding school.'

Thomas placed his newspaper on the chair beside him. 'Boarding school seems a little drastic. What about a second nanny? Would that help?'

'No! The noise and the commotion is making me quite ill. I can't sleep at nights, for worrying about how unruly the boys have become.'

'Mariah the boys are too young to leave home.'

'Thomas, the situation is intolerable. They need to be in boarding school. They can keep each other company so they won't be homesick.'

'Let me look into it,' sighed Thomas, picking up his newspaper again.

St Mary's Boys Boarding School in Ballygrove, Kildare was the school Thomas selected for their boys. But, as he informed Mariah over breakfast, there was a small problem.

'The school will only accept children from eight years old. So the boys won't be able to go for another year.'

'Isn't Jarlath eight?' asked Mariah, alarmed and puzzled.

'He is. But didn't we agree the boys should go together, to keep each other company?'

'Then find another school!'

'It appears that all boarding schools in Ireland have the same age stipulation.'

'Then Jarlath will have to go alone,' said Mariah firmly, as she poured herself another cup of tea.

On the day Jarlath was due to leave for St Mary's, Mariah developed a severe headache and couldn't get out of bed. In the drawing room after breakfast, a very upset little boy bade a tearful goodbye to Terrance, Tess, baby Ann and Nanny Mary.

On the footpath outside their home, Thomas helped his son into the waiting hansom cab while the driver strapped the boy's labelled trunk to the carriage.

'The school porter will help you with his luggage at the other end,' Thomas informed the driver, slamming the cab door.

'Aren't you coming with me, Father?' gasped Jarlath, peering out of the cab window.

'No, Jarlath. Your father has very important work to do!'

When the cab drew up to the front steps of St Mary's, the school porter unloaded the trunk and deposited it, and the eight-year-old boy that had come along with it, to St Jude's dormitory.

Jarlath stared in shock around the long, high-ceilinged room that was to be his home for the next nine years. Nothing about this place resembled the clean, comfortable High Street bedroom he had shared with Terrance. This room was cold and draughty and the plaster was marked with patches of damp. Ten shabby bunk beds jutted out from the walls, but there was no sign of any other occupants.

Jarlath sat down on the edge of the bed beside which the porter had dumped his trunk and sunk his head in his hands. Why had he been sent away from home? Why had his parents separated him from his brother and little sisters? He knew his mother did not like him, but he'd imagined his father was quite fond of him. Yet it was Thomas Dalton himself who had turned his back as the cab rumbled away. Jarlath bowed his head and let the tears run down his cheeks. He was very lonely and very frightened and couldn't imagine feeling any other way, ever again.

The following year, Terrance arrived at St Mary's.

And in that same year, after yet another difficult pregnancy, Mariah gave birth to another little girl: Alice.

CHAPTER THREE

In 1908, the year Alice was born, the population of Dublin city was 477,196. Dublin Castle was the seat of British rule and every day a swarm of government officials – locally known as spies and informers – emerged from the Castle to eavesdrop on the citizens of Dublin and report any signs of insurrection back to their superiors. Meanwhile the new middle class exodus from the inner city to the suburbs of Rathmines, Rathgar and Clontarf was well underway. Unemployment was high and every day hundreds of men gathered at the docks, seeking to emigrate to foreign countries. Suffragettes were protesting on the streets of the capital. Padraig Pearse, W.B. Yeats and Lady Gregory were living and working in the city and Admiral Nelson still stood proudly on top of his pillar in Sackville Street.

The youngest of the Dalton children was a skinny, quick-witted girl with a great mop of tangled fizzy hair. She was adventurous, light-hearted and was always ready to laugh, smile and learn new things; she was also opinionated and stubborn. For some unknown reason, Alice fascinated Thomas; he indulged her and permitted her freedoms that he had refused her siblings. She was allowed to invade his office in the rear of the High Street salon, where she would chatter to him about childish things. He didn't even mind when she trotted into the salon during business hours, plonking herself down in one of the leather and silver backwash hairdressing chairs to watch him at work on some fashionable lady's hair.

'I don't know what Thomas sees in the child,' complained Mariah to her friend Linda McDermott as they sipped cocktails in the Horse Shoe Bar in the Shelbourne Hotel. 'She's such an annoying little thing. Always asking questions. She is a bother.'

'Why are you talking to me about your children?' asked Linda, casting her eyes to heaven. 'You know how I feel about the little monsters.'

'And I don't blame you,' agreed Mariah, ordering a second cocktail.

On the afternoons when Ann had gone to her weekly piano lesson and Tess was with her badminton coach, Alice and her mother would find themselves alone together in the drawing room. Mariah would embroider and Alice would perch on the sofa, looking quietly around the room. She wondered why she was not allowed to press the keys on the piano or take down any of the books in the bookcase. If she made any noise at all, Mariah would glare at her. Then the little girl would murmur an apology and, on some pretence or other, she would leave the room.

Despite the problems with her mother, Alice enjoyed her life. She loved her dolls, jigsaws and board games and she loved playing with her sisters in the garden. And she loved Nanny Mary.

In September 1912, on the morning of Herbert Asquith's visit to Dublin, Alice was eating breakfast when she spat out a mouthful of crunchy toast and plunged her fingers into her mouth.

'Nanny, my tooth is wobbly and it hurts!'

'Open your mouth and let me see.' Nanny peered into Alice's mouth. 'It's just a baby tooth but your gum looks sore. We'd better visit the dentist.'

'What's a dentist?'

'A man who will help you with your tooth.'

It was a chilly morning and Nanny Mary and Alice stepped out into High Street. The little girl shivered and pulled up the collar of her dark blue wool coat. Unusually crowds of people were lined along the east side of Christ Church Cathedral, around Dublin Castle and all the way down Dame Street.

'Why are all these people here?' asked Alice, as they crossed Winetavern Street.

'That bloomin Asquith man must be still in the Castle,' said Nanny, as she guided Alice along the back of the waiting throng.

'What's an Asquith? Can we stay and see?' pleaded Alice, keen to delay her visit to the mysterious tooth-man.

'No we can't. And why would you want to see a British Prime Minister anyway?'

'I don't know. Who's that woman over there?' Alice pointed to a well-dressed woman who was standing on a step making a speech; she was attracting a lot of booing and rude laughter from the crowd.

A woman bystander smiled at the little girl. 'That lady is called Hanna Sheehy-Skeffington. She's a suffragette and one day you'll tell your children that you saw her making a speech, and they'll be impressed.'

'What's a suffragette?' asked Alice.

'Ssh,' said Nanny, pulling her away.

As Alice and her nanny pressed their way through the horde outside the Olympia Theatre, a middle-aged woman wearing a very wide-brimmed hat and carrying a large handbag pushed past, forcing her way to the front.

'The Prime Minister's carriage is coming!' shouted an excited onlooker.

'John Redmond is with him!' shouted another.

As the Prime Minister's carriage reached the theatre the woman in the hat opened her large handbag, pulled out a hatchet and threw it at the Prime Minister. The crowd gasped in shock and excitement. The hatchet missed the Prime Minster, bounced off the side of the carriage and plunged into the arm of John Redmond. The crowd surged forward; mounted policemen arrived and the woman in the wide-brimmed hat melted into the crowd. A small woman in a long green coat pulled a hammer from her bag and struck the large glass window of Burke's shop. A crack shivered up the glass; the pane groaned and buckled and finally crashed to the footpath, sending shards soaring through the air. The crowd scattered and two uniformed policemen descended upon the woman who had smashed the window.

'My name is Caroline Duffy!' the woman shouted. 'I'm a suffragette and if we have to wear out every hammer in the country smashing every pane of glass, we will get our vote!'

That was the signal, and suddenly well-dressed women all along Dame Street removed hammers from their bags and smashed more shop windows. Bedlam broke out; men, woman and children ran in all directions; horses reared up, carts were overturned and policemen with truncheons raised, shoved and pushed their way through the panicked crowds. Alice felt a sharp pain in her leg. She pulled open her coat; a small triangle of glass was protruding from her flesh above the knee. In shock, she stared at the blood oozing from her skin. The world went grey and Nanny Mary only just caught Alice as she fainted.

With the child in her arms, Nanny Mary pushed her way through the panicking people. Mounted policemen were trying to restore order but every few minutes another window would shatter and the panic would start again. Nanny carried Alice down Anglesea Street to Dr Fitzgibbon's surgery; a uniformed nurse opened the door and – after one look at the unconscious Alice – rushed Mary through the waiting room and into the doctor's surgery. There, Nanny laid Alice on the couch and Doctor Fitzgibbons – a young man with kind, deep-sunken eyes, waved a bottle of smelling salts under Alice's nose. With a snort and a sneeze Alice returned to consciousness.

'Where am I? Who are you?'

'I'm a doctor and you're a very brave girl,' said the young physician, as he examined Alice's leg.

'I don't think I'm brave,' Alice replied shakily. 'I feel sick.'

'Yes, you are brave. I've never met anyone braver. Now hold Nanny's hand and think about your favourite cake.'

Alice took Mary's hand while Doctor Fitzgibbons painted her wound with iodine. It stung a lot and Alice crushed Nanny's fingers hard. Then the doctor took hold of the glass sliver and slowly and carefully slid it out of the wound. The sudden sharp pain made Alice gasp. The doctor quickly placed a compress on the cut and pressed on it.

'The worst is over,' the doctor said. 'See, you are a very brave girl.'

When the bleeding stopped Doctor Fitzgibbons painted the wound with more iodine, put in a stitch and bandaged her leg.

At bedtime, as Nanny was brushing her hair, Alice asked, 'Why did the ladies break all the windows in Dame Street?'

Nanny Mary sighed. 'Because the ladies want the men to give them the vote.'

'What's the vote and why don't they just ask the men for it?'

'They have but the men don't listen to them.'

'But breaking windows is such a naughty thing to do.'

'It is, but when you're a grown-up sometimes you have to do naughty things to get people to listen to you.'

'I don't understand,' said the small child solemnly.

'You will, Alice,' said Mary, kissing her. 'One day, you will.'

Alice did her best to do nothing naughty, but her mother still found fault with everything she did and disciplined her over the mildest infraction – or imagined infraction – of family rules. When Alice's teacher noted on her report that the child sometimes had 'a little too much to say', her mother flew into an extraordinary rage.

'When you are in school, you have to listen! You are there to learn, not to give your opinion! Your opinions do not matter! You shouldn't even have opinions! If this happens again I will send you away to boarding school, like your brothers!' And, as Alice's eyes filled with tears, Mariah shouted, 'Now, go to your room!'

'But I haven't eaten,' whispered the child.

'And you won't, at least not until morning.'

Thomas was only in the door when Mariah told him of her altercation with Alice.

'My God, what kind of mother are you?' Thomas said and stormed up the stairs.

Mariah was already pouring a second glass of sherry when she heard her husband and daughter descending the stairs to the kitchen.

'You are undermining my authority with that child,' she snapped, when Thomas returned to the drawing room.

'You are too hard on her,' he countered.

'And you are too indulgent of her.' Mariah plunged a needle into her embroidery, angrily. 'You will ruin her.'

'We are her parents, not her jailers. The girl has spirit.'

'Yes – and that waywardness is what I'm trying to break. Her "spirit", as you call it, will be her downfall.'

'You're wrong. It will be the makings of her. She's a brave child.'

As Alice grew older, her world became more interesting. Like her sisters, she was sent to dance, music and horse-riding lessons. She also enjoyed going to church and listening to the chanting of the priests at high mass, and she adored her girls' sodality meetings. On the first Wednesday of every month, she would put on her brown sodality uniform, perched her beret on the left side of her head and – with her sodality medal pinned to the front of her blouse – walk with her sisters to St Audoen's Church. She always listened attentively to Father Patrick and loved his sermons. During Lent, however, when visiting priests came to tell them about saints being tortured and souls burning in hell, she closed her ears and thought of nicer things.

'Why do the visiting priests always talk about hellfire and brimstone?' she asked Tess after the first night of the Lenten Retreat.

Tess shrugged.

'What's brimstone?' asked Ann, pulling her beret down over her ears.

'I think it's some sort of hot rock,' suggested Alice.

'Why do we have to tell priests our sins in confession?' Ann whispered to her sisters.

'I make up my sins when I go to confession,' Tess said. 'I go to a different priest every week and I tell them the same sins. I tell them: "I told a lie, I hit my sister and I didn't say my prayers".'

'And do you always get the same penance?' Alice asked.

'No, sometimes I get three Hail Marys, sometimes two Our Fathers and once I went to old Father Hurley and he told me to say a Rosary. I never went back to him.'

One evening when Thomas was alone in the salon, the nine-year-old Alice slipped in to join him. For a while she sat quietly, watching him wax his moustache. Eventually, she spoke:

'Father, can you take the frizziness out of my hair?'

Thomas gave a final tweak to the ends of his moustache. 'Why would I do that? Your hair is beautiful.'

"Some of the girls in school make fun of it.'

Thomas stood up, came over and laced his fingers through her hair. 'You have lovely healthy hair. Each strand is puffy in the middle and pointed at the end, exactly as it should be. My mother had hair just like yours and everyone agreed that she was the most beautiful woman in Sligo.'

'The girls say I look like a wild woman and that my hair is electrified.'

29

Thomas laughed. 'Alice, there are two kinds of people in the world, sensible people and silly people. You and I are sensible people. The girls that make fun of your hair are silly people. They think by belittling you they diminish you, but they are wrong – they make you stronger. Your hair is beautiful, but if you like I'll take a little cutting and I'll experiment with it, to see if I can shape it a little. How about that?'

'Then will I look like other girls?'

'No, Alice, you will never look like other girls. How could you, when you're the most beautiful girl in the world?'

Alice's face broke into a broad smile and Thomas took a cutting of her gorgeous, frizzy hair.

When Jarlath and Terrance returned home after finishing boarding school, Mariah started to drink more heavily. At first it was a sherry before dinner which quickly became two sherries. The glass of wine with dinner became half a bottle and, because Thomas was rarely home for dinner and Mariah was usually in bed before he returned he failed to notice his wife's increasing consumption of alcohol.

One evening, Jarlath was sitting in the drawing room reading his Horse and Hound magazine when Mariah rose to her feet, staggered awkwardly and nearly fell. Jarlath rushed to her side just as Mrs O'Donnell appeared from nowhere.

'Best leave this to me,' announced the diminutive housekeeper, slipping her arm around Mariah's waist.

'Mother is ill! I'll fetch Dr Veale…'

'There's no need. Sometimes your mother gets a little light-headed. It's the medicine. Nothing to worry about, I'll look after her, you go back to your reading.'

Reluctantly, Jarlath returned to his seat and watched as Mrs O'Donnell coaxed his swaying mother out of the drawing room.

Alice liked seventeen-year-old Terrance. He talked to her, played with her and always had time for her. To Alice, he was perfect: tall, dark and handsome – just how a big brother should be. She didn't even mind that he called her 'mad hair'.

'How's "mad hair" today?' he teased, when they met on the stairs. 'What's the gossip?'

'There's no gossip,' replied Alice, smiling shyly.

'There's always gossip. What have you heard?'

'Well, Uncle Aiden told father that you're "moving in dangerous circles".'

'Uncle Aidan, the British soldier?'

'Yes – I overheard him talking to Father in the office. What does "moving in dangerous circles" mean?'

Terrance winked at her. 'It means I'm planning on running away to join the circus.'

'No you're not!' Alice did not know what dangerous circles meant but she was certain it had nothing to do with joining a circus. Yet before she could say another word, her older brother was halfway down the stairs.

Thomas was sitting in his office reading the latest edition of *Hairdressing Monthly* when Jarlath's shadow fell across him.

'Father, I'm worried about Mother,' said the boy solemnly, as he sat down in the chair facing the desk.

'Worried in what way?' asked Thomas, smoothing his right index finger across his moustache.

'Yesterday she nearly fell and Mrs O'Donnell said it was because of the medicine she was taking. But when I spoke to Mother afterwards, she told me she wasn't taking anything.'

'Then why does she think she nearly fell?'

'She doesn't think anything, because she doesn't remember it even happening.'

Thomas was startled. 'Doesn't remember?'

Jarlath leaned forward with his hands on his knees and said quietly, 'Father, I'm very sorry to have to say this, but I think Mother might have been drunk.'

Mrs O'Donnell and the assistant housekeeper Louise Kelly were in the basement packing away some unwanted furniture, when Thomas called down the wooden stairs:

'Mrs O'Donnell, please come to the drawing room!'

The two women exchanged looks; then Mrs O'Donnell shrugged, sighed and headed for the stairs.

'Why did you tell my son that my wife was taking medication when it was not so?' Thomas asked, as soon he had closed the drawing room door behind them.

The tiny woman drew herself up to her full height. 'Sir, I cannot answer that question without compromising your wife and I would never do that, so I suggest that you address that question to Mrs Dalton.' And she turned on her heel, leaving Thomas standing amazed and confused in the middle of the carpet.

Tony Murray was a bright, canny and aware man who was as thin as a wraith of grey smoke and as stern as a disappointed bishop. He was Thomas's accountant and also a good friend to the hairdresser.

'That's the building I'm interested in,' said Thomas, pointing to a mid-terrace, four-storied Georgian building across from where they were standing on Lower Leeson Street.

'That's a very large building,' said Tony, removing the monocle from his eye. 'Why do you wish to acquire such a large building?'

'Well, I don't suppose I can keep it a secret much longer. I plan to open Ireland's first academy of hairdressing and for that I need a prestigious premises in a good location.'

'An academy of hairdressing?' repeated Tony, astonished. 'I've never heard of such a thing.'

'Then you will soon enough. What's the condition of the building?'

'It's been maintained to a high standard. If you were looking for a business investment, I'd recommend it. But surely it's too big for any sort of an academy?'

'I'll only use the basement for the academy. The rest of the building, I'll rent out.'

'Thomas, you and your family are forever surprising me.'

'You're very kind...'

'It's not a compliment, Thomas.'

It took a few moments for Thomas to realise that his accountant and good friend was trying to tell him something. 'What on earth do you mean? What have you heard about my family that surprises you?'

'I've heard about Terrance and his involvement with the Irish Republican Brotherhood.'

Thomas felt quite faint. 'My son... involved with the IRB? Who told you that?'

'A chap I know from the Castle told me that Terrance regularly attends IRB meetings. Your boy needs to be careful, Thomas. The British are watching him. He's on their list.'

Home early for once, Thomas sat staring pensively into the drawing room fire, wondering what he was going to do about his second son.

'You're very quiet,' said Mariah loudly, as she poured herself another after-dinner brandy.

Thomas glanced disapprovingly at the glass in her hand.

Mariah caught the look and said defensively, 'It's just a little drink to settle my stomach.'

'Really? You seem to be having a lot of trouble with your stomach of late. Maybe you should talk to the doctor about it. Jarlath is worried about you.'

'He has no need to be.'

'I trust you're right. Is Terrance in the house?'

'I really don't know.'

'You should take more interest in your children,' Thomas said grimly.

'You mean like you do?' slurred Mariah, topping up her glass. 'The only one you really care about is Alice.'

Thomas caught Terrance in the hall, on the point of his son leaving the house. 'I'd like a word.' Thomas's voice was stern and abrupt.

Terrance glanced impatiently at his watch. 'I'm in a bit of a hurry, Father. Can we talk later?'

'No, we cannot.'

'But...'

'What's this I hear about you being in the IRB?'

The boy looked startled, then shrugged. 'I agree with their thinking. I don't think our country should be ruled by the British. I want rid of them.'

'That will happen in good time and it will be achieved without the involvement of the IRB or violence.'

'I don't think so.'

Thomas flushed. 'So you agree with violence?'

'Violence is the only language the British understand!'

'You want a repeat of 1916, is that it?'

'The Easter Rising lit a fire that will burn until the British are consumed by it!'

'Terrance, please think for a moment...' Thomas struggled to stay calm and in control. 'It is not wise to bite the hand that feeds you.'

'Is that the hand that turned Dublin into one of the biggest slums in Europe?' answered Terrance. 'Or is it the hand that causes mass unemployment and emigration? Or are we talking about the hand that turned a large part of our city into a whorehouse?'

'I won't have that kind of talk in this house!'

'No, you're a man of such high morals.'

'Who do you think is paying for your university education and your affluent lifestyle?' snapped the hairdresser, and flecks of spittle gathered at the side of his mouth. 'Unlike you, I can't afford to live in a romantic Celtic twilight! I have to live in a world of work and business!'

'Keeping your head down,' sneered Terrance.

'Don't you dare judge me!'

'Then don't you judge me!'

On the landing above, young Alice hovered listening to her beloved brother and equally beloved father argue, and the anger in their voices frightened her.

CHAPTER FOUR

In the quiet of her room Alice donned her prettiest dress and brushed her hair into submission. When she'd finished, she placed the brush on the dressing table, rested her hands in her lap and took a moment to think about what she was about to say to her mother. When she felt ready she walked down the stairs and knocked gently on the drawing room door.

'Come in,' came the sharp reply.

Alice opened the door, crossed the floor and stopped in front of Mariah.

'What is it?'

'I'd like to walk in the procession next Sunday,' said Alice, picking at a thread on the sleeve of her dress.

'Only common children walk in processions,' said Mariah, without lifting her eyes from her embroidery.

'Please Mother, all my friends are walking in the procession.'

'No they are not. I don't let you associate with common children, so why would I let you walk in a procession with them?'

'But Father walks in the procession.'

'I know he does and I don't like him doing it.'

'But I want to do it for God.'

Mariah lifted her head and her brown eyes darkened.

'You're not walking in the procession.'

Alice's lips started to tremble. 'But Mother...'

'If you're going to cry you had better go to your room.'

On Saturday morning, workmen hung yellow and white buntings along the street. Mrs Foley placed a statue of the Virgin Mary and a bowl of flowers in the drawing room window, as did every home along the route of the procession. Later that day when Nanny walked the children to the park, they stopped at each little grotto window and said a Hail Mary.

'How many Hail Marys are we going to have to say?' Tess whispered to Alice. 'This is worse than going for confession to Father Hurley.'

The following day at three o'clock, an altar boy opened the gates of the high altar of St Audoen's Church, the organ boomed into life and the annual May processions commenced. Carrying a huge brass crucifix and wearing a white surplice, the head altar boy led the altar boys down the aisle. Next followed sixty girls in their white communion dresses and then, in a long brown habit, came Thomas Dalton, leading the men of the third order out of the church. Finally, under a moving white canopy and carrying a statue of the Virgin Mary, came the parish priest, Father Mulcahy.

Wearing her white communion dress, Alice sat at her bedroom window and waited eagerly on the procession to arrive. When it did, she blessed herself; but when her father and the men of the third order walked past her window an overwhelming desire to participate overcame her. She jumped to her feet, raced down the hall and dashed into the street. The footpaths were crowded with people; some were saying the rosary, others were waving home-made white and yellow flags, and others were simply watching the spectacle. Alice ducked and dived behind the hordes of people lining the street.

At Christ Church Cathedral, when the procession took a left turn under the cathedral's covered bridge, Alice came abreast of her father. She pushed her way to the front of the crowd and waved frantically until Thomas saw and smiled at her. The procession continued and Alice walked along the edge of the crowd, parallel with her father. When the procession re-entered St Audoen's Church, Alice followed and stood in a small raised alcove at the back of the church. She listened to the congregation sing 'Hail Queen of Heaven' and when she identified her father's deep baritone voice she beamed with delight.

When a still excited Alice arrived home she came face to face with a furious, crimson faced Mariah.

'How dare you disobey me!' shouted Mariah, and she shook Alice by the shoulder and slapped her across the face. 'How dare you walk in the procession when I expressly forbade you to do so?'

Alice's hand shot to her cheek and tears filled her eyes. 'But I didn't walk in the procession...'

'Don't lie to me! This time you have gone too far, young lady!' Mariah was about to administer a second slap when a dark-robed figure filled the doorway.

'Alice, go to your room,' ordered Thomas, as he pushed her towards the stairs. To his wife, he said under his breath, 'Don't ever strike my daughter again. And for God's sake, stop drinking in the afternoon.'

Thomas was in his office leaning over his desk, studying the design drawings for his new academy of hairdressing, when Tony Murray strolled into the office.

'There you are,' said the tall accountant, as he placed his bulging leather bag on the desk.

'You're welcome, Tony. What brings you here today?'

'Do you mind if I close the door, Thomas? I can't stand the smell from the hairdressing salon. It's like being locked in a perfume factory.'

'So why are you here, Tony?'

'I came to get you to sign the last of the papers for the Lesson Street property. The lease holders have been notified of the new owner and the basement has been cleared.'

'Very good. The school equipment will be arriving soon and we'll be open for business in the New Year.' Thomas folded the architect's drawing and carefully stowed it in the top drawer.

'And is anyone out there interested at all?' asked Tony, as he spread the papers for Thomas' signature across the desk.

'Actually, they are. I placed an advertisement in the *Irish Times* and interest was extremely keen. We can facilitate about twenty five fee-paying students and it looks like we will be seriously oversubscribed.'

The accountant was astonished. 'Well, who would have thought? I've never heard of such a thing.'

One dull late summer day the girls were playing in the back garden when Tess suggested, 'Let's play the game the children in the flats play.'

'How do you know the games they play?' asked Ann.

'It's a secret, I can't tell you,' said Tess.

'Why can't you tell us?' demanded Alice.

'Because I promised Nanny I wouldn't tell anyone.'

'You've just told us,' Alice pointed out.

'You tricked me and besides you don't count.'

'Why did Nanny go into the flats?' asked a wide-eyed Ann.

'Nanny gave a woman there some of our old clothes,' Tess said in a hushed voice.

'What did the woman do with the clothes?' Alice asked.

'She gave them to her children.'

'Oh that's awful, they must hate that,' said Ann, making a sour face. 'Imagine having to wear other people's old clothes.'

'No, the children wanted the clothes, they were even fighting over them. Now do you want to play the game or not?' Tess said, bringing the conversation back to the important subject of play.

'What's the game called?' Alice asked, still thinking about the children fighting over the old clothes.

'It's called hop scotch. You draw squares on the ground in the shape of a cross and you write a number in each box. The first square is number one and the furthest square is ten. Then you throw a piggy and whatever square the piggy lands in, you hop to that square. Whoever gets the highest score wins.'

The girls were still playing their new game when Mrs Foley called them and asked them to go to O'Malley's shop to fetch a bottle of Bovril. As the girls exited the shop they saw some children from the flats scutting on the back of a horse-drawn cart. When Alice saw that one of the children was wearing her old yellow dress, she felt strange; and when she realised that the child was a boy, she didn't know what to think.

Saturday was a blistering hot summer's day and Nanny Mary decided to take the girls to St Patrick's Park to play in the shade of the trees.

As they walked up St Patrick's Street, they passed some of the children from the flats sitting on the side of a horse trough cooling their feet in the water. Alice noticed the little boy wearing her yellow dress and was about to point him out to Ann when a uniformed policeman appeared from nowhere. The children scattered but the constable caught the small boy in Alice's dress and shouted into his face.

'What's your name, boy?'

'What do you want to know for?' screamed the boy as his bare feet kicked wildly at the policeman.

'Don't you kick me, you little brat. I know you, you're Eanna de Búrca. We'll see how cheeky you are after you've spent the night in jail.'

That night as Alice lay in her bed she thought about the little boy in her yellow dress and wondered if the policeman had really put him in jail.

A shabbily dressed young woman in a brown weather-beaten over-coat with a soiled fox-fur stole draped around her shoulders made her way around the packing crates and the sinks that littered the floor of the hairdressing academy-to-be. When she reached the half-open office door, she patted her hair into place and knocked tentatively on the door.

Thomas Dalton looked up from his desk. 'Come in?'

'It's a bit of a mess, isn't it?' said the young woman in a very Dublin accent, as she gazed around.

'Ah, you must be the cleaner. I want you to gather all the packing material and other rubbish and put it in the bin out back. Sweep the floor and then come back and I'll give you some more instructions.'

Thomas's eyes returned to the invoices but the young woman remained standing in the doorway.

'What is it?' Thomas asked, without looking up.

'I'm not the cleaner,' explained the young woman. 'My name is Bridie Halpin and I want to be a hairdresser.'

Thomas glanced up again and this time took in the young woman's worn coat and her unwashed hair. 'You want to be a hairdresser, Miss... err?'

The woman nodded; she took a step forward. 'Call me Bridie, everyone does. I don't want to spend all me life selling fish in Moore Street. I want to be a hairdresser.'

'You sell fish in Moore Street?'

'Yes, me and me Ma do, but you see I'm good at the hairdressing. I do me Ma's and me Aunt Julie's hair and they always look beautiful. But I think there are a few things I don't know about the hairdressing lark.'

'Miss Halpin, I don't consider hairdressing to be a lark and I really don't think you're a suitable candidate for the academy.'

'Why?'

'Are you questioning me?'

'Is it because I'm not posh? Is that it?'

'No, the class is oversubscribed and besides it's very expensive.' Thomas stressed the word 'expensive'.

'How expensive? How much is it?'

'You're persistent, I give you that much. The course costs five pounds and there is equipment and books to buy.'

At the mention of books, Bridie's back stiffened and her eyes dulled. 'That's all right. I don't mind books.'

'So you can read and write, Miss Halpin?'

Another slight pause. 'Oh yea.'

Thomas slid a blank sheet of paper across his desk. 'Write your name and address on that and I'll contact you if a place opens up.'

Bridie took a step away from the desk. 'Maybe you're right, maybe the hairdressing lark's not for me. Sorry to have taken up your time, sir.'

A disappointed Bridie Halpin buttoned her coat and held her head high as she walked briskly out of the office. Thomas shook his head and resumed studying the invoices on his desk.

Every Christmas, the Dalton girls were allowed to write to St Nicholas and ask for one present. The selection of that present was the biggest decision that they had to make all year, and Nanny Mary and the children would spend endless hours walking the streets looking in every toy-shop window for that one toy that was special enough to ask St Nicholas to bring to the house on Christmas morning.

On the 8th December 1918, the Feast of the Immaculate Conception, Nanny Mary took the girls to South Great George's Street to see the displays of toys in Pim's department stores windows. She dressed the children in their warmest clothes and when everyone was ready they stepped out into the bright cold day. As they waited to cross the road at Winetavern Street, the girls were fascinated by the sparks that flew from the hooves of the horses as the creatures struggled to pull their heavy-laden carts up the hill.

'Give us a look at your new teeth, Anto?' a bald-headed boy in ill-fitting clothes shouted at a passing cart driver.

'I'll give you, new teeth,' the driver shouted and cracked his whip in the air.

The boy laughed, jumped off the railings and grabbed hold of the back of the cart.

'Get off the cart or I'll give you a good crack on the arse with me whip!' yelled the driver.

'The man said "arse",' Ann whispered in shock, while Tess and Alice giggled wildly.

'Go on Anto,' begged the boy. 'It's Christmas – give us a scut.'

'All right, but if you fall off and kill yourself, don't blame me.'

After the cart had passed, Nanny and the girls crossed the street. As they walked around the railing of Christ Church Cathedral, the church choir within erupted into song. The footpaths of South Great George's Street were crammed with busy shoppers, excited children, noisy street entertainers and glorious hot chestnut vendors. Alice and her sisters peered eagerly into every toy shop and every window display caused them to rethink their St Nicholas present.

'Children, we have to go to Whitefriar Street Church and visit Mr Flanagan,' said Nanny Mary when they reached the bottom of Aungier Street.

'Does Mr Flanagan live in the church?' asked Ann.

'No, he's doesn't. Mr Flanagan doesn't have a home. Mrs Foley made up some sandwiches and asked me to give them to him.'

'Is Mr Flanagan a tramp?' asked Tess.

'He's a poor unfortunate, Tess, and you should never call a person a tramp. It's not nice.'

Nanny and the girls walked up Whitefriar Street and when they entered the church Ann stopped and stared in startled astonishment at the life-size statue of the crucified Christ.

'It's only a statue,' Nanny said as she took Ann's hand and led her further into the church.

Bathed in the soft glow of candlelight, the church looked warm and comforting and while Nanny Mary looked for Mr Flanagan, the children studied the many stained-glass windows. When Nanny found Mr Flanagan, he was fast asleep on a pew near the back of the church.

'Mr Flanagan,' Mary said as she shook the sleeping man. 'I've brought you something to eat.'

Mr Flanagan eyes blinked open. Dazed, he looked around and when his gaze fell upon Mary holding out a grease-proof paper package he smiled.

'Ah Mary, the blessings of God on you.' He tore opened the package and took a bite of a dripping sandwich.

'He's eating in the church,' Ann whispered to Tess and when Mr Flanagan burped, Tess went into a fit of giggling.

'Tess, you're in church and you're being rude, stop giggling and say you're sorry to Mr Flanagan,' said Nanny.

'But he's a tramp!' Tess exclaimed.

'That's all right Mary, they're only youngsters,' Mr Flanagan said between bites. 'This is a lovely bit of grub. Who are the children?'

'These are the Dalton children, Tess, Ann and Alice. I look after them. And I apologise for their manners. I thought they were well brought-up young ladies, but I must have been wrong.'

'Would you like to come to our house for dinner on Christmas Day, Mr Flanagan?' Alice said, as Tess rolled her eyes. 'And I'm sorry my big sister called you a tramp.'

Mr Flanagan looked serious. 'That's very gracious of you, Alice. But you see I have a standing arrangement with the British Viceroy that every Christmas Day we have dinner together in his lodge in the park. But thanks very much and I don't mind if your sister calls me a tramp. Sure everyone has to be something.'

'Mr Flanagan, if you can't come to my house, can I bring some food to you?'

'That would be lovely, thank you,' replied Mr Flanagan. 'The dinner with the Viceroy is rather late in the day, and I'm often a bit peckish beforehand.'

That evening after dinner, Alice told Mrs Foley about meeting Mr Flanagan and how she had promised to bring him food on Christmas Day; she said she didn't really believe about the late dinner with the Viceroy. Mrs Foley smiled and reached out her big arms to embrace Alice.

'You're a kind-hearted little one. We can spare some food for Mr Flanagan on Christmas Day. I'll make up something special and you can bring it to him.'

CHAPTER FIVE

Ten days before Christmas Day the children were peering in the window of Cleary's Department Store in Sackville Street when they finally identified the presents that they wanted.

Tess was the first to glimpse her heart's desire. 'Look, over there, the Set of Books for Girls – that's what I want St Nicholas to bring me.'

'Oh, I want them too!' cried Ann.

'No, I saw them first – find your own present!'

'Then what will I get?'

'Oh, look!' Alice's eyes had fallen upon a sad-faced, droopy-eyed rag doll and her quest had also ended. 'Look! The Dismal Desmond doll there beside the Meccano set! That's what I'm asking for!'

'That's what I want too!' cried Ann.

Alice looked hurriedly about the shop window. 'How about that Noah's Ark filled with wooden animals?'

'That's a boy's toy,' Ann said, with a frown.

'Is it? Look over there, look at the tea set! There, beside the big red spinning top! See, it's beautiful! I think I'm changing my mind...'

'No, I want The Tea Set!' cried Ann enthusiastically. 'It's lovely, we can have tea parties.'

That night Alice wrote her letter to St Nicholas and asked for a Dismal Desmond doll for herself, The Tea Set for Ann, and the Set of Books for Girls for Tess. The following morning she left the letter in the post tray in her father's office and every night for the next ten nights she prayed to St Nicholas and hoped that her prayers would be answered.

Christmas morning was a beautiful, fresh frosty morning. Snow was gently falling and a mantle of white had already formed on the window ledge outside the girls' bedroom. Alice was the first to wake and as she lay in her bed waiting for the house to come alive, she listened to the soft rhythmic clip, clop of horses' hooves and the muffled rumble of cart wheels on the snow-covered cobble stones outside her home.

'Alice, are you awake?' Ann whispered through the darkness. 'Do you think St Nicholas has brought our presents yet?'

'I don't know,' Alice whispered back.

'When will we get them?'

'We'll get them after breakfast and stop talking about them. You're getting me too excited.'

An hour later the house began to stir. First Alice heard Mrs Foley trudging down the kitchen stairs, then she heard the tinkle of Mrs O'Donnell's keys as she passed the bedroom door and then, after what seemed forever, Nanny Mary threw open the bedroom door and cried, 'Wake up everybody! It's Christmas morning!'

For the first time in a long time Jarlath, Terrance, the three girls, Mariah and Thomas all sat down together for breakfast. Mrs Foley produced a feast of bacon, sausages, eggs and a mound of freshly toasted bread. After breakfast, Jarlath donned his riding clothes and left to join the Christmas Day hunt in County Wicklow and Terrance went off to meet his university friends. Alice, Ann and Tess waited anxiously at the locked door of the drawing room for Mother to arrive with the key.

'Better get this over with,' Mariah murmured to Mrs O'Donnell, as the two women slowly descended the stairs from above.

Hurry, hurry up and open the door! Alice wanted to scream, but she bit her tongue. Mrs O'Donnell placed the black key in the lock, slowly turned it and the lock clicked... Mariah stepped in front of children, blocking the doorway.

'Girls, each armchair has a name pinned to it. Find your name and you'll find your St Nicholas present.'

And at last the door was open and the children skipped into the drawing room. Alice stopped at the grand piano and scanned the three armchairs in the centre of the room. A small white card was pinned to each armchair; when she found the one with her name, her heart sank.

'I got it!' Ann screeched. 'It's The Tea Set, the one from Cleary's window!'

'I've got the Set of Books for Girls!' screeched Tess.

But Alice just stared at the game of Snakes and Ladders which sat on her armchair. Where, oh where was Dismal Desmond? She blinked back tears, trying to understand why St Nicholas had disappointed her, until she felt a gentle tap on her shoulder. It was her father and he was pointing over the side of the chair. Alice craned to see where he was pointing; her eyes lit up and she scooped the Dismal Desmond doll off the floor.

'Father, it's exactly what I asked St Nicholas to bring me!'

'Well, that's wonderful,' replied Thomas, as he took his seat by the fire.

The children played with their new toys, ate biscuits and drank sweet lemonade. Thomas lit a cigar and a stern-faced Mariah sat opposite him and stared into her past.

Alice went up to her mother with the soft toy in her arms. 'Look mother it's a Dismal Desmond. I thought St Nicholas had forgotten me, but he was just teasing!'

Mariah came slowly back to the present, glaring at the doll in her daughter's arms, then she rose and crossed the room to Nanny Mary.

'Go to the breakfast room and wait for me there,' she said through clenched teeth.

'Yes, Mrs Dalton,' replied Mary, wondering what she had done wrong now.

Two minutes later, a furious Mariah stormed into the breakfast room.

'I told you what present to buy each child!'

'And I followed your instructions to the letter, Mrs Dalton,' said Mary.

'Then where did Alice get that stuffed toy?'

'I bought it,' Thomas said, appearing in the doorway and drawing on his cigar. 'Mary, please return to the children.'

Mariah's eyes flared, as she waited for the nanny to scuttle from the room. 'Why do you have to undermine me?' she demanded sharply, the moment they were alone. 'It is I who decides what's best for my children.'

'You instructed Mary to get a board game when you knew Alice wanted that stuffed doll. Why did you do that?'

'I wanted her to learn she can't get everything she wants in life. Lord knows I didn't.'

'Mariah, there are times when I have no understanding of you.'

For the rest of the morning, Mariah was angry and annoyed. She spoke dismissively to the servants and harshly to the children. When Thomas frowned at her, she scowled and when it was time for the family to go to high mass she refused to leave the house.

Alone, Mariah drifted around the house in a haze of apprehensive desperation. She knew the black creature was near and it was readying for an attack. She sat in her chair in the drawing room and while she waited for her terrifying visitor she twisted a handkerchief in her hand until her fingers were sore.

When the family returned from church, Alice went down to the kitchen and asked Mrs Foley if she would make up the promised food parcel for Mr Flanagan.

'I will of course,' replied Mrs Foley. 'Come back after you've eaten and I'll have it ready for you.'

After their Christmas dinner, the Dalton family gathered in the drawing room for coffee and Christmas cake. When everyone was finished, Alice asked Nanny if she'd bring her to Whitefriar Street Church to give Mr Flanagan the food parcel.

Nanny looked worried. 'I doubt Mr Flanagan will be in the church today. It's not as if he lives there.'

'I know that, but I think he might be there today.'

'Perhaps he'll come to the house – remember you asked him to come?'

'No, he doesn't know where we live.' Alice fixed Nanny Mary with her beautiful brown eyes. 'Nanny, please. I promised St Nicholas that if he brought me a Dismal Desmond I'd bring Mr Flanagan food on Christmas Day. So you see, I have to find him. I have to keep my promise.'

'I don't know what to do, Alice,' Nanny groaned, glancing at Mariah. 'I have so many extra duties. No, I'm sorry but I can't take you to the church today.'

'I'll take you there,' said Thomas, who had been listening. He was glad of the opportunity to temporarily remove himself from his home. 'Get your coat.'

Delighted, Alice put on her new wool coat, leather boots and fur hat. Thomas donned his own heavy winter overcoat and top hat and took a tartan umbrella from the hallstand. Out on the street, he looked for a hansom cab but after a few minutes without success he decided they should walk. As they passed City Hall, a blustery cold wind swirled around them and rain poured down on the snow covered streets. Thomas unfurled his umbrella but the wind blew the cold rain under the umbrella and beat it into their faces. Wet and shivering, Alice clutched the parcel of food tightly in her hands.

'Are you sure you want to continue?' Thomas asked, hoping his daughter would abandon her quest. 'There's still a good way to go?'

'Father, I have to find Mr Flanagan. I promised St Nicholas!'

And so they continued their journey. By the time they reached Pim's Department Store, the rain was falling so hard they had to shelter. Standing in the shop's doorway, Thomas watched the rain turn the snow into slush and watched the river of slush and rain race along the gutter and swirl into the sewers. A procession of Christmas revellers rolled past, the carriage drivers cracking their whips and the horses dipping their heads against the rain and wind. Across the street, Alice saw a grey bearded homeless man shuffling along the footpath.

'Mr Flanagan!' she shouted and bolted across the road between the carriages.

'Alice, come back!' yelled Thomas, as a rain-blinded horse reared up in panic. 'Alice!' He rushed across the street, but a young woman from the opposite pavement got there just ahead of him; snatched Alice from under the flailing hooves and retreated with her to the far side of the road. Reaching the pavement, Thomas swept his terrified daughter into his arms.

'Don't ever do anything like that again!' he cried.

'I'm sorry,' sobbed a pale-face Alice.

'It's all right, you're safe now.' He held her tight as he looked around for the young woman who had helped his daughter but she had disappeared into the Christmas crowd. He took his trembling daughter into a nearby shop doorway and as they sheltered from the rain, he racked his brains to think where he had seen that young woman before... Something about that weather-beaten coat and the cheap fur stole... He had seen her before. She was the young woman who came into his hairdressing academy looking for a place on the course! The girl who couldn't read, the girl he had insulted, humiliated and rejected.

On St Stephens' night, Alice awoke to dreadful sounds of groaning, choking and gulping for air. Terrified, she burrowed down under her blankets. The groaning and gulping grew louder in the pitch-black room.

'What's making that awful noise?' hissed Tess from the other bed. 'Is it an animal?'

'It's coming from Ann's bed,' whispered Alice.

'Go see what's wrong with her!' ordered Tess, still hiding under her bedclothes.

Reluctantly, Alice emerged from her blankets, tiptoed to Ann's bedside and turned on the Quick-Lite gas lamp. Her sister's face was completely white; she was drenched in perspiration and her body was trembling. Suddenly Ann's body arched upwards; she shuddered and shook violently as if possessed.

Alice gasped in fright. 'Tess, there's something really bad happening to Ann!'

At last, Tess slid out of bed, took one look at her younger sister and exclaimed, 'I'm getting Nanny! I'm getting everyone!'

Moments later Nanny, Mariah and Thomas were in the room; Nanny Mary pressed the back of her fingers to Ann's forehead. 'She has a very high fever. We need Dr Veale here at once.'

'I'll go!' cried Thomas, running from the room and down the stairs.

Nanny turned to Mariah, who seemed transfixed by the sight of her daughter writhing in the bed. 'Mrs Dalton, we need to cool Ann down immediately. Please hold her arms down to stop her from hurting herself while I go and fetch a bowl of water to make a cold compress.'

Mariah blinked and took a step backwards. 'No. No. I couldn't do that. You hold her down and I'll get Mrs Foley to bring you a bowl of cold water. And I'll call Mrs O'Donnell to help.' She lurched from the room and as she stumbled her way down the stairs she could be heard muttering to herself: 'This is very upsetting, very upsetting. '

Thirty minutes later Dr Veale removed the stethoscope from his ears and replaced it in his well-worn, brown leather bag.

'It's a lung infection. The next forty eight hours will be critical. But first, we need to separate her from the other children to prevent contagion.'

'You think she's contagious?' gasped Thomas. 'Alice, go down to the drawing room quickly! You as well, Tess...'

'I'll prepare the guest room,' said Mrs O'Donnell hurrying away, keys jangling.

The doctor took six small sachets of powder from his leather bag and handed them to Nanny Mary. 'Dissolve one of these in a cup of warm milk and give it to the child to drink. It will help fight the infection and enable her to sleep. Repeat the dose every four hours and make sure she drinks plenty of water. We need to keep her hydrated.'

'Where is my wife?' Thomas asked Mary after Dr Veale had left.

'I think she went to her room sir,' replied the nanny softly.

'Thank you Mary. I don't know what we'd do without you,' Thomas replied in an equally sad voice.

The following day, while Nanny Mary was having her lunch in the kitchen, Alice crept up the seventeen steps to her sister's new quarters in the guest bedroom. She opened the door very quietly and stole into the darkened room. While she waited for her eyes to adjust she listened to the sounds of her sister's ragged breathing. Ann's face slowly came into view, deathly pale in the low light; strands of her hair were stuck to her forehead and there were black hollows beneath her eyes. The shaking and trembling had stopped and she was no longer gulping for air but she was still perspiring profusely.

Alice placed her hand on Ann's forehead; her sister felt so hot it was like she might burst into flames. Alice's lower lip quivered and tears welled in her eyes.

'What are you doing in here?' Nanny demanded, when she and Mrs O'Donnell entered the bedroom. 'You know the doctor said you shouldn't be in here!'

'Why is Ann so hot?' asked Alice.

'She has a fever,' Nanny replied and placed a fresh cold compress on Ann's forehead. 'Alice, I know you're worried about your sister but you have to leave. Now.' When Alice didn't move, Nanny took her hand and walked her to the bedroom door. 'Run downstairs and ask Mrs Foley for a drink of milk and a biscuit. It will make you feel better.'

'But...'

'Go!'

'Yes, Nanny.'

'Illness is so frightening for children,' sighed Nanny as she rejoined Mrs O'Donnell at Ann's bedside.

'I suppose it is,' agreed Mrs O'Donnell. 'I only hope Ann doesn't go the way of baby Róisín. Mariah took the child's death very badly indeed.'

'I have a dead sister?' gasped Alice from the doorway.

"What are you still doing here?' Nanny rushed to Alice, put her arm around her and brought her down the stairs to the kitchen. 'Mrs Foley, Alice is very upset. Could she stay with you for a while?'

'Of course she could,' said Mrs Foley and she sat Alice at the kitchen table.

'Mrs Foley, did you know I had a sister that died?' asked Alice, wide-eyed.

Mrs Foley looked sad. 'Did your mother finally tell you? Róisín was her name, the poor little thing, and she was only a few days old when she left us.'

'Mother didn't tell me. I overheard Mrs O'Donnell speak of it. I never knew I had a dead sister. Did she sweat like Ann?'

'She did. But sick people often sweat.' Mrs Foley stroked Alice's hair. 'The doctor has given Ann medicine and she'll soon be feeling better. Why don't we say a little prayer for her?'

'I did last night. I said ten Our Fathers and ten Hail Marys.'

'Well that was a very good thing to do.'

The kitchen door opened and Mariah swept into the room and Alice's tummy twisted into a knot.

'Alice, what are you doing here bothering Mrs Foley? You should be off playing with Tess.'

'Mrs Dalton, Alice is no bother,' said the cook.

Alice stood up from the table. Her voice quavered. 'Mother, why didn't you tell me I have a dead sister?'

'Good God! Mrs Foley, whatever possessed you to tell Alice about Róisín?'

'I didn't Mam, it was Mrs O'Donnell who mentioned her.'

The following morning Mrs O'Donnell stood in front of Thomas in the breakfast room, arms folded and tapping her foot as if being in his company was a waste of her valuable time.

Thomas was angry but spoke in a level voice. 'My daughter is very upset, Mrs O'Donnell. Why did you talk about baby Róisín in her presence?'

'I didn't know the child was present. I thought she was downstairs.' Mrs O'Donnell's gaze wandered towards the window where rain was falling.

'In future be more careful of what you say around my children.' Thomas's voice grew increasingly stern. 'The children are Nanny Mary's responsibility. Please leave them to her.'

'No disrespect sir, the children are Mrs Dalton's responsibility and I take my instructions from my mistress.'

Thomas struggled to stay calm. 'My wife may be your mistress but I am your employer and I will dispense with your services if I judge them to be unsatisfactory. Can I be any clearer than that?'

'No sir,' Mrs O'Donnell replied, looking like she'd bitten on a lemon. She waited for a moment but Thomas, clearly deciding to quit while he was ahead, said nothing more and Mrs O'Donnell dipped her head and left the room, both annoyed and unusually subdued.

For the next two days Ann's fever raged unchecked. Alice couldn't concentrate on anything: not school, not her music practise, not even her dancing lesson which was usually the highlight of her week. How could she dance without Ann? She could barely concentrate on her prayers. Each night before she fell asleep she thought about her dead sister Róisín and although she had never met her, she missed her.

On the third day Ann's fever broke and very quickly the house returned to normal.

CHAPTER SIX

It was the first Monday of the New Year and Moore Street was thronged with shoppers. Shrill-voiced traders extolled the quality of their wares and haggled with customers over prices. Wearing his new brown trilby hat and chamois gloves and with the usual white carnation in his buttonhole, Thomas Dalton slowed as he passed the flower stalls, inhaling the perfume of the roses, hyacinths and tulips. But when the coppery odour of meat drifted across his nostrils, he quickened his pace and averted his eyes from the hanging carcasses of skinned rabbits and plucked chickens.

At the fish stall, however, he stopped. The woman behind the stall was weather-beaten and wore a bloodied apron, yet her hair was beautifully cut and shaped.

'Lovely fresh mackerel, ray and whiting!' the woman said as she plunged a sharp, short, serrated knife into the soft belly of a mackerel and expertly removed the fish's internal organs. 'What can I get you son?'

'I'm looking for Miss Bridie Halpin. Might you know where I'd find her?' asked Thomas.

'She's on the last stall. Mister, are you sure you wouldn't like a nice piece of cod? Nothing like a nice bit of fresh fish to keep you healthy?'

'I'm sure, thank you,' Thomas replied with a tip of his hat and he moved on down the street.

Bridie Halpin was emptying a tray of mackerel onto her stall when Thomas saw her.

'Miss Halpin!' Thomas doffed his hat.

'Oh, Mr Dalton.' Bridie rubbed her hands down the side of her oil-cloth apron. 'Did you want some fish?'

'No, not today. I wonder if I might have a word with you.'

'If you like.' Bridie stood with her hands on her hips.

'In private,' added Thomas.

Bridie turned to the older woman working beside her who despite having broken teeth was also beautifully coiffed. 'I'll only be a minute Ma!' she said loudly into the woman's ear, then stepped out from behind the stall. 'So, what do ya want to talk about?'

When Thomas realised that this was the extent of the privacy he'd been granted, he removed his hat and coughed.

'Miss Halpin, I'd like to thank you most sincerely for helping my daughter on Christmas Day. What might have happened without your intervention I dare not contemplate? Thank you most sincerely.'

Bridie turned pink and looked at the ground as he was speaking. When she realised he was waiting for her to reply, she shuffled with embarrassment. 'Eh, it was nothing, anyone would have done it.'

'No they wouldn't and they didn't, but you did. Miss Halpin, are you still interested in joining the hairdressing course?'

'I don't know.' Bridie shifted her weight from one foot to another.

'Well, a place has opened up and I thought I might offer it to you.'

Bridie eyes brightened and then dulled. 'Mr Dalton, I don't have the money anymore. I bought me Ma an overcoat for the Christmas.'

'You wouldn't have to pay the fees,' promised Thomas, smiling broadly.

Bridie recoiled. 'Mr Dalton, what kind of girl do you think I am?'

Thomas could feel himself flushing bright red. 'Good God, girl, what are you suggesting?'

'I'm not the one suggesting anything! You're the one who said I wouldn't have to pay and no-one in the world gets something for nothing!'

Flustered, Thomas grasped for an explanation that would satisfy her. 'No, no, no – I'm here because someone who has already paid has dropped out and as the fees are non-refundable, I'm offering you her place...'

But Bridie had already retreated back behind the stall. 'Eh, sorry Mr Dalton but you see me Ma needs me to be here on the stall because she can't hear the customers too well.'

'Nonsense!' Bridie Halpin's mother was clearly not as deaf as her daughter believed her to be. 'Bridie Halpin, don't you dare use me as an excuse not to better yourself. Mister, I can see you're an honest man and hairdressing is all this young one ever talks about, day and night it's hairdressing...' Bridie's mother waved her filleting knife in the air for emphasis. 'I'm sick of hearing about your hairdressing school. Bridie, give us all a rest and go to the bloomin' school. I'll get that lazy sister of yours to help me on the stall, it's about time she started to earn her keep, the fat heap. And for the hundredth time – I'm not deaf, young lady!'

Blushing, Bridie leaned across the stall to Thomas and murmured, 'Mr Dalton, I'm really not that good at the reading and the writing.'

'Don't worry about that,' said Thomas, equally quietly. 'Classes begin on the twentieth of January. Be at the academy at nine o'clock. Classes will take place in the morning and in the afternoon you will train in a salon.'

Bridie was still suspicious. 'Mr Dalton, you're not giving me the place just because I helped your daughter, are you?'

'Certainly not, you are an impressive young person who thinks and acts swiftly, particularly in an emergency situation. By the way, you did an excellent job of cutting your mother's and your aunt's hair.'

Bridie blushed as Thomas doffed his hat and marched away. Watching him go, his head up and shoulders squared like a military officer, Bridie's face broke into a big smile and she was still smiling long after she had finished gutting every fish on the stall.

The thud of the hall door closing and the clap of her father's shoes on the hall's highly polished parquet floor told Alice he was home.

'Did you find the lady who helped me on Christmas Day?' Alice asked as she raced down the stairs.

'Yes I did.'

'Oh Father thank you! When will I meet her?'

'She's starting in the academy later this month and I'll organise a time and place for you to meet her.'

It was late afternoon and the Bailey Bar on Duke Street was crowded with university students, office workers and would-be-poets. A dapper man in a tweed suit, paisley waistcoat and bow-tie sat down beside Terrance and dumped his leather bag on the seat between them.

'Why did you pick here for us to meet?' he asked, glaring around the busy bar. 'These are not our type of people.'

'Sometimes an unsuitable place is the safest place,' Terrance replied and surreptitiously slipped a brown envelope into the open bag.

'We are not playing a game. Choose a neutral location next time,' snapped the man and left.

Terrance was ordering another pint when his brother Jarlath joined him. 'Who's your friend in the fancy waistcoat?'

'Nobody.'

'This isn't your usual watering hole.' Jarlath lowered his voice. 'I've heard some rumours about you.'

'You mean your nosey, well-heeled friends are gossiping about me,' Terrance replied with a smirk.

'It's not funny. They said you were involved in a raid and some men were injured.'

'Don't believe everything you hear.'

'You'll get yourself killed doing what you're doing.'

'You worry too much.'

'I don't worry at all.'

'Good.' Terrance leaned close to his brother and whispered, 'Up the rebels.'

Everyday life in the Dalton household was growing more difficult. Thomas felt that he treated Mariah with great respect and civility but he also felt that his politeness and good manners weren't always reciprocated. They quarrelled often and partly as a result, Thomas's working day grew longer and he often remained at the salon until late into the evening. He also took to eating at his club and spending overnights there. For her part, Mariah spent most of her days in bed and her evenings sitting in the drawing room staring vacantly into the fire.

And so Nanny Mary became the stabilising force in the girls' lives. She woke them in the morning, laid out their clothes and walked them to school. In the afternoons, she picked them up from school and supervised their homework. After their evening meal, she bathed them and put them to bed. When the girls fought or argued, the final word always rested with Nanny and once she had adjudicated an argument no one disputed the decision.

On the morning of Alice's eleventh birthday she woke to the peeling bells of Christ Church Cathedral. Tess's bed was empty, the curtains were open and shafts of bright sunshine streamed through the window. Lying in her warm bed, Alice stretched her arms and thought: *Today is my birthday and it's going to be a happy day.*

'Get up sleepy-head,' said Tess rushing into the room and pulling the bedclothes off her sister. 'Or are you going to spend all your birthday in bed?'

After school, Nanny took the children to St Patrick's Park to meet with the McDermott children and their nanny. The two nannies had grown up together in the small harbour town of Ballyvaughan in County Clare and were best friends.

'Are you still going out with that little fella that joined the British army?' Mary asked as she searched in her handbag for a handkerchief.

'Of course I am, and you don't have to be sarcastic about it.' Maisie stopped talking when she noticed Alice and young Susan McDermott listening to their conversation. 'Ear-wiggers never hear anything good about themselves. Off you go.' Maisie waited until the children were out of ear shot before she spoke again. 'Last week when you read my fortune in the tea-leaves, I don't think you told me everything you saw?'

'I did, I told you everything.'

'You never said anything about me marrying Michael?'

'I didn't see anything about you marrying your bloomin' soldier.'

Across the park Alice and Susan had joined their older sisters and the five girls all chased each other around the bronze statue of Sir Benjamin Lee Guinness.

Suddenly Tess stopped running, raised her hand in the air and said, 'Let's play 'See the Devil.'

'I don't know that game. How do you play it?' asked Emma McDermott.

'It's easy. All you have to do is to run backwards around this Protestant church three times and you'll see the devil.'

'That's sounds fearsome. I'm not playing that game,' sulked Emma.

'I wouldn't like to play that game,' agreed Ann. 'Let's play Hide and Seek. Tess, you cover your eyes, count to ten, we'll run and hide and you come and find us.'

With a screech, the children scattered. Ann and Emma ran behind the cathedral and Susan and Alice sprinted to the small island of bushes in the centre of the park. Laughing and giggling, the girls pushed their way through the thick bushes but froze when they heard a groan.

'What's that?' asked Susan, her eyes darting from side to side.

Another groan. Alice's heart thumped against the cage of her chest. Susan grabbed Alice's hand and nodded towards a crumpled overcoat at the base of a large bush. Alice pushed out her right foot and touched the coat; it moved and an old man's face peered out from under the ragged coat, his fingers combing through his grubby beard. The girls gasped and the old man scrambled away from them. 'Don't tell on me!' he begged. He grabbed his small cloth bag off the ground and held it close to his chest. 'Don't tell the man on me!'

'No, we won't tell on you,' Alice reassured him, holding Susan's hand tightly.

'Why are you hiding in here?' quavered Susan.

'I'm not hiding. This is where I sleep.' He staggered to his feet and when he was at his full height he was over six foot tall; he was very thin with weary eyes that were filled with sadness. Alice fumbled in her pocket, found a half-penny and held it out to the man. The man reached out and when his finger brushed against her palm, Alice flinched, pulled her hand away and the coin tumbled to the ground. Ashamed of herself, she quickly picked it up and placed it in the man's hand.

'Thank you,' he said and dropped the coin into a pocket of his baggy trousers. 'I have children,' he added, and scratched his head. He looked around over the bushes as if searching for someone and then wandered off.

On the other side of the park, Nanny Maisie glanced at the clock on the church tower and jumped to her feet, crying, 'Jesus, we'll be late. It's nearly four o'clock!'

'Late for what?'

'For the changing of the guards! I told you, it's Michael's first time to be duty drummer!'

'And I told you I'm not going to watch British soldiers marching about...'

'If you want me to go with you to your *Cumann na mBan* meeting on Wednesday night, you'll come.'

Mary frowned and a few minutes later the five children and the two nannies had joined a small crowd outside the Palace Street entrance to Dublin Castle.

'What are the soldiers doing?' Tess asked, standing on her tippy-toes and craning her head sideways.

'The soldiers of the Royal Irish Rifle Regiment, the ones wearing the long green coats, are handing over the keys of the castle to the soldiers of the Irish Fusiliers, the ones with the big black hats and the red jackets. My Michael is the drummer with the Fusiliers.'

'I don't see a drummer,' Ann said, looking along the line of bearskin-hatted Irish Fusiliers.

'He's called a duty drummer but he's playing a bugle today,' Maisie said proudly.

'Why do they call him a drummer if he plays a bugle?' asked Alice.

'I don't know and stop asking questions,' snapped Maisie. 'Let me enjoy the ceremony in peace and quiet.'

The short soldier at the end of the line raised a gleaming bugle to his lips and music rang out around the castle grounds.

'I love Michael's bearskin hat, it makes him look so tall. What do you think, Mary?'

'I think he looks like a bloody British soldier. If my father caught me watching this lark, he'd tan my hide.'

'Is that so, well I won't be able to go with you to your meeting on Wednesday night, I'm meeting Michael.'

'If I had of known that...' snapped Mary, but Maisie seized Emma and Susan by their hands and marched away.

'Why are you annoyed with Nanny Maisie?' asked Alice, as they walked along Dame Street. 'Don't you like soldiers?'

'I don't like British soldiers and I don't want to talk about them.'

Alice grimaced at Ann and not another word was said about Maisie, her boyfriend or British soldiers.

When Alice opened the door of Brennan's Bakery in Parliament Street, the glorious aroma of baking wafted into her face. The smell of fresh soda bread and the sweet aromas of cakes and pastries combined with the scent of caramelizing sugar, jellied fruits and jams made the girls' mouths water. Then, covered from head to toe in a light dusting of flour, Mr Brennan – baker extraordinaire – walked into the shop.

'What can I do for you, ladies?' he smiled at the three girls.

'Is my cake ready?' Alice asked.

She had scarcely finished speaking when Mr Brennan, as if from nowhere, produced a most beautiful iced sponge cake with the words 'Happy Birthday Alice' written in pink icing.

'It's beautiful!' Alice declared and all eyes watched as Mr Brennan carefully placed the iced cake into a blue and white cardboard box. Then, with box in hand Alice, Nanny Mary and the girls left the palace of cake, sugar and jam and proceeded home.

Nanny pushed open the front door of their home and after the girls had hung up their hats and coats. Alice brought the cake downstairs to the kitchen.

'I'd like to put my birthday cake in the pantry, please!' announced Alice to Mrs Foley.

'That would be the place for it,' agreed the portly cook. 'I have the birthday candles and when you're finished your evening meal, I'll light the candles and bring the cake to table.'

'Thank you, Mrs Foley! This is so exciting!'

'It is, isn't it?' Mrs Foley took Alice's small face in her big hands and dropped a kiss on the girl's forehead.

Alice was bounding up the stairs singing to herself when she crashed into Mrs O'Donnell.

'Ups-a-daisy,' said the housekeeper, helping Alice to her feet. 'Could have been a nasty little accident, must watch where we're going.' Mrs O'Donnell's face grew serious. 'Alice, you must be quiet around the house. Your mother is sleeping.'

'Mother will be at my birthday party, won't she?' asked Alice, suddenly fearful.

'I don't think so,' replied an overly honest Mrs O'Donnell. 'Your mother needs her rest.'

Head bowed, Alice squeezed past Mrs O'Donnell and carried on up the stairs to her room.

'Why is our mother so different to other mothers?' Alice asked Tess, who was lying on her bed reading.

'I think our mother's a bit mad,' Tess said, putting down her book.

'Mother's not mad, she's sick. Dr Veale said so.'

At dinner that evening, Alice wore her new light blue chiffon dress and sat at the top of the table and almost forgot about her mother not being present. Ann and Tess were giddy because Terrance and Jarlath had joined them. Jarlath said little but Terrance made a big fuss of his sisters. Another surprise for Alice was that Nanny Mary sat at table. When the meal was over, Mrs Foley brought the iced cake complete with ten flaming candles to the table.

Everyone sang Happy Birthday and just as Alice was about to blow out the candles her father arrived. Alice blew out the candles and Mrs Foley sliced the iced cake. Later, as Terrance was leaving the house, he handed Alice a small wrapped parcel and said, 'Open it later, mad hair.'

When Nanny finished brushing Alice's hair, she placed the brush on the dressing table and pulled back the bed covers.

'You were annoyed with your friend today,' said Alice, lingering at the dressing table mirror to try on the blue velvet hairband that Terrance had given to her.

'I told you I don't want to talk about that,' Nanny replied. 'Now stop admiring yourself and get into bed.'

'You read her tea leaves,' said Alice, taking off the hairband and climbing in between the sheets. 'What did you see in her fortune?'

'None of your business.'

'Tell me my fortune!' Alice held out her hand.

'You're too young, your fortune isn't writ yet.'

'It's my birthday!'

'All right, just this once,' Mary gazed into Alice small hand. 'I see dancing in your future and... And a handsome dark-haired young man and...' Mary's face went ashen and she stopped talking. 'I was right, your future isn't writ yet. Now lie down and go to sleep.'

'What did you see, Nanny?'

'I saw nothing and anyway everyone knows telling fortunes is a load of codswallop.'

Alice lay down, Nanny tucked the bedcovers around her and – unusually – she placed a kiss on Alice's forehead, just as Mrs Foley had done earlier.

CHAPTER SEVEN

Alice was a thinker. In school she was an attentive student who, as some of the nuns saw it, 'expressed her opinions too readily.' One of her teachers, Sister Rena – or Sister Blush, as the students nicknamed her – considered Alice to be 'far-too-talkative.' One day, the red-cheeked nun sent Alice to the head nun's office to be disciplined for talking in class. Head bowed and fearful, Alice walked down the long grey corridor to the dreaded office. She had heard horrible stories about Sister Concepta, or "Sister Killer" as she was known to the girls. Alice suspected most of the stories were just talk but they still worried her. The office door was closed but through the translucent glass she could see the nun's robed figure towering over a much smaller figure and could hear the angry rumblings of the nun's voice. Nervously, she took a seat on the bench outside the office, beside an older student Suzanne Furlong who was already waiting.

'Sister Concepta is in a bad mood,' the older girl said in a hushed tone. 'Some idiot girl called her "Sister Killer" to her face by accident. She's in the office now.'

'Oh, poor her!' exclaimed Alice.

The girl blinked at her. 'Oh wait – you're Alice Dalton, aren't you?'

'Yes...'

'I'm talking about your sister, Ann.'

At that moment, the deep voice of Sister Concepta boomed out 'Stand still, girl!' and Alice and Suzanne looked towards the translucent glass panel. Behind the glass, the nun's hand flew through the air and smacked the smaller figure across the face. Ann staggered, and a furious Alice jumped off the bench and flung open the office door.

'Don't you hit my sister again!' she shouted.

'How dare you come in here without permission!' boomed the tall, coarse skinned nun, trying to close the door on her. 'Take your foot out of the door, you insolent child!'

At that moment, a breathless young Sister Bernadette came rushing down the stairs. When she saw Alice confronting the mighty Sister Concepta she stopped and then remembered why she'd been rushing down the stairs in the first place. 'Sister Concepta, you're needed in the infirmary, Nuala Flaherty has broken her arm!'

'Sister Bernadette, return to the infirmary immediately and please don't run, it sets a very bad example for the students,' barked Sister Concepta. Then, when the young nun continued to stare at Alice in disbelief and admiration, she snarled, 'Sister Bernadette, I said return to the infirmary!'

The young nun shook her head and ran back up the stairs. Sister Concepta ushered Alice and Ann out of the office. 'I'll deal with you two later. Return to your classrooms.'

Alice took her sister's hand and instead of returning to their classrooms, the girls walked out of the school and into the chill of a damp spring day.

Jarlath Dalton was perusing the many international hairdressing awards on the walls of his father's office when the door clattered open and Thomas swanned into the room.

'Hello Jarlath!' said Thomas in surprise as he hung his over-coat on the wooden coat stand. 'What are you doing here?'

'I'd like a word, Father,' said Jarlath, placing a highly-polished, foot-long, ornate wooden box on the desk.

Thomas raised his eyebrows at the box. 'What have we here?'

'Vials of France's finest and most expensive perfumes!' Opening the lid, Jarlath revealed a row of six tiny bottles filled with different coloured liquids sitting on a plush red velvet cushion. 'Fleur de France, Psyka, Lily of the Valley, Caron Narcisse Noir, Parfum Inconna and Aimez-Moi.'

'Interesting,' nodded Thomas. 'And what do you propose to do with them?'

'I have a business proposition for you. I would like to open a special *parfumerie* section in each of our hairdressing salons.'

Thomas eyes widened at his son's use of the word 'our' but Jarlath didn't seem to notice. The youth closed the lid and tapped the wooden box. 'The profit margin on perfume is substantial. All that is needed in each salon is a dedicated staff person and a vitrine.'

'A vitrine?' murmured Thomas.

'It's a glass-panelled cabinet designed especially for displaying fine merchandise such as perfumes.'

'Splendid. It's good to know your education wasn't completely wasted.'

Jarlath scowled. 'This is not the time for levity Father,' he said irritably. 'This is a serious, important proposal.'

'Proposal? I don't see any proposal.'

'But I just told you…' Jarlath was taken aback.

Thomas sighed, sitting down in his chair behind the desk. 'I mean a proper proposal Jarlath. Paperwork, estimates of the material costs, sales projections, projected profit margins, staff costs, suppliers et cetera, et cetera.'

Jarlath rolled his eyes. 'I don't have paperwork Father. But it goes without saying, it will be successful.'

'It does not go without saying. Right now this is little more than an idea. You need to show me that what you're proposing is a viable business opportunity. Do the work and I'll consider it.'

'Consider it?' cried an indignant Jarlath.

'Yes.'

'I might have known you wouldn't support me,' whined Jarlath as he slammed out of the office.

It was then that Thomas realised that he just had his first adult conversation with his eldest son.

A cold wind chilled a hatless and coatless Alice and Ann as they took a short cut home through St Stephen's Green. They walked briskly through the People's Gardens, over the tiny stone bridge and along the park's large pond.

'Do we have to tell Nanny and Mother about the Sister Killer bit?' Ann asked. 'We could say that the school gave everyone a half day.'

'No we couldn't say that because that would be telling a lie. We have to tell the truth.' Alice was still young enough to believe that her mother could see into her head and knew when she was telling a lie.

Ann looked miserable. 'I wish we had our coats and hats, I'm freezing.'

'Well we don't, so we'd better walk more quickly.'

They were passing Brown Thomas's store when it started to drizzle and by the time they reached City Hall the heavens had opened and rain was pouring down.

'Girls, look at you, you're soaked and you're freezing cold!' Nanny said when the downstairs maid brought the two girls to her. 'Let's get you out of those wet clothes!' She hurried the girls to their bedroom, dried them off and gave them fresh clothes. 'Now tell me what happened?'

Ann looked to Alice and Alice fidgeted with her fingers.

'Girls, what happened?'

'Sister Concepta hit Ann and she was so upset I brought her home,' said Alice, hoping that was a sufficient explanation.

'But why did your teachers let you walk home unaccompanied without your hats and coats?'

'The teachers don't know we left school,' admitted Ann.

'Well I never heard the likes. What your mother will make of all this, I don't know.'

'What am I to make of what?' Mariah asked, appearing at the girls' bedroom door. 'Alice, Ann – why are you not in uniform and why are you not in school?'

Alice flinched but she knew she had to tell the truth. She stuttered and stammered and it seemed like her voice was disconnected from her body but she persevered, gained confidence and soon the words were tumbling out of her mouth. When she had finished speaking, she waited for her mother to scold her but to her great surprise Mariah's eyes filled with tears and for the first time in Alice's short life, her mother leaned down and kissed her on the cheek. Overcome, Alice tried to kiss and hug her mother back but Mariah straightened up and turned away. 'Mary, take the girls to the kitchen and ask Mrs Foley to give them a bowl of broth and tell Mrs O'Donnell I'd like to see her right away.'

It was the first Wednesday of the month and Thomas and his prosperous friend John Swords were having their usual long lunch in the Shelbourne Hotel. Like Thomas, John was a successful self-made businessman and a dapper dresser; unlike Thomas, he was an astute observer of the human condition and prided himself on his close family relationships. Whenever Thomas needed guidance or advice on business or family matters, John Swords was the first person to be consulted. And now Thomas's family and business affairs had collided.

'It seems you have something on your mind?' suggested John after they had ordered lunch.

'You're right, I do.'

'And...?'

Thomas opened a starched linen serviette and placed it on his lap. 'Jarlath, my eldest, made a business proposition to me this morning.'

'That's encouraging.'

Thomas sighed. 'No – it was little more than an idea and not a particularly good one at that.'

'What are you going to do?'

'I haven't got the foggiest idea. What would you suggest?'

'Let him try his wings. You've always wanted at least one of your sons to join you in the business. Well now you have your chance. Invest a small amount on his behalf but then let him do the work and find out for himself if the venture is viable or not.'

Thomas shook his head. 'Jarlath doesn't have the tempera-ment for business. Hard work is not his forte.'

'Then you do have a problem,' John said as their hors d'oeuvre of six oysters on the half-shell arrived.

It was still raining when Mariah, helped by Mrs O'Donnell, alight-ed from the carriage and walked up the seven steps to the con-vent school. As the two women entered the austere, grey vestibule, Mariah shuddered. When she saw the life-size statue of the Virgin Mary, her muscles tightened. And when Sister Concepta swept around a corner into the hall, her legs went weak.

Recognising her visitor, the head nun came to a startled halt. 'Mrs Dalton, to visit the school without an appointment is quite irregular! You really should make an appointment!'

Mariah glared at the nun, saying nothing, feeling her churn-ing emotions transform to contempt. In the silence, the bell went for end of class and students poured into the corridors.

Sister Concepta smiled feebly, adjusting her rosary beads. 'But you're here now and I suppose there is something you wish to dis-cuss. Please follow me to my office where we will have peace and quiet.'

'No, we'll talk here,' answered Mariah. Her voice was so intense that passing students glanced at her and an elderly sister paused to watch, interested, her arms full of books. 'You assaulted my daughter.'

The head nun flushed. 'This is not the place to discuss such matters Mrs Dalton...'

'You slapped my daughter across the face!'

The whole vestibule fell silent. Sister Concepta poked her face into Mariah's face and sniffed loudly. 'Mrs Dalton, you have drink taken,' she announced witheringly. 'I must ask you to leave immediately.'

White hot rage thundered through Mariah; she drew back her hand and slapped Sister Concepta so hard that the nun staggered back and collided into the elderly nun behind her. The schoolgirls screamed, the elderly nun dropped her books and Sister Concepta grabbed hold of the banisters to stop herself from falling.

'Tell me Sister, do you feel disciplined or do you feel assaulted?' demanded Mariah, standing over the cowering nun. 'Well? Which is it?'

'Girls go to your classrooms immediately!' cried the young Sister Bernadette as she shooed the students away. As the girls scattered and the elderly nun picked up her books, Sister Bernadette placed herself between Mariah and Sister Concepta. 'Please leave Mrs Dalton.'

'No! I'm not finished yet!' Mariah glared at the trembling school principal with disgust and revulsion. 'You call yourselves brides of Christ. Well, you're not – you're brides of the devil!'

'Please do something to stop this madness!' Sister Bernadette begged Mrs O'Donnell, who was clearly relishing the scene.

'It's not madness. You *are* shameful, all of you!' announced the little housekeeper but she took Mariah's arm. 'Mrs Dalton I think you've said everything that needs saying here.'

Ten minutes later, an exhausted Mariah sat gazing out the window of her carriage as it swayed down Grafton Street. She was experiencing a rare moment of clarity and honesty. 'They haven't changed, have they, Eunice? They're just as cruel as they were in that dreadful school we attended all those years ago in Cliftden.'

'I looked after you then and I'll look after you now Mariah.'

'Will the sun ever shine on us?' Mariah asked – not of Mrs O'Donnell but of some distant ghostly presence.

The house was unusually dark when Thomas arrived home. The fire in the drawing room was cinders, the dining room was empty and the breakfast room was set for breakfast. Thomas saw a light in the kitchen, went downstairs and found a fretting Mrs Foley sitting by the stove saying a rosary.

'Oh, Mr Dalton. Thank God you're home.' The cook stood and blessed herself. 'It's been a dreadful day. So many awful things have happened.'

Thomas opened the drinks cupboard, removed a bottle of brandy and poured a small amount into a glass. He handed the glass to Mrs Foley and stood by the still warm stove.

'Thank you Mr Dalton, I don't normally take a dram but today was such an awful day, I will.' Mrs Foley's tubby fingers raised the glass to her lips and she took a sip of the golden liquid.

'When you're ready, tell me about the day,' said Thomas, standing at the mantelpiece.

When Mrs Foley finished telling Thomas about the day's events, he poured a second brandy for Mrs Foley and a larger one for himself.

'This is appalling, my daughter running away from school and my wife assaulting a nun? What has happened to order and decorum?' Feeling weak, he sat at the kitchen table. 'Where is Mrs Dalton?'

'She's resting. Mrs O'Donnell is with her. I'm no friend of Mrs O'Donnell but she was of powerful service to Mrs Dalton today.'

Thomas quietly opened the bedroom door and entered the darkened room. Mariah was lying in bed; her face was pale and her eyes were red and puffy. Mrs O'Donnell was seated in a chair beside the bed and when Thomas's shadow fell across her, she turned towards him.

'Mr Dalton it's been a dreadful day.'

'So Mrs Foley has already informed me. I believe you were of great service to Mariah. I thank you for that.'

'I did my job,' Mrs O'Donnell replied. 'I've given Mrs Dalton some of her old medicine and she's quite groggy.'

'Thank you Mrs O'Donnell. Get some rest for yourself. I'll look after my wife.'

'Goodnight Mrs Dalton.'

Mrs O'Donnell patted Mariah's hand and quietly left the room.

'Thomas, you're home,' sighed Mariah when he placed his hand on her shoulder.

'What in God's name took hold of you Mariah?' he asked. 'Whatever possessed you to strike a nun?'

'It was awful,' said his wife, gazing up at him. 'It all came back to me.'

'What came back to you?'

'I heard the babies crying.'

'What are you talking about?'

'I was back in the orphanage in Cliftden where I was reared.'

'Orphanage? Mariah, you were reared by your aunt in Galway.'

'No, I wasn't. I was reared in an orphanage, an industrial school. I never knew my parents and the nuns refused to tell me who they were.'

Thomas's back stiffened and he took a step back from the bed. 'Mariah…'

'I can still see the grey grimy walls of the orphanage,' she sobbed, 'and that awful steamy airless laundry room. I can hear the cries of the infants, I can even taste the awful food we fed them. Goody, it was made of stale bread, buttermilk and sugar.'

In the half-dark, Thomas listened in cold, remote, fearful silence.

Maria covered her face with her hands. 'Once I grew attached to a little baby girl, her name was Lily. She was lovely and then they sold her. They never told me anything and when I asked I was told to never mention Lilly's name again. I missed little Lily and losing her hurt so much that I swore I'd never let myself get that close to another living being.' For a moment, she reached out as if to touch Thomas but he remained ram-rod straight, his arms by his sides. Mariah sighed and withdrew her hand. 'One night I wet my bed and Sister Gloria made me carry the wet mattress on my back down the fire escape and all the time she made the children chant "Mariah Mulroney wet the bed". Eu... Mrs O'Donnell helped me carry the mattress across the yard to the boiler house and because she helped me, Sister Gloria beat her unmercifully. Mrs O'Donnell is right, they are not the Sisters of Mercy they are the Sisters of No Mercy.' Mariah's voice faded; her eyes closed and she drifted into sleep.

Thomas stood gazing at his wife's slumbering form, shaken to the core. He was appalled at how she had deceived and lied to him all these years. If Mariah didn't know who her parents were then who was she? What kind of woman had he married? To what unwholesome family might his children be related? He shuddered and felt ill. If Mariah had lied to him about her identity, then was he even married to her in the eyes of God? And what would Canon Mulcahy say and what would he do?

CHAPTER EIGHT

Most nights as Alice lay in her bed waiting on sleep her mind would wander aimlessly, but tonight she had lots to think about. In the week following the incident with Sister Concepta, Nanny Mary had supervised Alice and Ann's lessons at home. But this morning Nanny had dressed them in new, different uniforms and had taken them to Mary Immaculate School.

Why do we have to go to a new school? wondered Alice. She knew it was wrong to shout at Sister Concepta and she knew she shouldn't have walked out of the school, but Caroline Ivory took money out of the black babies' box and Yvonne Murray broke the window in the sports hall and they were allowed stay in the school.

Then she thought about the kiss her mother had given her and how it made her feel warm. She remembered the softness of her mother's lips on her cheek and the smell of powder on her mother's face. *Mother is so very pretty when she smiles but why doesn't she smile more often? Is it because she can see into my head and knows that sometimes I don't like her? Why does Mrs O'Donnell say Mother needs lots of rest and why when she gets loads of rest does she never seem any better?*

Then she pondered the strange thing Ann had said to her before in the garden: 'Father always talks to you and never talks to me or Tess. Sometimes I think he doesn't even know my name.' Alice was still thinking how awful it was for Ann to feel like that when she drifted into sleep.

On Tuesday, when Nanny was walking Alice and Ann home from dancing class, they met up with Maisie in St Patrick's Cathedral Park. It was a cold and frosty afternoon and the white fading sun was dipping behind the cathedral. When Nanny Maisie saw Nanny Mary she rushed over and threw her arms around her friend and burst into tears.

'Johnny is being sent to Wales for infantry training,' she gasped through her tears. 'I don't want him to go to war and come back like Johnny One Leg.'

'Why don't you girls go and play?' said Mary, flicking her eyes in such a way that Alice knew the two nannies wanted to be left alone.

'We'll go for a walk,' Alice said.

'Don't go too far,' said Mary, and turned to her friend.

'Have you ever been inside a Protestant church?' Alice asked Ann as they stood looking up at the huge oak door of the largest church in Ireland.

Ann was shocked. 'No! It's a sin to go inside a Protestant church.'

'I don't think it's a sin just to look,' said Alice, and she pushed opened the door to peep inside.

'What can you see?' whispered Ann, hovering behind her.

'I can't see anything...' Alice took a step into the building.

'Don't leave me!' In a burst of fretful energy, Ann grabbed her hand and the two sisters entered the cavernous church together.

'It's really big,' said Alice, gazing around the empty stone interior. 'It looks different from our church. There's no statues.'

'What's that over there?' Ann pointed at a free-standing, very old black wooden door with a rectangular hole cut in it.

Alice went to look. 'It's called the Door of Reconciliation,' she said, reading a small plaque to the side of the door. She peered through the hole.

'What's in there?' gulped Ann.

'Nothing, just the rest of the church.' Leaving the door, Alice sat into a pew and looked around the semi-dark cathedral. 'Do you know who Johnny One Leg is?'

'No, just what Nanny Maisie said about him. We'd better get back before Nanny Mary starts looking for us.'

Weeks after Mariah's altercation with Sister Concepta, Thomas was still trying to come to terms with the horror of it all. He felt angry as well as sad that his wife had never confided in him about her dreadful childhood – yet he knew in his heart that if she had, he would not have married her. After a lot of careful consideration, he decided to believe that Mariah had been baptised in Cliftden and that her parents were married – but as he couldn't be sure he decided not to mention the sorry story to Father Mulcahy. After all, what Mariah said might not have been true at all; it might have been her imagination or it might have been her medication talking. Another thing that bothered him was the violence of Mariah's attack on the nun but the gossip that had found its way to the salon embarrassed him, and its nastiness shocked him. What must the world think of him, being married to such a woman? Late in the evening, sitting at his desk in his small office, he also wondered what God might be thinking of him.

Dressed in a riding jacket, jodhpurs and with a riding crop tucked firmly under his arm, Jarlath stood outside Thomas's office door, summoning up the courage to face his father. At last he knocked on the door and without waiting for a reply, entered the office and slapped his three page business proposal on the desk.

'What is it?' asked Thomas vaguely; mentally he was far away, still absorbed in his own worries.

'The proposal you demanded,' growled Jarlath, throwing himself into the chair facing the desk. 'I think a fifty-fifty split is fair.'

Jolted back to the present reality, Thomas picked up the three sheets of paper. 'I see.'

'And I nominate Larry White to be the dedicated perfume salesman in our High Street salon,' declared Jarlath.

'Larry? He is my finest stylist.'

'Yes, he's a good man. That's why I choose him.'

'He's a very good man.' Thomas was about to add that was why his son's suggestion was so preposterous, when he remembered John Swords' advice. 'Jarlath, I have been thinking about this idea of yours. If it's going to succeed it will need someone who really believes in it and wants it to work.'

'Exactly!' Jarlath looked pleased that his father was coming round to his point of view. 'I think our business will benefit from…'

'So, I propose that you be the sole perfume salesman.'

'Me?' Jarlath was astonished. 'But I know nothing about sales!'

'I know and that's why this is an excellent opportunity for you to learn. I'll ask Larry White to keep an eye on you to make sure you address the customers properly. I propose we have a trial of your idea in the High Street salon and if it is a success I will consider extending it to my other salons.'

'A trial? You'll consider?' Jarlath was sputtering with surprise and fury. 'I didn't agree to a mere *trial* Father. Remember, we are equal partners in this venture.'

'That's not the way I see it,' said Thomas, gently but firmly. 'And the split won't be fifty-fifty, it will be seventy-thirty. You get thirty per cent of the profits after all costs, taxes and expenses have been recovered.'

'That's outrageous, Father.'

'Is it?' Thomas quietly flattened his hands on the desk. 'I'm taking all the risks. I'm providing the premises, I'm buying the unique cabinet and the stock. What are you contributing? I have made you a very generous offer. Have I your agreement on thirty per cent after all costs have been deducted?'

Jarlath scowled. 'But I thought we were…'

'One other thing, you keep referring to "our" business when it is in fact "my" business, so please desist from doing that.'

'We haven't talked about my salary?' muttered Jarlath in the petulant voice of a child who has just been reprimanded.

'There is no salary. Is there anything else?'

Thomas was fully expecting Jarlath to leave in a huff but instead his son remained where he was, staring at the floor between his feet. 'Actually, Father, there is a family matter…'

'Yes?'

The youth shuddered. 'There is a nasty rumour circulating at my club that the reason my sisters are attending a new school is because our mother assaulted a nun.'

Thomas remained silent, stony-faced.

Jarlath stared. 'What, is it true? Good God! What a ribbing my friends will give me.'

'Is that all you can think about, what a ribbing you'll get?' Thomas shook his head sadly. 'Aren't you worried about your mother?'

Jarlath shrugged. 'Mother doesn't care about me. I haven't spoken to her in weeks. Have you?'

Thomas suppressed a rush of guilt. 'Never mind about me. She is your mother, and you should care for her.' And when Jarlath stood to leave, he added harshly, 'Do not spend a penny on the perfume project without clearing it with me. And one other thing, never come into the salon wearing those ridiculous clothes again. This is a place of work, not leisure.'

Thomas was smoking a well earned cigar in the summerhouse, soaking up the pleasant winter sun through the glass, when Alice, Ann and a new friend invaded his quiet.

'Who is your friend?' Thomas asked Alice, when Ann and the new girl left the summerhouse to pick snowdrops at the bottom of the garden.

'That's Wendy Brimcombe. Her family moved into the McNeela's old house,' Alice replied.

'Oh, the Brimcombes.' Thomas's face darkened. 'They're Protestants, aren't they?'

'I don't know.' Alice noted the negative tone in her father's voice. 'Is that bad?'

'Not bad exactly, but don't invite the girl into the house again.'

'What shall I say to her?'

'Don't say anything, just don't invite her. Actually, I'd prefer if you didn't associate with her at all.'

It was late January and after a few sunny days the city was back in the grip of freezing arctic weather. Bridie Halpin stood on the steps of the Dalton Academy of Hairdressing and stared at the frost-covered brass plate on the Georgian door. Then, adjusting the collar of the long coat she had given her mother for Christmas, she turned the handle and stepped over the threshold. There were a few older people standing around the foyer talking, but the most noise – the excited chatter of young people socialising – streamed from an open door at the end of the hall. Bridie crossed the foyer and was looking apprehensively into the crowded room when a young woman about her own age came up beside her.

'Is this the hairdressing school reception?' she asked.

'I think so,' replied Bridie cautiously.

'Goodness. I never saw so many posh people in my life. I feel like a bit of a fool in my home-made dress,' said the young woman, opening her coat.

Bridie beamed with relief; she had met a kindred spirit. 'I think your dress looks lovely!'

'Thanks. It's just something my mother ran up. I'm Kate Murtagh, I'm from Mallow, that's in Cork.'

'I'm Bridie Halpin. I'm from the Liberties, that's in Dublin.'

'I love your coat,' said Kate, rubbing the sleeve of Bridie's mother's coat. 'It feels lovely and cosy.' She lowered her voice. 'There's a short fat man over there looking at us. He looks like a villain from a melodrama with his frock coat and waxed moustache. All he needs is a top hat. Oh God, now he's looking at us. Jesus, he's coming over to us.'

'That's Mr Dalton,' whispered Bridie, but before she could explain further, Thomas was standing in front of them.

'Miss Halpin, you brought a friend?' Thomas held out his hand.

'No, she's not my friend – I mean, I just met her,' Bridie replied, shaking Thomas's hand. 'This is Kate Murtagh.'

'Ah, Miss Murtagh from Cork, I believe – welcome. I'm very pleased to meet you. Why don't you two join the other students at the registration table?'

'Mr Dalton, there you are,' cried the effervescent Lady D'Arcy of Abbywell, interrupting Thomas's conversation with Bridie and the smiling Kate. 'I have been singing your praises to Lady Nolan of Borris and she is most anxious to meet you.'

'Enjoy the proceedings,' Thomas said to Bridie and Kate as Lady D'Arcy whisked him away across the room to meet the venerable Lady Nolan.

The following Monday at nine thirty in the morning, Bridie and Kate sat in the back of the classroom in the Dalton Academy of Hairdressing and waited for the class to begin. Sitting in front of them were twenty other excited students; some were silent, some pretended to be looking for something in their handbags and a few were chatting. Thomas entered the room and the classroom fell quiet.

'Welcome to all of you,' Thomas said. 'Over the next two years you will be taught to master the skills of ladies' hairdressing. First you will learn the rudiments and the fundamentals of basic hairdressing. You will learn how to clean, brush and comb hair, and you will be taught how to apply lotions and powders. You will learn how to cut and curl and to execute simple *coiffures de ville*. In the second year you will be taught the techniques of professional conditioning, styling, layering, colouring, perming and straightening. You will learn how to pin hair and help the master hairdressers execute their creations. And you will learn that hairdressing is not work nor a job, nor even a craft – it is an art. Let us begin.'

That afternoon when Bridie and Kate arrived in High Street for their salon training, Thomas greeted them and asked an alarmed Bridie to accompany him to his office. When he opened the door an excited, shiny-eyed Alice jumped to her feet.

'Hello! You're Miss Halpin, aren't you?' cried Alice, beaming her brightest smile.

'Yea I am,' blushed Bridie.

'I've been waiting so long to meet you!' The young girl rushed over to gaze up admiringly into Bridie's face.

'Alice,' instructed Thomas, 'say what you have to say and let Miss Halpin go about her business.'

Alice swept out her hands like an opera singer about to sing and curtsied.

'Thank you, Miss Halpin, for helping me on Christmas morning. You are the bravest person I've ever met.'

Noticing that Bridie was speechless and blushing furiously with embarrassment, Thomas intervened. 'Alice you've said your piece, better run along now,'

'But I want to talk to Miss Halpin!' Alice protested.

'You can do that some other time,' said Thomas. 'Off you go.'

Alice sighed, took one last look at Bridie, waved her hand and reluctantly left the office.

That evening and most evenings after that when the salon closed for business, Alice visited Bridie. Thomas noticed the joyous way the young woman talked to the child and how she laughed at Alice's childish jokes and happily admired Alice's new dance steps. Bridie, thought Thomas, definitely had a natural rapport with children – yet he also noticed that she was very shy around adults. During the day while she was working in the salon, she only ever exchanged words with her friend Kate; she seldom spoke to other staff members and never to customers. In class, Bridie and Kate always sat in the back of the class and Bridie never asked questions.

On Wednesday morning after his morning lecture, Thomas approached the fishmonger's daughter.

'Miss Halpin, I know you are enjoying your studies but I wonder why you only ever speak to your friend Miss Murtagh?'

'I never know what to say to other people sir.'

'What do you talk to Miss Murtagh about?'

'We talk about anything and everything sir.'

'Well that's what you should talk to other students about and to customers.'

'But...'

'Miss Halpin, if you're going to be a hairdresser it's essential you talk to people.'

'I'll try better sir.'

'Oh, you'll do better than that. Next Wednesday I want you to talk to the class.'

Bridie looked horrified. 'I couldn't do that. I wouldn't know what to talk about sir!'

'That's easily remedied. I want you to tell the class about the strangest or the oddest person you ever met.'

'*What?*' In her shock, Bridie forgot to add "sir".

That evening when Alice visited the salon Bridie wasn't very talkative. She hardly spoke and busied herself cleaning combs and disinfecting scissors and other paraphernalia.

'What's the matter Bridie? Why are you not talking to me? Did I do something wrong?'

'No you did nothing wrong love,' said Bridie gently, perching on the edge of a hairdressing chair. 'Mr Dalton told me I have to talk to the class next Wednesday and its driving me demented. He said I had to talk about the strangest person I ever met.'

'That sounds fun! Who are you going to talk about?'

'I don't know any strange people.'

Alice sat looking at the ceiling, deep in thought. 'I know, what about your boyfriend? You could talk about him?' She was only suggesting this idea to find out if Bridie actually had a boyfriend, and her plan worked: Bridie laughed immoderately.

'No, I couldn't. If he heard that I talked about him he'd kill me, especially if I said he was strange, which he's not.'

'What about your grandfather – you told me he once worked in a circus? You could talk about him.'

'He wasn't strange either.'

Alice thought again and when she got her next idea she jumped out of the chair in excitement.

'I know exactly who you can talk about. Did you ever hear of a man called Johnny One Leg?'

Bridie's eyes lit up. 'Yes, he lived near us! He was strange, for sure...'

'Then tell the class about him! But tell me first.'

Bridie looked suspiciously at Alice. 'Why?'

'Because it would be good practice!'

Thomas and Jarlath sat in silence as their carriage swayed and shook its way around College Green. Thomas tried to think of something to say to his son but just before he gave voice to his thoughts he lost confidence in what he was about to say and remained silent.

'I don't know why you insisted on me being here,' complained Jarlath when the carriage stopped outside Gerard Bierne's premises in Merrion Square. 'Why did you ask Mr Bierne to locate a vitrine when I had located a perfectly good one?'

'If I had purchased that vitrine your venture would never have turned a profit.'

'It's not always about money.'

'In business, it's always about money.'

Alighting from the carriage, Thomas rang the bell and the immaculately coiffed, beautifully groomed Gerard Bierne opened the door.

'Come in!' he cried with a great flourish of his hand.

'Gerard, allow me to introduce you to my son Jarlath.'

'Delighted to meet you Jarlath. You're a handsome dog just like your father.' Gerard laughed hugely at his own joke while Jarlath looked at the man as if he was an idiot. 'Good news Thomas! I have found a superb, well-preserved vitrine in a stately home in County Wicklow. It's an original Martin French cabinet, it's in beautiful condition and it will fit in perfectly with the rest of the salon's décor... Oh, don't worry, it is well within the cost parameters you set!' Gerard handed Thomas a sheet of paper. 'Here is an etching I made of the unit.'

'It looks perfect,' said Thomas, smoothing his moustache with one finger. 'What do you think, Jarlath?'

'Whatever you think Father.' Jarlath took his pocket-watch out of his waistcoat and flipped it open. 'Would you mind if I scarpered? I was asked if I would be a second on the polo team and I simply couldn't refuse.'

'Surely you'll stay for tea?' murmured a disappointed Gerard, fiddling with his cravat.

'I'm afraid not Mr Bierne,' said Jarlath and a moment later he was gone.

Gerard Bierne was clearly annoyed. 'I abhor sports as much as sports people abhor common sense,' he remarked to Thomas, as he dispensed Earl Grey tea from his mother's finest china teapot.

Bridie Halpin's mind wandered as she sat in class listening to Thomas's description of the most common varieties of hair and the best way to cut the different types. *When is Mr Dalton going to call on me to do this bloomin' talk and what will I do if the students laugh at me? Maybe he'll forget about me. Maybe he will.* Then she heard Thomas call her name. She looked up and Mr Dalton was beckoning her to join him. Bridie broke into a cold sweat, her stomach churned and her hands were clammy. She walked up and stood in front of the class; twenty one pairs of eyes were staring at her; she looked back at them, drew a deep breath and started her talk – just the way she'd practised it over and over with Alice.

'Mr Dalton said I was to tell yous about the strangest or oddest person I ever met, so I'm going to talk to yous about Johnny One Leg. Well, he was a man and his real name was Johnny Farrell but everyone called him Johnny One Leg. You see, they called him that because he lost his right leg in the war and the army gave him a wooden one. He wasn't an old man but he was an unfortunate. He used to stand at the railings of St Patrick's Cathedral, near where I live, and shake and shout. He use to shake something awful and his wooden leg would bang off the railings and he'd shout, "Away with you, you bloody bastards" or sometimes he'd shout, "You bloody Huns". Then he'd stamp the ground with his wooden leg and wave his stick in the air. One day I saw him asleep in the park and I was surprised how young and good-looking he was. My mother said he wasn't thirty. Then one day he wasn't there, he was gone and we only knew he was dead when Mrs Lacey found his leg on the road. She said the leg was in a rubbish bin and when the corporation men came to empty the bin, the leg fell out and that's how it ended up on the road. That's the strangest man I ever met, Johnny One Leg.'

When Bridie finished speaking the students stared open-mouthed at her. Then her friend Kate Murtagh started to clap and a few seconds later everyone in the class was applauding. Bridie smiled proudly, bowed and resumed her seat.

The bedroom windows were rimmed with ice and the street outside the bedroom was quiet. It was late at night and Ann and Tess were sleeping. Alice lay in her warm bed and wondered why Father did not say a single word to Mother all through dinner and why he was sleeping in the guest bedroom nearly every night now. Father had been furious when he'd overheard Tess calling mother a 'looney'. 'Never call your mother that, it's very insulting and it's incorrect, your mother is ill, she is suffering from melancholia.' Tess had been so frightened by the anger in her father's voice that she hadn't said another word all evening.

Later, when Alice went to the drawing room and looked up 'melancholia' in the encyclopaedia, she was confused. The encyclopaedia said it was depression but when she looked up depression she learned that it was a low atmospheric pressure which produced cloudy, rainy and windy weather.

Trying to think about something more cheerful, like playing with her friends, she found herself wondering why her father had asked her not to play with Wendy Brimcombe. Were Protestants really bad people? The Protestant church that Ann and she had visited was nice. It was a bit dark and gloomy and different from a Catholic church but it still felt like a church. Wendy's mother was nice too; she always walked Wendy to dancing class and even though Wendy wasn't very good at dancing, her mother always acted like she was. Alice wondered what it would be like to have a mother like Wendy's mother: someone who would give you a hug when you felt you needed one or someone you could talk to and tell things to. Alice shook her head and decided to think about something else but before she did, sleep overcame her.

CHAPTER NINE

I t all started with a commotion. Alice, Ann and Tess were playing hopscotch in the garden when they heard a hullabaloo
on the street outside their home. The girls raced up the stairs to
their bedroom and pushed and shoved each other to get the best
position at the window. On the footpath below were three men,
a horse and cart and a big wooden crate. One of the men, a tall
flamboyantly-dressed fellow in a colourful tailored suit, was ges-
ticulating with a handkerchief and calling out instructions to the
driver of the cart.

'I knows what I'm doing,' the driver growled. 'I've been doing
this job for many a year.'

'That's exactly why I employed you my good man,' the deb-
onair gentleman declared, as he polished his monocle with his
white handkerchief. 'I'm only trying to be of help.'

'I am not "your good man" and I don't need your bleedin'
help,' snapped the driver.

'There's no need for that kind of low language,' retorted the
gentleman, shocked.

'Mr Bierne, I'm not your good man and you've getting on my wick. I'm having no more of it.' The driver turned to his assistant. 'Gem, get back on the cart; we're taking the crate back to the yard.'

'No you're not!' declared Gerard Bierne as he grabbed the horse's bridle. The horse flared its nostrils and flattened its ears, but Gerard clung to the bridle. 'I won't allow you to leave!'

'Leave the bleedin' horse alone! You'll upset the animal,' yelled the driver. 'He's like a child, if he gets upset...'

The horse shuddered and Gerard Bierne leapt back in horror as a great gush of hot yellow urine splattered off the cobblestones and sprayed his high-waisted, stylish trousers.

'Good God, I'm soaked in horse piss!' groaned Gerard, almost in tears. 'And these trousers are new!'

'I told you not to upset the animal' bellowed the driver.

Giggling and guffawing, Ann and Alice clasped their hands over their mouths while Tess collapsed on the bed in a fit of laughter.

'What's all the shouting about?' cried a clearly annoyed Jarlath, rushing out of the salon. 'You there, bring that crate inside.'

'God help me,' grumbled the driver. 'Now I have two fecking eejits telling me what to do.'

'What did you say?' demanded Jarlath.

Thomas Dalton hurried out of the salon and spoke briskly and quietly to the driver. Then he brought the miserable Gerard into the salon, leaving Jarlath alone on the kerbside.

'Go on, off with you son,' said the driver to Jarlath. 'Let a man do his work.'

Lady Agatha Gains considered herself a cultured and educated woman. She was president of Royal Dun Laoghaire Ladies' Society for the Betterment of the Poor, treasurer of the Royal Botanical Society and a member of countless other national and local philanthropic organisations. As she sat in the salon having her hair washed, set and dried, she looked to her friend Lady D'Arcy of Abbywell and said, as if she was uttering a universal truth, 'My dear, you must know Ireland doesn't have any history.'

Bridie Halpin was connecting the hot air supply to the dryer cap on Lady Agatha's head and thought this was an ideal moment to start talking to customers.

'Ah but you're wrong there Mrs,' she explained earnestly. 'Ireland has lots of history. We have the Druids, the Brehon Laws, St Patrick, the 1798 rebellion, Charles Stewart Parnell and lots more.'

The salon fell silent. Lady Agatha stared with a faintly puzzled frown into the near distance. 'I'm sorry, did someone speak?'

'Yes, it was me, I said...'

'Miss Halpin,' cried Thomas, rushing across the salon, 'Mr White needs your assistance in the storeroom, immediately!'

Bridie looked quizzically at her employer – she knew Larry White was still at the academy. Frowning, Thomas jerked his eyes in the direction of the storeroom. Still puzzled, Bridie walked away – but paused at the door, listening.

'Lady Agatha, please forgive my new trainee's youthful enthusiasm,' gushed Thomas, pretending to adjust the hairdryer.

'Thomas, you really must instruct you employee to speak only when spoken to. It's very disconcerting. And your staff shouldn't have opinions.'

'You're perfectly right, Lady Agatha, but the girl is young and has so much to learn.'

Lady Agatha's next comment plunged like a dagger into Bridie's heart, but Thomas's casual reply pushed the dagger even deeper.

'Mr Dalton, youth is no excuse, you must let her go.'

'Lady Agatha, you have a solution for every problem.'

That evening as Bridie was leaving the salon, Thomas approached her.

'You're going to sack me, aren't you?' asked Bridie glumly.

'Good heavens, no!' smiled Thomas.

'But should I give up the hairdressing?'

'Certainly not, you're one of the finest natural hairdressers I've ever known.'

Bridie's heart lifted a little. 'But Lady Agatha said...'

'Don't worry about Lady Agatha – she has a memory like a sieve. Bridie, it's wonderful that you've started to talk to customers but it might be wise to let them instigate the conversation.'

'Does that mean that I should keep my opinions to myself?'

'Let me put it this way – it is not always advisable to speak one's mind to certain people. Lady Agatha is a self-obsessed woman who is quite convinced that she is the font of all knowledge.'

'She said that Ireland...'

'Miss Halpin, our job is to dress our clients' hair, not to disillusion them or worse, educate them.'

Bridie smiled. 'Goodnight, Mr Dalton.'

Bridget Halpin pulled the salon door behind her. It was six in the evening and the street was busy with people hurrying home from work. Behind her, Alice's head popped out of her own front door and watched Bridie set off toward Christ Church Cathedral. A moment later, Alice settled her hat comfortably on her head, emerged onto the footpath and promptly collided with a perambulator.

'Why don't you look where you're going?' barked a grim-faced nanny in uniform who was pushing the pram.

'Sorry,' cried Alice, leaping out of the way.

She followed Bridie up the street, and the clacking of horse hooves and the clattering of the steel-rimmed wheels of delivery carts pounded in her ears. Bridie crossed the street. Alice tried to follow but the slow procession of carts, cabs and bicycles forced her to remain on the footpath. By the time a break occurred in the traffic, Bridie was nowhere to be seen. Dodging a bicycle, Alice dashed across to the corner of Nicholas Street and caught sight of Bridie entering a four-story, red-brick block. Alice ran to the building and peered into its dark foreboding hallway. At the other end of the hall, Bridie opened a door and bright golden sunlight flooded in. Alice ventured into the grimy interior; the smell of stale urine made her gag. Holding her nose, she walked quickly through the shadows and out into an enormous courtyard.

Most of the huge yard was given over to clothes lines flapping with wet grey bed sheets, well-worn clothes and some rags. Nearby, a group of children were skipping. They had attached a rope to a lamppost and a boy was swinging the rope in a circle while the girls leapt over it, chanting the skipping rhyme: 'Proddy woddy, ring the bell, when you die, you go to hell.'

A cheer erupted, and Alice turned to look further down the courtyard. A group of about twenty adults and children were staring up at the building, and Alice gasped when she saw a barefoot boy climbing up a drainpipe high above their heads.

'Good on you, Gerry!' shouted a hunched old man from the front of the crowd, as Alice drew near.

'Mags Ahern should be shot,' complained a rotund woman in curlers as she pulled her black shawl tight around her enormous body. 'That's the second time this month the aul one has locked herself out of her flat.'

'And poor little Gerry O'Hara has to go climbing the bloomin' drainpipe and squeeze through her kitchen window to let her in,' nodded a rake-thin woman.

'Sure, Gerry doesn't mind. Doesn't Mags give him a few coppers for his troubles?' grinned the old man.

'Gerry's a bleedin' little monkey,' laughed another.

The boy was within reach of the window ledge when two rivets tore from the wall and the upper half of the drainpipe swung away from the building. The crowd gasped as the boy clung to the swaying pipe.

'Oh Jesus, Gerry's a goner,' cried the rotund women, as she made the sign of the cross.

The boy slowly and carefully reached toward the windowsill, the tips of his fingers grazed the ledge then gripped it. He pulled himself closer, got his whole arm over the sill and climbed in. The crowd cheered and clapped and young Gerry O'Hara appeared in the window and took a bow. Alice joined in the cheering but stopped abruptly when a red-headed boy snapped the hat off her head.

'Give me that!' she demanded furiously, as she lunged at the boy and jerked the hat out of his hand.

'You don't belong here, you're posh!' accused the boy.

A shadow fell on Alice and the crowd tightened around her.

'What are you doing here?' demanded a big, rough-looking man.

'I'm looking for my friend,' Alice replied defiantly, looking up at the big man.

'The likes of you doesn't have friends here,' declared the rotund woman, staring at Alice as if she was an exotic animal in a zoo.

'Yes I do,' insisted Alice.

'Who's your friend then?'

'Me – she knows me!' cried Bridie Halpin pushing her way through the crowd. 'Leave the child alone!'

'Ah, the fancy hairdresser girl,' jeered the rake-thin woman.

Bridie took Alice by the hand and led her away through the crowd.

'That boy took my hat,' whispered Alice.

'You're lucky that's all he took,' said Bridie sternly.

Alice was trotting up the stairs from the kitchen when she heard Bridie's voice in the garden. Intrigued, she stopped and peered out of the small side window that opened onto the garden. Bridie and Terrance were just outside, deep in conversation. As Alice watched, Bridie took a buff-coloured envelope out of the pocket of her smock and handed it to Terrance, who nodded and disappeared into the house by the back door. As Alice continued on up the kitchen stairs, she could hear her brother racing up to his bedroom.

'Hello, Miss Halpin,' said Alice as Bridie re-entered the house after Terrance.

'Oh!' Bridie looked startled. 'I didn't see you there Alice.'

'Is Terrance your boyfriend?' Alice asked with a cheeky smile.

'Good Lord, why would think that?'

'When you gave him that letter you looked at him like you really liked him.'

Bridie was clearly horrified. 'Now listen to me, Miss Alice – firstly, Terrance is not my boyfriend and secondly, I didn't give him any letter.'

'But I...'

The shriek of a police whistle and the clattering of boots on the pavement outside the house interrupted their conversation. Bridie tensed, her eyes on the hall door. A policeman shouted and the boots grew closer; Bridie blessed herself. The boots clattered past, the whistle sounded in the distance, and the girl relaxed.

'What's the matter, Bridie?' whispered Alice, scared and excited. "Why were you so upset?'

'Nothing's the matter, I'm not upset. And remember, there was no letter and don't ever tell anyone there was.'

'Why am I not to tell anyone?'

'Because it's a secret.'

'I don't like secrets, friends don't have secrets.'

'Sometimes they do. I didn't tell anyone that you followed me home, did I?'

'Well...'

'So you see, friends do have secrets. You will keep ours, won't you?'

Alice forced a smile. Bridie plunged her hands into the pockets of her smock and as she walked away, Alice noticed the young trainee was trembling slightly.

Alice climbed the stairs and stopped on the landing outside Terrance's room. Through the half-open door, she saw her brother wrap a revolver in an oil-stained cloth and place it in his leather bag. Shoving open the door, she marched into the bedroom. 'Is that a real gun you just put in your bag?'

A startled Terrance turned towards her. 'Don't be silly. Where would I get a gun?'

Stepping around him, Alice put her hand on the bag but Terrance placed his hand on top of hers.

'Let me look,' said Alice, trying to open the bag.

'No. Alice, I'm in a hurry, someone is waiting on me. I want you to go to your room and forget what you thought you saw.'

'What was in the letter Miss Halpin gave you? She said it was some sort of a secret.'

'Yes, it is a secret. Now please go and let me do what I have to do.'

Reluctantly, Alice left him and went to her room. A few minutes later, she heard her brother hurry down the stairs and when she looked out her window she saw him close the front door behind him, jump on his bicycle and set off down the street. Leaving the window, she lay face down on her bed, worrying. She didn't understand what was going on; she just knew it was something terribly wrong.

John Swords and Thomas Dalton sat in Bewley's Oriental Café and ordered coffee. John flicked a glance towards a man sitting on his own in the rear of the café and said softly, 'I know that man. He's a Castle man. He followed you into the café just now.'

'So?' asked Thomas guardedly.

John lit a cigarette and inhaled deeply. 'I heard of a compositor who printed some illegal pamphlets for the Shinners. The men from the Castle arrested him and smashed the man's fingers so badly he never composited another word, let alone a pamphlet.'

'Why are you telling me this?'

'Thomas, don't pretend you don't know. Your Terrance is active with the IRB.'

'Ah.'

'You need to take this seriously, Thomas.' A jet of smoke shot from John's nose. 'You and your son are under constant surveillance. Thomas, the men from the Castle are not to be trifled with.'

Thomas sighed. 'I am not trifling with anyone. For the life of me, I do not know why Terrance has so little respect for the lawful authorities. Frankly, it's embarrassing.'

John leaned forward and spoke very softly. 'Terrance is a Republican and he views the lawful authorities, as you put it, to be unlawful. He doesn't understand why Irishmen and Irish women can't be the masters of their own destiny in their own country. He doesn't understand why the British authorities spy on us or why they make laws to kill our Irish culture, heritage and language. Need I say more?'

'Good Lord, John. Don't tell me you're a Republican too?'

'No, I'm an Irishman and like you I'm a father.' John glanced over Thomas's shoulder. 'We should leave. The man from the Castle has moved closer to us.'

All day Alice worried about having to keep Bridie's and Terrance's secret. At the end of the day, she pushed open the salon door. Bridie's coat was hanging on the rack so she knew her friend was still on the premises. To avoid inhaling the astringent chemicals used to perm and colour hair, she took a deep breath and held her nose as she strolled into the salon. Plopping herself onto the high-backed chair in one of the cubicles, she admired herself in the ornate mirrors.

'I'll have a perm and make sure the waves are even,' she said to an imaginary hairstylist. Then, in the mirror, she saw the vitrine's door was ajar and she jumped down to go and look. There were lots of pretty bottle filled with different coloured perfumes. She was about to open a pink bottle when Jarlath swanned into the salon.

'What do you think you're doing?' he barked and snatched the bottle from Alice's hand. 'Never go near the vitrine again. Now get out of here.' He was replacing the perfume bottle in the cabinet when Bridie and Kate walked into the salon. 'Ah girls, good timing, I want you two to clean and polish the vitrine.'

'Mr Dalton said we could go home after we tidied up the stockroom,' said Kate.

'And I'm telling you to clean the vitrine. If you don't, you won't have a job tomorrow.'

'They don't have "jobs",' said Thomas, appearing in the salon behind the crestfallen young women. 'They are trainees and they are here to learn their craft. Girls, go home.'

Bridie hastily pulled on her overcoat, Kate threw her scarf around her neck and grabbed her coat and the two young women scurried out of the salon.

'Never again tell a trainee to do your work,' Thomas scolded Jarlath, unable to keep the annoyance out of his voice.

'I was just looking for a little help,' sulked Jarlath. 'I'm very busy.'

'You were not looking for help, you wanted someone to do your work. Last week you only spent three days in the salon and this week, two days.'

'This is Spring Show week, Father,' Jarlath explained, unable to comprehend his father's annoyance.

'Yes, and that makes it one of our busiest weeks. You have missed wonderful opportunities to sell your perfumes. If you continue to run your business in such a cavalier manner, you won't have a business for very long.'

Alice, who had retreated to the cubicle, was surprised and shaken by the anger in her father's voice.

That night Alice lay awake and wondered what was in the letter Bridie had given to Terrance and why her friend had asked her to keep it a secret. She decided that they were in love and didn't want anyone to know about it. *Maybe they're going to elope,* she thought, and a big smile lit up her face. Then she remembered the look of fear in Bridie's eyes when she'd thought the police were going to knock on the door, and she felt sad again. Why did Terrance have a gun and what was he going to do with it? Alice stared at the moving shadows on the ceiling and tried to empty her head. *Why doesn't father like Jarlath? I know he can sometimes be awful, like he was when he grabbed the perfume from my hand. He's not as nice or as handsome as Terrance but sometimes he can be all right.* Then she wondered why her mother was sick so often and why she felt something burning in her stomach whenever she spoke to her mother. She was thinking about the boy who climbed the drainpipes and how the people in the courtyard had turned nasty to her, when she fell asleep.

CHAPTER TEN

A cold metallic moon was shining its blue light on the city as Terrance Dalton cycled over a strangely deserted Baggot Street Bridge. A gunshot rang out. Terrance's bicycle skidded from under him as he fell to the ground. Seconds later two British soldiers were standing over him pointing their Enfield rifles at his head.

'Hands on head and get to your feet slowly,' ordered one of the soldiers.

Terrance rose and a young bespectacled soldier handcuffed him. A dark green military lorry thundered over the bridge and stopped. Terrance was bundled into the back of the lorry and driven at speed to Great Brunswick Street Police Station. The desk sergeant, Sergeant Kelly of the Dublin Metropolitan Police – a huge man with a pugnacious face and a gruff manner, glared at Terrance, while a pock-marked younger policeman removed the handcuffs. Terrance's arms were forced upwards while the young policeman ran his hands down each of Terrance's legs. He examined Terrance's tie and the inside collar of his jacket and ordered him to remove his shoes and socks.

'No weapons, sir,' the policeman said, when he had finished his inspection.

Sergeant Kelly fixed his unnerving dark eyes on Terrance and tapped the counter with a wooden ruler. 'Your bag smells of gun oil.'

'No sir, that's bicycle oil.'

'Is it now?' asked the desk sergeant sarcastically. 'And what were you doing on Baggot Street Bridge?'

'Falling off my bicycle, sir.'

'Oh, we have a comedian here.' The sergeant struck Terrance across the face with the edge of wooden ruler. 'What were you doing in Baggot Street?'

Terrance flinched but answered coolly, 'I was on my way home from visiting a friend.'

'What's your friend's name and address?'

'Jim Mooney and he lives at 8 Lower Baggot Street.'

'I'm going to check on your Mr Mooney and if he doesn't back up your story, you're in trouble. In the meantime, consider yourself a guest of His Majesty.'

Terrance was thrown into a nine foot by four foot damp, windowless cell. There was no chair or bed, so he sat on the floor with his back against the wall and waited. Four hours later, the cell door clanked open and the Sergeant Kelly growled, 'You can go. But I know you were up to something. I'll be keeping an eye on you.'

'What about my bicycle?' Terrance asked.

'If you're lucky it's still on the bridge,' the younger policeman said, and threw Terrance's bag at him. 'Now get out of here before the sergeant changes his mind.'

Terrance was unlucky; when he got to the bridge his bicycle was gone.

Nanny Mary closed the bedroom curtains, Alice gathered her drawings and paintings and stowed them in a box under her bed while Ann removed her glasses and carefully placed them in a case on her bedside table. Then Alice and Ann knelt by their

and plumed horses. After that, there was a break in the traffic and Nanny and the girls, carefully avoiding the many mounds of horse droppings, crossed the street. They were peering into the windows of Brown Thomas's department store, when Alice saw Terrance walking up the street towards her with two other men. She waited eagerly, but before the three men reached the store, they turned aside down a narrow lane.

Alice ran to the corner of the alley and called to her brother. He seemed not to hear her, so she followed him down the shadowy, litter-strewn laneway. Close to the end, a door opened and Terrance and his companions stepped in. Alice ran and pounded on the now-locked door.

'Terrance! It's Alice!'

Footsteps came up behind her and she turned with a gasp. A long-haired, unshaven, dark-faced man was shuffling towards her; he smelt of beer and stale sweat and his face was dirty and his lips cracked and broken. A pigeon diving for a bread crust fluttered its wings in Alice's face, she swung her arms wildly, screamed and two large hands grabbed her from behind.

'Jacko, you're frightening the girl,' said Terrance, as he leaned over Alice's head to press a coin into the old man's hand.

'Jacko wouldn't frighten anyone,' said the man, his tired eyes filled with confusion. 'Jacko likes children.'

'Jacko, go and get yourself a cup of tea,' said Terrance, still holding Alice's shoulders with his big hands.

Shaking his head and muttering to himself, Jacko shuffled away down the lane.

'Are you all right?' asked Terrance, bending down and looking into Alice's small, frightened face.

'I think so. I didn't like that man.' With her fingers, she dabbed a tear from the edge of her eye. 'You didn't come home last night. Are you coming home tonight?'

'No, I'm not and I won't be home for a long time. How did you ever find me?'

'We were out shopping with Nanny and I saw you.'

Terrance escorted Alice to the top of the lane and checked up and down Grafton Street. 'They're looking in the window of Brown Thomas's. Run back to them before they notice you're gone,' he said.

'But I want to talk to you.'

'Alice, I'm sorry, but I don't have time to talk. The police are searching for me.'

'Oh...' Alice blinked up at her brother.

Terrance touched her cheek. 'Don't worry, Alice. But don't tell anyone you saw me – not even Nanny.'

Nanny and the children were still engrossed in their window shopping when Alice rejoined them, and when she looked back to wave to Terrance he was gone.

Thomas was intrigued when Ashley Pringle, the vice president of the Hibernian Club asked him to join him for a drink, not in the club's bar but in the nearby Shelbourne Hotel's Horseshoe Bar.

However, his heart sank when – after two short minutes of what Ashley clearly considered sufficient small talk – the vice president turned the conversation to Terrance.

'I thought it better to have this discussion away from the club, Thomas, because many of our members are disturbed by the reports circulating about your son.'

Thomas looked the man straight in the eye. 'The "reports" as you call them, Ashley, are idle gossip and I am not going to give them credence by commenting on them.'

'I understand,' said Ashley – although he was clearly put out that Thomas wouldn't confide in him. 'Still, it might be good to clear the air?'

'There is no air to clear. Let's change the subject. Have you heard about the latest hair fashion sweeping Paris?'

'What?' Ashley was now not just hurt but also quite confused.

'It's very interesting. Men who are going to war, present their lady love with a small strand of their hair and the lady has it artistically preserved inside a medallion.'

Ashley shuddered. 'Why would anyone do such a gross thing?'

'It is said to bring good luck. I have a chap coming from London to demonstrate to my staff how to prepare and preserve hair from the ravages of time and mites.'

'Ravages of time and mites?' repeated Ashley, bewildered.

'Have to keep abreast of the times,' said Thomas and sipped his drink.

Ashley did not enjoy the time he spent with Thomas Dalton. He had never approved of Catholics joining the club. He had voted against Thomas's application and after the conversation he'd just had, he was more than ever convinced that he had done the right thing. But how was he going to explain to the club's board members that he had spent an afternoon with Thomas yet had been unable to ascertain whether the hairdresser shared his son's Republican views?

Thomas strolled into the Royal Hibernian Hotel; he was there to give a talk to members of the Irish Association of Professional Hairdressers. When he entered the ballroom, two detectives followed him and positioned themselves at the back.

'I see you have brought your friends,' John Swords murmured, joining Thomas as he made his way through the room.

Thomas smiled brightly. 'It seems the Castle is very interested in ladies' hair fashion.'

'Very amusing. Did you talk to Terrance?'

'No, he hasn't been home.'

'How long do the detectives usually stay?'

'They leave when I leave and they follow me home. There's usually a couple more of them waiting for me there, ready to take over.'

'Quite a following you have.'

'Well I hope they enjoy my talk on new trends in Parisian hairstyles,' said Thomas, as they reached the front of the room.

After his talk, the two detectives dutifully followed Thomas home and for the next few weeks they and others dogged, shadowed and tagged him wherever he went. Every morning a detailed record of every place the hairdresser visited and every person he spoke to was lodged in the records office of Dublin Castle.

A few days later, Alice and Ann were sitting on the stairs waiting for Nanny to bring them to dance class when a loud knocking echoed through the hall. A clearly annoyed Mrs O'Donnell answered the door and an unusually dishevelled John Swords dashed past her into the drawing room. A moment later, Tess came out of the drawing room and closed the door behind her.

'Tess, what's happening?' hissed Alice. But Tess put her finger to her lips and remained standing outside the door, listening with her ear to the crack.

'Terrance has been arrested,' Tess could hear John Swords saying breathlessly. 'There's talk they plan to charge him with murder.'

'Tell me everything you know!' cried her father in alarm.

'Terrance was arrested in McGlone's pub in Capel Street this morning. Apparently there was a killing. He was taken to Dublin Castle.'

'Oh good God. John, will you come with me to the Castle?'

'I will but I can tell you, they won't let us see him.'

'I have to try.'

Tess leapt aside as her father rushed out into the hall and grabbed his coat, hat and cane. John followed, jamming his hat onto his bald head and seconds later, the two men were marching down High Street towards Dublin Castle.

'Terrance is in jail in the Castle and Father and Uncle John are on their way to see him now,' Tess told Alice and Ann, after the three of them had retreated to their bedroom.

'The Castle's a terrible place,' sobbed Alice.

'Do you think they'll put us all in jail?' wondered Ann.

When Thomas returned home and told his wife that their son was incarcerated in Dublin Castle, Mariah's eyes rolled up in her head and she fainted.

CHAPTER ELEVEN

The fat solicitor leaned back in his chair, fondling his wide lapels with sweaty fingers. 'Mr Dalton, your son is now in the custody of the Metropolitan Police. I have requested that he be released immediately but they have refused to do so.'

'Good God.' Thomas stared at Paddy Williamson across the file-strewn desk. 'Then what is to be done?'

'The law moves slowly in these matters Mr Dalton. We simply have to be patient. All I can tell you with certainty is that your son can be held for up to seventy two hours and then the authorities must either release him or bring him before a magistrate to be charged with an offence. If the latter, I will immediately file for bail.'

Thomas Dalton tugged at the ends of his moustache, his eyes on the file-strewn desk. 'Do we even know what is supposed to have happened?'

The lawyer sighed, taking a yellowing handkerchief from his pocket and wiping his gleaming brow. 'Not officially. But reliable sources inform me that yesterday morning a man was shot and killed in McGlone's Public House in Capel Street. The man was an informer, although it is not known if he was working for the Castle, the police or the military.'

'What has that to do with my son?'

'Terrance was present in the public house at the time of the killing. He did not fire the weapon but he is suspected of supplying it. Mr Dalton, you have to understand that your son could be charged with murder or accessory to murder.'

Thomas gripped the arms of his chair so tightly his knuckles went white. 'What evidence do they have to justify such a charge?'

'You were not listening to me, Mr Dalton. Your son has not been charged with anything. He has merely been arrested. If he is charged with an offence, the prosecution's evidence will be disclosed at the committal proceedings and not before then.'

'My son is innocent!' protested the desperate father. 'At the very worst, he was duped into doing something foolish!'

A shadow crossed the solicitor's moon-shaped face and his voice became suddenly officious. 'That is your opinion, Mr Dalton. However, the law must deal in facts, provable facts. As I said, we simply have to be patient.'

Thomas called his other children into the drawing room and explained the situation to them as optimistically as he could, ending on the reassuring thought that it was all no doubt a matter of mistaken identity.

His children weren't reassured and each in their own way tried to comprehend what was happening.

Jarlath expressed the view that Terrance was a Republican and a bloody fool. Ann announced tearfully that if Terrance had killed anyone, it must have been an accident. Tess was bubbly; she clearly thought it was all very exciting. Alice stayed silent; she remembered how upset Terrance had been when he read the letter that

Bridie had given him and how frightened she'd felt when she'd seen the gun in his bag.

The committal proceeding was heard in court three of the Four Courts and took less than two minutes. Wearing his smartest uniform, Sergeant Kelly of Great Brunswick Street Police Station stood in front of the presiding magistrate and said, 'The plaintiff Terrance Dalton is a person known to the police, and the Crown has a prima facie case against him and asks that he be indicted on two charges – murder and accessory to murder.'

Terrance grabbed the edge of the dock as his knees buckled under him. Watching his son, Thomas felt a cold hand grab his heart.

'How do you plea?' asked the magistrate, matter-of-factly.

'Not guilty,' stammered Terrance.

'Very well,' said the magistrate. 'I commit you for trial in four weeks.'

The obese Paddy Williamson struggled to his feet. 'Your honour, my client is a man of good reputation. Contrary to that which Sergeant Kelly has inferred, my client has no criminal record and has never previously appeared before a court. I respectfully request that bail be granted.'

The magistrate looked to Sergeant Kelly, who shook his head.

'Bail denied.' And without returning his gaze to the perspiring solicitor, the magistrate pounded his gavel and barked, 'Next case!'

In stunned disbelief, Thomas watched his handcuffed son being led away into the bowels of the court building. Paddy Williamson waddled across the courtroom and sat beside him. 'I'm sorry, Mr Dalton. It is very hard to achieve bail in these circumstances. Now, I don't want to intrude on your moment of private grief, but there are matters to attend to.'

'Matters?' Thomas was still in a state of shock.

'Terrance will need a barrister to represent him in court. Might I suggest Mr Leslie Laurence? He specialises in this area of law.'

'Whatever you think, Mr Williamson.'

'Another thing – the less savoury part of this business. This case will attract a considerable amount of interest so you will need to prepare your family. They should not talk about the case to anyone, and especially not to journalists. Newspapers can be quite nasty.'

A weary Thomas left the court building. As he beckoned a hansom cab, he saw two policemen usher Terrance into a waiting Black Maria and drive him off in the direction of Mountjoy Prison.

That evening, Thomas gathered his entire family together and told them Terrance was in Mountjoy and his trial would commence in four weeks. He ended his little speech by emphasising that they must not talk to anyone about Terrance or the trial.

Mariah collapsed in tears and Mrs O'Donnell ushered her away, up to her bedroom.

'How did Terrance look?' asked Alice, breaking the sad silence.

'He looked extremely worried,' said Thomas. But then, seeing the panic in his youngest daughter's eyes, he added more gently, 'They seem to be treating him well. And they'll soon let him go when they find out he's innocent.'

'If he is innocent,' said Jarlath, off-handedly. Thomas scowled at him and he added quickly, 'Which I believe he is, so yes of course he'll be set free.'

The family gathering broke up and as they were leaving the room, Tess whispered to Jarlath, 'I don't believe any of this. I think there is something Father hasn't told us.'

Thomas remained alone in the drawing room, deep in thought. A few minutes later, his oldest son returned and asked if he could have a word. When Thomas nodded Jarlath paced the room, readying himself to speak. Finally, he threw himself into a chair opposite his father.

'Father, it's time that the perfume concession be extended to all salons. I am prepared to take full control of this venture and for that I would like to be made a junior partner in the Dalton business.'

Thomas raised his head from his hands. 'This is not the time to be talking about business, Jarlath.'

'Father, you always said business comes first.'

'For God's sake, your brother is in jail awaiting trial.'

'Father, when I agreed to the test period for my venture, it was with the understanding that you would give me a decision in four weeks. It is now six weeks. When are you going to extend the perfume concession to the other salons?'

Trying to control his annoyance, Thomas pressed his palms together as if in prayer. 'Never. The answer is never. The venture was not a success. I'm closing it down.'

A stunned Jarlath stared at his father. 'That's outrageous, the money has poured in!'

'Jarlath, you have little understanding of business. Money did not "pour in". The venture did not generate enough cash to even cover the cost of the perfume stock. If you had looked after your project, if you had been in attendance more often, perhaps the result might have been different. I have cancelled all further perfume purchases and I intend to put the vitrine in storage. Now please leave me, I have much to consider.'

Jarlath went red with rage. 'You mean, you want to think about Terrance, don't you? It's always about him or Alice! It's never about me or how I feel! I'm your eldest son and you treat me like I don't exist!'

'Jarlath, this is a very trying time. This dreadful publicity is already damaging the business, salon visits have declined by nearly fifty per cent – and who knows what will happen after the trial?'

Jarlath jumped to his feet and, on leaving the drawing room, slammed the door.

Bridie Halpin was about to leave for home when Alice rushed into the salon. 'Miss Halpin, what was in that letter you gave Terrance?'

'I thought that was our secret,' gasped Bridie, glancing furtively around the salon.

'I told you I don't like secrets!'

'Alice, keep your voice down. Even talking about that letter could get Terrance in a lot of trouble.'

'Terrance is already in a lot of trouble.' Alice's face was pale with concern. 'Did he kill someone?'

'No, of course he didn't kill anyone.'

'Then why is he in prison?'

Bridie looked away. 'I don't know.'

'Terrance had a gun, I saw it in his bag.'

'Stop, don't tell me anymore. Alice, you need to remember your brother is a good man and you need to trust him.'

'I do trust him but he's all alone in prison and people are saying awful things about him.'

Thomas stood at the main entrance to Mountjoy Prison, an enormous barrier of grey metal; he pulled on the bell chain. After an endless few minutes he heard the jangle of keys; a lock clunked open and a portal in the entrance opened. Thomas stepped through the portal and the warden locked it behind him and escorted him to a wall of iron bars which rose from floor to the ceiling. He signed a register and the warden opened a small gateway in the wall of bars. Thomas stepped through the opening and this procedure was repeated again and then again. When Thomas finally saw Terrance he was taken aback. His son had lost weight, his skin was sallow and he looked like he hadn't slept in days.

'Hello Father,' Terrance said softly. 'Thank you for coming.'

Before Thomas's next visit to Mountjoy Prison, he asked his eldest son to accompany him.

Jarlath refused. 'I simply can't, Father. If I went with you it could be interpreted as my sharing Terrance's Republican views. I could lose my place on the polo team.'

'But Terrance is your brother. He would benefit greatly from a visit from another family member.'

'Really? Then why not take Alice?' asked Jarlath coolly.

Terrance's detention and forthcoming trial affected everyone in the Dalton household differently. The girls were constantly upset by their brother's plight, Jarlath seemed unconcerned. Mariah's depression deepened and Mrs O'Donnell grew more protective of her. Thomas's acquaintances avoided him and many of their wives stopped attending his salons. At his club, disapproving eyes stared at him and all casual conversation ceased when he entered the room. Thomas took to spending his evenings at home and his only visitor was John Swords.

One week before the trial, Thomas was abruptly summoned to the smoke-filled chambers of barrister-at-law, Leslie Lawrence. Wearing a finely-tailored suit that hung neatly on his thin frame, Mr Lawrence stood up and extinguished a cigarette in the already overflowing ashtray on his desk.

'Mr Dalton! How good of you to come at such short notice.' His voice was hoarse. 'The empanelling of the jury will happen next week. It is the most crucial part of the trial and it will take at least two days with dozens of persons summoned. The crown barristers will of course try to jury pack.'

'Jury pack?'

The barrister's head jutted forward on his long thin neck. 'It means the Crown will try to ensure the jurors chosen are sympathetic to the Crown and thus more likely to convict the accused.'

'Does fairness not count?' protested Thomas.

'We're not talking about fairness, we're talking about the law. To minimise the Crown's attempt to jury pack I would like to interview many people. It will take time to achieve a balanced jury.'

'Do as you must,' said Thomas resignedly.

'Mr Dalton, time is expensive,' coughed the barrister, drawing deeply on yet another cigarette.

The following day, Thomas made arrangements to sell two of his properties in Rialto.

The trial lasted six slow days and the sixth day, the day of sentencing, was the longest day in Alice's life. It began with rain beating hard against her bedroom window. When she awoke her first thoughts were of Terrance. Was he cold? Was he frightened? Everyone in the Dalton household was unusually quiet; even the usually talkative Tess said little. On her way to her bedroom to fetch her school bag, Alice decided to visit her mother. She knocked gently on the dark wooden door and entered. Her mother was sitting up in bed watching the rain clatter against the window.

'Hello Mother,' Alice said.

'Who's that?'

'It's Alice. I came to see how you are?'

'I am as well as can be expected. Terrance is to be sentenced today, isn't he?' Mariah spoke as if in a trance. 'He was always such a trouble that boy, such a trouble.'

'Poor Mother...'

Mariah's eyes slowly focused on Alice. 'Your father always had a soft spot for you. I wonder why? You're not even pretty.'

Alice's tummy cramped and bile gathered in the back of her throat.

'Alice, will you hurry up!' called Nanny Mary up the stairs. 'We'll be late for school!'

'Goodbye Mother,' Alice said, as a tear leaked from her eye.

After school, Nanny and the children visited Whitefriar Street Church. Kneeling in a pew in front of the high altar, Nanny handed each of the girls a half-penny. Each girl rose and put her half-penny in the donation slot in the candle stand and took a three-inch yellow wax taper. Lighting the wicks, they wedged the smoking candles into holders on the top of the stand. Then, heads bowed, they returned to their pew and pleaded with God not to send their brother to prison today.

When they got home, loud voices were coming from the drawing room.

'Five years! Five years and all the evidence they presented was the unreliable word of an informer!' Thomas's voice was shaking with anger.

'Jesus, Mary and Joseph,' Mariah was wailing. 'My son in prison, I can't bear to think of it!'

Alice's heart nearly stopped and Ann and Tess burst into tears. Nanny gently pulled the drawing room door closed and ushered the sobbing girls upstairs. In a strange void of numbness, the children played but they were unable to enjoy their games and they fought and eventually had to be separated.

That night a howling wind rattled the window of Alice's bedroom so loudly that it woke her. She lay in her bed and listened to the wailing wind and the sounds of the sleeping house. She listened to the ticking of the clock and gurgling of the water pipes. She listened to the creaking of the floorboards and the swishing of the lace curtains as they billowed in the breeze. When she could stand it no longer, she got up and closed the window. She was returning to her bed when she heard a faint moaning and the eerie patter of shoeless feet scurrying down the stairs.

'Who's that?' whispered Ann in the dark.

'You're awake! Did you hear it too?' Alice got into Ann's bed for warmth, but after much excited talk they both got out and crept onto the stairs. Their mother's bedroom door was open and when they looked in, her bed was empty. A gush of cold air surged through the house; the girls peered over the banister; the front door was wide open.

Rain beat steadily into Mariah's face as she stumbled barefoot down High Street. Her wet hair flapped wildly about her face, her dressing gown was open wide and her light white nightgown fluttered in the gale. Frightened and confused, she stared around her as she stumbled on.

It was midnight and Judy and Stuart Brimcombe were returning home from the Lord Mayor's Ball. As their hansom cab trundled up High Street, Judy Brimcombe saw the disoriented Mariah stumbling down the street. The Brimcombes stopped the cab and Judy got out and talked to Mariah. After a few minutes of muddled conversation, Judy convinced the fretful Mariah to allow them to take her home.

Thomas was standing helplessly out on his front steps, wondering which direction his wife had taken, when a cab drew up and Stuart Brimcombe leaned out of the window.

'Mr Dalton, your wife is here with us!'

'Oh, thank God!' cried the hairdresser with relief. 'Thank you so very much sir!'

'I'm here! I'm coming!' Mrs O'Donnell rushed to help Mariah out of the cab.

'Eunice, where am I?' a perplexed Mariah asked, taking her hand.

'You're home, Mariah,' sighed Mrs O'Donnell, as she helped her mistress into the house.

'Thank you so very much sir,' Thomas said to Stuart. 'I don't know who you are but I am forever in your debt.'

'Think nothing of it. My name is Stuart Brimcombe and this is my wife Judy. I believe your daughter Alice is friends with our Wendy.'

'Of course, little Wendy,' Thomas said, remembering his dismissive comment to Alice about Protestants.

'Goodnight, Mr Dalton and I hope your wife will be feeling better in the morning,' Judy Brimcombe called as the cab pulled away.

The following morning, after Dr Veale had finished examining Mariah, he took Thomas aside.

'Your wife's melancholia is deepening. Medicine will help but what she really needs is professional care in a hospital which specialises in problems like hers.'

'You're saying I should commit my wife to a mental asylum. That is out of the question,' snapped Thomas. Then he softened. 'I'm sorry to be so brusque, Doctor, but it's been a very trying few weeks.'

'I understand.' The doctor handed Mrs O'Donnell a written prescription. 'One spoonful, three times a day, I will return in a few days and see how she is progressing.'

Mrs O'Donnell held out a spoonful of thick yellow medicine and Mariah shook her head like a child.

'The doctor said it will calm you and help you sleep,' encouraged Mrs O'Donnell.

'It doesn't calm me and it doesn't help me sleep. It makes me see things.'

'Mrs Dalton, this is a new medicine. I'll sit here until you fall asleep.'

Mariah eventually took the medicine. The housekeeper placed the spoon and the small green medicine bottle on the bedside table, then took her mistress's hand and sat with her until she fell asleep. An hour later, Mariah's eyes blinked open. She lay in the dark and waited. Her breathing deepened and her heart thumped against her ribcage. A creature formed in the blackness and then leapt into her body.

The following morning, Alice was in the kitchen and overheard Mrs O'Donnell tell Mrs Foley that Mariah didn't like her new medicine. *That's why Mother was in such a bad mood, that's why she was so awful to me – it was the medicine,* Alice comforted herself, and she left the kitchen and ran up the stairs.

'You're not thinking of disturbing your mother, are you?' asked Mrs O'Donnell, following her.

'Yes I am!' Alice declared defiantly. 'She's *my* mother.'

'*Your* mother needs rest.' Mrs O'Donnell blocked Mariah's bedroom door. Alice waited for a moment but when she realised the housekeeper wasn't going to move, she gave up and carried on up the stairs to her own room. She was packing her school bag when she heard Mrs Foley call Mrs O'Donnell down the stairs. Alice grabbed her bag and raced back to her mother's bedroom. She turned the doorknob and crept in. The room was dark except for the light that glowed around the edges of the thick curtains. A bilious odour made Alice gag and in the half-light she saw a pale form sprawled over the edge of the bed. She crept closer. It was her mother – her back arched, her head and shoulders nearly on the floor, her face white, eyes blank and her lips covered in yellow foam. A scream erupted from Alice's throat and seconds later Mrs O'Donnell was in the room.

'I didn't do anything!' wept Alice. 'I didn't do anything!'

'Quiet, child,' hissed Mrs O'Donnell as she attempted to lift Mariah back into the bed. When she realized she needed help she rushed back out onto the landing and called down the stairs.

In a whirl of movement, Thomas, Nanny Mary and Mrs Foley raced up the stairs. Mary ushered Alice out of the room and Mrs Foley helped Mrs O'Donnell lift Mariah back into bed.

Thomas placed his ear to his wife's mouth. 'She still breathing, I'll fetch the doctor!' He raced back downstairs.

An hour later, the house was calm again. Mrs Foley was cooking in the kitchen and the children were in school. Mariah was sleeping deeply and Mrs O'Donnell, Thomas Dalton and Dr Veale were gathered at her bedside.

'She consumed all the medicine in the bottle,' the doctor said. 'She will be uncomfortable for a while, her stomach will be upset, but there's no long-term damage.' He turned to Thomas, his face very serious. 'What your wife did was deliberate and dangerous, and for her own protection she must be institutionalised.'

'If I do that my wife will never forgive me,' sighed Thomas, gazing into Mariah's pale sleeping face. 'But if it will help her, I'll sign the papers.'

PART 2

Ten years later

CHAPTER TWELVE

The Crossley motor-taxi lumbered into Primrose Street and the children playing on the road screamed and shouted as they ran for the safety of the footpaths. Not many automobiles visited Primrose Street and on this airy spring day the Crossley motor was the only automobile in the entire neighbourhood. Leaving a trail of blue silvery smoke, the huge motor turned into a slightly wider street, motored along the row of yellow-bricked terraced houses and stopped.

'Are you sure we're at the correct address?' Ann asked the driver. 'It's a very small house.'

'The address you gave me was 5 Primrose Avenue' stated the heavy-set taxi driver as he pointed to the green door with a brass number '5' screwed to it. 'This is Primrose Avenue and that, if I am not mistaken, is Number 5.'

'Well then, this is where we want to be,' Alice said and handed the taxi driver the fare.

Alice, Tessa and Ann stepped out of the vehicle and were startled to find themselves surrounded by a group of children, who had followed the vehicle down the avenue.

'We seem to be a bit of a novelty,' said Alice, amused.

'Hooligans,' muttered Tess.

'I do wish Braiden had come with us. I'd feel a lot safer,' whispered Ann.

'Oh for goodness sake, they're only children and they're curious,' smiled Alice, and she lifted the brass knocker on the door of Number 5, and let it drop.

The door swung open and a dishevelled young man in a collarless shirt and corduroy trousers looked at the three refined, well-dressed young women and smiled doubtfully. 'Well, well, who have we here? Are you proselytizing or are you lost?'

'Mr Gilbert?' asked Alice, ignoring the young man's smart remark.

'That's me.'

'We'd like to talk to you.'

The young man shifted his weight from one foot to another, thrust his hands into his trouser pockets and leaned against the door frame. 'Fire away.'

'In private,' said Alice, glancing at the children gathered around her and her sisters.

'Have you nothing better to do then to be gawking at people?' The young man said as he stepped out of the house and shooed the children away.

'Who are they and what do they want?' demanded a small boy with a squeaky voice.

'None of your business, Jamie Nolan – go home!'

After the children reluctantly dispersed the young man turned back to Alice. 'Now, what can I do for you, ladies?'

'We are still standing on a public street, Mr Gilbert. Do you think we could have a little more privacy?'

The young man raised his eyebrows. 'Very well, we can talk in the parlour.' And he pointed to a door halfway down the hall.

The parlour was small and smelt of stale tobacco smoke. A red, two-seater settee and a small coffee table were placed along one wall. To the left of the street window was an armchair and – taking up another wall – was an upright piano. The sisters stood and the young man opened the window.

'It's a bit stuffy in here, we had a card game last night. Sit down, please.'

Alice and Ann perched on the edge of the settee and Tess stood by the piano. The young man pulled a packet of Gold Flake cigarettes from his shirt pocket and offered it around to his visitors. When the women declined, he plucked a cigarette from the pack and placed it between his full lips. 'Now, what do you want to talk to me about?'

'Mr Gilbert, we'd like you to play the piano for our dancing school,' Alice said and glanced at the piano. The young man struck a match on the side of the matchbox; it burst into flames. 'We were hoping you would be ready to start next week, when we start practising for our end of term display.'

A jet of smoke billowed from the young man's nostrils.

My fiancé Braiden Doyle said you played for the Keogh Sister's display last month,' Ann interjected, clearly convinced that the mere mention of Braiden's name would win the young man over.

'Braiden Doyle, is your fiancé?' the young man said and drew heavily on his cigarette.

'We'll pay the going rate,' added Tess.

'I'm sorry but you've been misinformed, I don't play the piano.'

'We were told that you played the piano for concerts and displays?'

The young man laughed. 'I don't play the piano but my brother George does.'

'And who are you?' asked Tess

'I'm Dessie, George's older brother. 'Who are you?'

'I'm their older sister, I'm Tess.'

'Well hello, older sister Tess,' said the young man, and shook her outstretched hand.

'Hello yourself, Dessie.'

'Could we talk to George?' Alice asked frowning at Tess.

'Yes, I'll get him. But I tell you, he won't play for your display. The Keogh sisters you just mentioned nearly drove him mad, he vowed never to play for a dancing school ever again.'

'Oh, but we're nothing like the Keogh sisters,' murmured Tess, glancing up at him from under her lashes.

'May we talk to George?' asked Alice, irritation creeping into her voice.

'Certainly, I'll get him – I think he's in the east wing.' Dessie grinned at Tess. 'It was a pleasure meeting you, older sister Tess.'

'The pleasure was all mine,' replied Tess and made a point of watching the young man leave the room.

'What did he mean, George is in the east wing? Little houses like this don't have wings,' puzzled Ann, adjusting the steel-rimmed glasses on the bridge of her nose.

'I think he was making a joke, Ann,' sighed Alice.

'Well, I didn't think it was very funny,' snapped Ann.

'But he is very handsome.' Tess was studying a framed family photograph on the top of the piano. 'Goodness, the whole family is good looking! What a pity they're Protestants.'

'Protestants?' choked Ann. She pressed her hand to her breast, almost unable to draw breath. 'So that's why there are no holy pictures on the wall and no painting of the Pope! We're in a Protestant house!' She lowered her voice. 'I don't think Father would like us to be here...'

'What would your father not like?' asked the pale faced young man standing in the doorway.

Alice looked in the direction of the voice and immediately sat up straight. The young man was handsome and there was a calm and gentleness about him that was as fascinating as his physical appearance. He smiled at Alice and she felt the warmth of his smile wash over her.

'Hello, I'm George. My brother said you were looking for a piano player?'

'Yes, that's right,' Alice replied trying not to stare at the young man. 'We'd like you to be our accompanist...' Her voice trailed off; she didn't finish her sentence – she simply stopped talking.

'Your accompanist, I see,' said George as he sat on the arm of the settee next to Alice. 'And who are you?'

When Alice remained tongue-tied, Tess jumped in: 'We are the Dalton sisters and we have a children's dancing school. I'm Tess, I'm the prettiest. Ann wears glasses but has a fiancé and Alice is just Alice, no boyfriend, no ambition, no life.'

'I beg your pardon, I do have ambition,' protested Alice, finding her voice. 'Wasn't it my idea to start the dancing school?'

'Don't get upset, your sister is only joking,' said George, not taking his eyes off Alice.

'And how would you know that?' asked Tess.

'Easy. You had to be joking when you said you were the prettiest of the Dalton girls.'

'Oh, that's cruel. Tell me which of us does your little mind think is the prettiest – or need I ask?' smirked Tess.

'A gentleman would never answer that question.'

'A gentleman would never say I wasn't the prettiest.'

'Very true,' George replied. 'How should I answer that question, Alice?'

Alice's cheeks burned hot and she fell quiet again. She never experienced anyone quite like George. He was the most interesting person she had ever met – calm, confident and captivating.

'George Gilbert, you're a caution,' Tess laughed. 'You're flirting with my little sister. You're every bit as bad as they said you were.'

'Then I'm glad I didn't disappoint. Alice, tell me about this display of yours?'

'It's our dancing school's annual display,' she said weakly. 'It's very important to us and we'd like you to be our accompanist.'

'What happened to your last piano player?'

'Ann has always played for our displays, but she's doesn't want to do it anymore.' Alice's eyes never left George's face.

George turned to Ann,. 'So Ann you are a musician. Pleased to meet you!' Ann flinched back in her seat and George turned back to Alice. 'I had a terrible experience with the Keogh Sisters a while back. They nearly drove me mad, always changing music and music cues. I swore I'd never again play for a dancing school.

We are nothing like Keogh sisters,' interjected Tess.

'As much as I hate to disappoint you Alice, I have to say no.'

Alice suspected she was being teased and she decided to play this young man at his own game. 'Then maybe we should find another accompanist,' she said, getting to her feet.

George smiled. 'Don't give up so easily! How about this – Alice, if you'll come with me to a concert this Sunday, I'll play for your school.'

'That's blackmail,' replied Alice, a grin tugging at the corners of her mouth.

'That's true. Or you could call it a date.'

'No, I'd call it blackmail.' Alice's grin widened. 'But I'll go.'

The three young women climbed back into the waiting cab. Tess removed a compact from her bag and slid the soft puff around the cake of powder. 'Well, little sister, you work fast,' she said, admiring herself in the compact's little round mirror while dabbing the puff on her face.

'What do you mean?' protested Alice in mock-annoyance. 'He blackmailed me into going out with him.

'Alice, he's a Protestant.' Ann blessed herself. We shouldn't have even gone into that house.

'We needed a piano player,' Alice snapped. 'And now we have one.'

'You know very well this has little to do with us needing a piano player,' said Tess. 'But you can have him, he's not my type.'

'Everyone in trousers is your type,' sniffed Ann primly.

Tess lowered the compact. 'And you know all about men, don't you Ann? Look at who you're engaged to – Braiden Doyle, for God's sake.'

'What do you mean by that?' asked Ann. 'Braiden is rich and very nice.'

'I'm only teasing you. Braiden is a perfect specimen of manhood,' said Tess insincerely. 'But Alice, all teasing aside, Ann is right – going out with a Protestant is not the done thing. Even I wouldn't think about doing that.'

'Stop powdering your nose, we're in public,' said Alice crossly. 'We needed a piano player and now we have one, that's all. So as usual Tess, you've got it all wrong.'

'I saw the look on your face,' said Tess, as she snapped the compact shut. 'You like that Protestant piano player but you're playing with fire.'

Thomas Dalton and John Swords sat in the bar of Jury's Hotel on Dame Street. The depression was hitting the business community hard. John had lost considerable sums of money on his investments and Thomas's housing portfolio was performing poorly. His salons business had bounced back after the scandal over Terrance, but now they were half empty again. Emigration and unemployment were rife and the government was floundering.

'When is this depression going to end?' wondered Thomas as he stirred his gin and tonic.

'God knows, I had to sell three of my properties last month to service my bank loans,' said John, taking a gloomy mouthful of his vodka and orange.

'I closed the hairdressing academy for the same reason – overheads too high. But at least my girls have found a use for that part of the building with their dancing school.'

'Good for them, finding something useful to pass their days.'

'Yes, and it's a pleasant surprise to get a return on all those music and dance lessons. I always thought they were a waste of money at the time.'

'I hear Mariah is a lot better these days? Kay said she met her at a charity sermon in the pro-Cathedral last week and she looked well.'

'Yes, she is nearly her old self again.'

'That's wonderful. You must be very happy.'

'Not really. She still hasn't forgiven me for committing her to hospital all those years ago, even though it helped her at the time.'

'You said you had some good news to tell me' said John, feeling a little uncomfortable with the turn the conversation had taken.

'Oh yes!' A spark of excitement flickered in Thomas's eyes. 'The chairman of the Society of Irish Hairdressers has informed me that I have been selected to represent Ireland at the Earl's Court Hairdressing Exhibition in London later this year!'

'Well, congratulations! That is good news, and it will certainly bring the ladies flocking back to your salons.'

'Only if I win, John. Only if I win.'

Alice adjusted the collar of her new high-necked white blouse and straightened the waist of her stylish red and black-striped satin skirt. She applied a little powder to her cheeks, and then exited the ladies' cloakroom.

The foyer of the Round Rooms of the Rotunda was buzzing with excitement. The glamorous, the influential and the erudite of Dublin society had gathered for this special concert for the world-famous pianist, Arthur Rubinstein.

George was on the far side of the foyer, queuing at the cloakroom with Alice's coat and while he waited, he stole a glance in Alice's direction. She was at the foot of the stairs, adjusting the fall of a stray curl on her neck. Suddenly, she turned and caught him looking at her. She smiled and he felt himself blush.

'Are we upstairs or downstairs?' she asked, as he rejoined her.
'Downstairs,' said George.

'You blushed when I caught you looking at me,' Alice whispered mischievously into his ear.

'Are you always so frank?'

'I think it's always best to be honest.'

They entered the curved Round Room and Alice quietly admired the room's elegance and the magnificent crystal chandelier that hung from the stucco ceiling.

'Oh this room is so beautiful, I love it!'

'So do I, particularly tonight,' answered George, looking at Alice.

'You're a very forward young man.'

'I think it's always best to be honest.'

'Now you're being bold,' said Alice, pretending to be miffed.

George liked everything about the slim, handsome young woman beside him. He liked her beautiful wild hair, particularly the loose strands that fluttered around her small face and slim neck. He liked the way she looked at him and gently teased him, but most of all he liked the way she smiled at him.

They took their seats, the lights dimmed, the audience settled and to wild applause, the world-renowned classical pianist Arthur Rubinstein emerged onto the stage and took his seat at the Steinway grand. In the moments before the pianist's finger touched the piano keys, George placed his hand gently over Alice's fingers and her skin prickled with excitement. Moments later, when she glanced at him, his handsome face and dark eyes were completely engrossed in the beauty of the music and the skill and artistry of the pianist.

'Why don't you walk me home? It's a lovely night and I love to see the city by night,' said Alice, when they emerged from the Rotunda.

'I really enjoyed that concert. He's such a wonderful pianist,' said George, buttoning his overcoat.

'And very good looking too,' teased Alice, with a grin.

'I think you must have a thing for piano players.'

'Not really – I just said that to get a rise out of you.'

'So it's going to be like that, is it? Let me see if I can get a rise out of you.'

'Go ahead.'

'Not now, it wouldn't be fun now. I'll get you when you least expect it.'

He took Alice's hand and again she felt a surge of excitement that frightened and delighted her. It was a warm, balmy night and cabs, carriages and trams rattled and swayed up and down O'Connell Street. The footpaths bustled with the crowds of people flowing out of theatres, pubs and picture houses. Approaching O'Connell Bridge, Alice dropped a few coppers into a beggar's hat and leaning on the parapet they watched people walking in and out of the pools of light as they travelled over the Halfpenny Bridge,. Then they strolled chatting and laughing together along College Green, up Dame Street and around Christ Church Cathedral. When they reached Alice's home, they lingered on the pavement and the last few words of their conversation drifted into the cloudless night. Finally, they stood in silence just looking at each other. Then George suddenly stepped away from Alice.

'I hope this won't disappoint you but I don't kiss girls on a first date.'

'And what makes you think I do?' asked Alice pertly. 'Besides, it wasn't a date – you blackmailed me into going out with you, remember.'

George smiled, leaned in and quickly kissed her on the lips. 'Got you!'

'George Gilbert, you are dreadful!' protested Alice, and the sides of her lips curled into the beginnings of a smile.

'I'd like to see you again, Alice,' said George.

'And why wouldn't you?' she asked and opened the front door. 'I'll see you at the rehearsal on Wednesday night. Goodnight!'

Alice closed the door behind her, ran up the stairs to her room and smiling joyously sat on her bed.

Jammet's Restaurant in Nassau Street was particularly busy on the night that Thomas took Mariah there to share his good news about the Earl's Court Hairdressing Exhibition. He meant to wait until the very end of the meal, but after their turtle soup and Sole Jammet, Thomas – unable to contain his excitement any longer – blurted out his good news. Mariah's eyes brightened and for the first time in a long time she placed her hand on his.

'Congratulations, Thomas. That's wonderful news. It's going to be exciting, working together again.'

Thomas's face stayed smiling but his eyes didn't.

Thomas and his chief stylist Larry White sat in the High Street salon after the close of business and talked.

'It gives me no pleasure to say this but Mariah's hair is too fine and dry to give you even the slightest chance of winning at Earl's Court,' said the hairstylist. 'Her hair is too weak to support the elaborate design needed to win a competition at that level. And even if by magic you did devise a way to do it, the hair is so dull and lifeless it would detract from the design. If you want to be a prize-winner you'll need a model with strong, healthy hair.'

'Have you any idea who I might use?'

'I do and so do you.'

'I do,' said Thomas. 'God help me.'

Alice was running through a dance routine with a group of little girls when George entered the dance studio. He stood by the piano and watched Alice counting out the beats and calling out directions to the children. George lifted the lid of the piano and played to Alice's count. She looked over at him and smiled. He winked at her and she continued counting. When the children had completed their routine, Alice strolled over to the piano.

'You're early.'

'I'm eager.'

'I thought you were George.'

'You're too quick.'

'And you're too forward. And by the way, I'm still annoyed about that kiss the other night.'

'No you're not. How about joining me for a cup of tea, after the rehearsal?'

'I might, but no kissing this time,' Alice replied.

'What kind of person do you think I am?'

'I know what kind of person you are. I'll go get the sheet music for the display,' said Alice and as she walked away George played the opening sequence of Wagner's *The Ride of the Valkyrie.*

Alice ignored the musical comment but when she reached the changing room she leaned against the wall; her hand went to her mouth and she stifled a happy giggle.

CHAPTER THIRTEEN

Alice was sitting in the summerhouse reading when a very pale Mrs O'Donnell stepped into the garden, pulled a handkerchief from her pocket and coughed into it. For some time Alice had noticed a gradual change in the housekeeper's appearance. The tiny woman's face had become grey; she had lost her fine posture and she looked like she was disappearing into her knitted cardigan. When she stopped coughing, Mrs O'Donnell leaned against the wall and drew several shallow breaths.

Alice closed her book. 'Are you unwell, Mrs O'Donnell?'

'Oh Alice, I didn't see you there. It's just the flu, better not get too close.'

'Mrs Foley told me you might be taking a little holiday.'

'Yes I hope to, but I have to get your mother's permission.' The housekeeper crumpled the handkerchief in her fist, but not before Alice noticed that it was spotted with blood.

In all the years Mrs O'Donnell had been the housekeeper for the Dalton family she had only ever taken one holiday, so when she requested a second holiday within three months Mariah was greatly surprised. She closed her Woman's Own magazine and placed it on the coffee table beside her. 'Why do you need another holiday so soon after the last?'

The little housekeeper wiped her forehead with her handkerchief. 'Would you mind if I sit while we talk about it, Mrs Dalton?'

'Very well.' Mariah indicated the seat facing her and Mrs O'Donnell sat on it. 'How much time off will you require?'

'Two months,' sighed Mrs O'Donnell. 'I have been feeling unwell for some time now and Dr Driscoll has recommended a short stay in hospital.'

'For two months?' Mariah frowned, disapprovingly. 'Mrs O'Donnell, during your last holiday things got a little chaotic in the house. You see, we depend on you. You are part of this family.'

'I appreciate you saying that, Mrs Dalton, but Dr Driscoll has told me I have a touch of consumption. He said I need time to rest and recuperate and that there is a bed for me in St Mary's from the first of the month.'

'I see.' Mariah was clearly peeved. 'Well, if you must, you must. But before you go, please find me a temporary replacement housekeeper and personal maid.'

Mrs O'Donnell nodded and waited to see if there was anything else – perhaps a word of affection or sympathy. But Mariah returned to her magazine, so the housekeeper rose and left the room.

A spring sun dressed Stephen's Green in luminous yellow light. It was Saturday morning and the park was filled with people strolling along the paths or sitting on the grass or feeding the ducks on the artificial lake. A crowd gathered around the bandstand when a pipe band started to play traditional Irish airs. Alice and Ann Dalton were among the audience; they sat under an oak tree, listening to the pipers.

'Which one of the Dalton girls did you say you liked?' Dessie asked his brother George, pointing out the two sisters in the distance.

George grinned. 'Who said I liked either of them?'

'Let me see… You broke your new rule about never playing for a children's dance school again and you have an idiotic look on your face the whole time. Yes, I'd say you like one of them.'

'Ah, shut up.'

'Now the question is, which one?' Dessie looked quizzically at his brother. 'I'd say it's the one with the wild hair. She's petite and has that slightly uppity expression you like and she has a nice pair of legs too. Let's go talk to her.'

'We haven't time, we're late already.'

'Jimmy will wait, another minute or two won't hurt. Come on.'

Before George could reply, Dessie was off – dodging in and out of the crowd. Smiling, George followed.

'How is my brother's piano playing?' asked Dessie as he joined Alice and Ann under the tree. 'Is it up to standard?'

'He's quite adequate,' replied Ann coolly, and she repositioned herself away from Dessie.

'Well if it isn't the Gilbert boys,' said Alice.

'The one and only,' replied George, opening his arms wide like a circus performer. 'You know my brother Dessie.'

'Yes, we know your brother,' frowned Ann.

'Alice, George told me all about you,' Dessie said, and added with mock surprise, 'He said you're very bossy in the school.'

'I never said anything of the sort,' laughed George.

'What *did* you say about me?' asked Alice.

'I told him nothing.'

'No, George is the strong silent type. I'm the sensitive one in the family.'

'He's about as sensitive as a slab of granite. Come on Dessie, we're ten minutes late already.'

'Sorry girls, I hate to break your hearts but the man insists,' said Dessie.

George tipped his cap to Alice and, walking backwards, said, 'See you, Alice of the beautiful hair.'

'See you, George of the silly grin,' smiled Alice.

'Promise me you won't go out with him again,' Ann said as soon as George and Dessie were out of earshot.

'I'll do nothing of the sort. You worry far too much about what Father will think. Leave Father to me.'

Later that evening when Thomas returned home, Mariah told him about Mrs O'Donnell's request for a second holiday. 'Apparently she has a touch of consumption and wants to rest. I don't know what I'm expected to do without her. I think she's being a bit selfish about it, actually.'

'Consumption?' Thomas went white, his eyes went dark and he sat in stunned contemplation. Then he bolted out of the room and bounded up the stairs to the top of the house, where he knocked loudly on Mrs O'Donnell's bedroom door.

Wearing a hairnet and patterned flannel dressing gown that looked at least two sizes too large for her, the housekeeper opened the door.

'Is Mrs Dalton all right?' she asked, alarmed. 'Is something the matter?'

'Yes, there is something the matter,' replied Thomas curtly. 'My wife has just informed me that you have TB.'

'Just a slight touch of it,' replied Mrs O'Donnell defensively, pulling her dressing gown tighter around her shrinking body.

'You have my sincere sympathy, Mrs O'Donnell.' But Thomas's voice was neither sympathetic nor sincere. 'Now I want you to pack your bags and leave this house immediately.'

Mrs O'Donnell turned white. She pressed her hands to her face and when she lowered her stubby fingers, her pale almost colourless eyes were moist with tears.

'Mr Dalton, I'd like to stay until the end of the month?'

'Absolutely not, you leave immediately.'

'I'd like to talk to Mrs Dalton.'

'No.' Thomas shook his head.

'But Mrs Dalton asked me to find her a temporary replacement housekeeper...'

'That is no longer your concern.' His face was flushed. 'Mrs O'Donnell, I will give you an additional month's wages but you must leave the house within the hour. If you wait until morning I will have you forcefully removed and you will leave with nothing.'

The tiny housekeeper made one last bid for reassurance. 'Then I will return after my treatment is complete?'

'Certainly not.' Thomas spoke with such absolute cold resolve that the housekeeper knew it was foolish to argue. Within the hour, she had packed her bags and left the house.

When Mariah awoke she was surprised that Mrs O'Donnell was not at her bedside. She rang the bell and when it went unanswered, she dressed herself and went in search of her housekeeper and lady's maid.

'Have you seen Mrs O'Donnell?' Mariah asked the upstairs maid when they met on the landing.

'No, Ma'am,' replied the maid.

Mariah went up to Mrs O'Donnell's bedroom and opened the door; the bed was stripped and the room was devoid of the housekeeper's clothes and possessions.

'I dismissed her,' said Thomas, when Mariah inquired at the breakfast table about the housekeeper.

'Well, I'm going to reinstate her.' Mariah shook out her linen serviette. 'After all, the woman only asked for a holiday.'

'You will do nothing of the sort. This has nothing to do with a holiday, the woman has TB.'

Mariah was confused. 'Mrs O'Donnell hasn't got TB, she has a touch of consumption.'

'Consumption is TB and you can't get just a touch of it. When I was a child, a village in the next parish was completely devastated by TB. Within ten months of the disease arriving not one man, woman or child was left alive.'

'Oh...' His wife looked put out. 'But what am I to do?'

'I will arrange to have her room fumigated and everything she left behind burned.'

'I've known Mrs O'Donnell for a very long time...'

'You need not worry about her. I have given her money.'

'I mean, who can replace her? She was both my housekeeper and my personal maid. It will take two new people to do all her work.'

Thomas looked down and drew a breath. 'That is something else we need to discuss, Mariah. The depression has greatly affected my businesses. As you know, I have already closed the hairdressing academy. I have also had to sell much of my property portfolio to service my bank debts. I've closed two salons and I run the remaining two with reduced staff numbers. In spite of all that, our financial situation continues to deteriorate.'

'That's not my fault,' said Mariah quickly.

'No dear, it is not your fault. But the realities of our changed circumstances must be faced.'

'But how?' A perplexed Mariah looked at her husband.

'We have to economise dear. We have to greatly reduce the number of servants we employ.'

'Are you suggesting we get rid of Mrs Foley as well as Mrs O'Donnell?' asked Mariah, appalled.

'Goodness, no – not unless you wish to take over Mrs Foley's kitchen responsibilities.'

'Don't be ridiculous, Thomas.'

'Still, someone has to go.'

'I suppose, the upstairs maid...'

'Mariah, that would help, but we need make more extensive changes. With the exception of Mrs Foley, we are not in a position to employ any servants at all.'

'But who's to run the house?' Mariah cried in alarm.

'You will, dear.'

'But I know nothing about running a house!'

'You will soon learn and the girls will help with the housekeeping duties.'

Mariah stared at him, bewildered and angry. 'Why do I have to make all the sacrifices? How is any of this affecting you?'

'Among other things, I have cancelled my club memberships and I have sold my carriage.'

'We have no carriage?'

'No.'

'Oh...' Mariah was nearly in tears. 'But Thomas, I can't manage without any help. Mrs O'Donnell promised to find me a personal maid before she left...'

Thomas shook his head.

His wife pressed her hands to her pale cheeks, thinking hard. 'Very well. Then one of our daughters will have to become my maid. But which one? Oh dear... Tess is intolerable, Ann is engaged to that dreadful Braiden Doyle. Alice! She's the only one left. Alice will have to become my personal maid. If she prefers, we'll call her my companion.'

'You and Alice were never close,' murmured Thomas, touching his forehead with his handkerchief.

'Be that as it may, it is her Christian duty to look after her mother. Anyway, enough of this horror. How are the plans for London?'

'Everything is coming along very nicely,' Thomas replied, shifting uncomfortably in his seat.

It was Saturday morning and George Gilbert tapped his foot as he waited outside Tara Street railway station. Alice was nearly fifteen minutes late and he was getting a little worried. To impress her, he was wearing his brother's new grey pleated trousers, a white shirt and his favourite navy jacket. He had just finished checking his watch for the sixth time when he saw Alice's wild hair moving through the crowd. He relaxed and his face broke into a broad smile.

Moments later, a slightly flushed, out-of-breath Alice stood in front of him. 'You waited!' she cried, her eyes shining with life.

'Of course I waited.'

'The silly tram broke down, and I was sure you'd be gone. What time is the next train to Bray?'

'Five minutes.'

'We'd better hurry!'

She took his arm and they half-ran to the train, hurrying down the platform until they found a third-class carriage. By the time they had taken their seats, the train was already pulling out of the station in a cloud of grey smoke and white steam.

Forty minutes later, George and Alice were walking hand in hand along the sun-drenched esplanade. Seagulls swooped and dived through the blue sky; paddling children jumped up and down in the sea as white-topped cresting waves whipped pebbles around their small feet. In the park alongside the esplanade, families picnicked and traders peddled their wares. On the jetty, fishermen helped people onto their boats for tours around Bray Head and a carnival at the foot of the Head pumped out hurdy-gurdy music inviting all comers to join in the fun. Alice and George followed the footpath to the top of the Head. After a while, George became out of breath and sat on the grass. Alice sat down beside him and they watched a steam train as it chugged along the coastline.

'That section of the rail line is called Brunel's Folly,' George said, leaning closer to Alice.

'I hope you're not thinking of stealing another kiss,' said Alice and placed her hand on George's chest.

'I ask you, would I do something like that?'

'I know you would.'

He moved closer. 'You're right. No more stealing of kisses. My father used to say, "George you can't just steal things, you have to earn them".' George looked into Alice's face. 'Tell me what do I have to do to earn a kiss?'

'Let me think about that. Hm. I know! Tell me three things I don't know about Bray and you can have a kiss.'

'That's hard. I might just pass on the kiss.'

'No you won't.'

'All right, let me see. In 1649, Oliver Cromwell stayed in Bray on his way to Wexford.'

'Very good. That's one. Two more to go.'

'Bray straddles the borders of County Wicklow and County Dublin.'

'I knew that but I'll pretend I didn't. One to go.'

'Sorry, that's everything I know about Bray.'

'George how can you say that?' asked Alice in mock indignation. 'I'm seeking knowledge here.'

'Very well – this section of the mountain is called Alice's Delight.'

'No it's not,' she replied and kissed him gently on the lips. 'And Bray Head is not a mountain, it's a hill.'

'Really? I didn't know that,' replied George, pulling Alice close and kissing her again.

Alice and George were walking along the esplanade on their way back to the train station when dark clouds rolled across the blue sky and sprinkled light rain on them. Umbrellas popped open and people quickened their pace. Suddenly the light rain turned into a deluge and Alice and George rushed across the street into the nearest tea rooms. It was shabby; paint was peeling off the walls and the oilcloth tablecloths were faded and even soiled.

'I don't think I'd like to eat here,' Alice whispered, hanging back. 'Let's go to the Bray Head Hotel.'

'It's raining and don't be such a snob,' George said and he pulled Alice across the steam-filled room to the only vacant table. 'This is where real people eat. What would you like?'

'I'd like to leave.'

'How about tea and scones?'

'I'll have tea but only if they have teacups,' said Alice.

A long-necked, exceptionally thin older waitress arrived at the table. Flicking her long grey hair off her face, she pulled a notepad from the pocket of her stained apron.

'What do yous want? And before you ask, we have teacups. But don't expect to be served in a hurry. I'm on me own here today.'

'We'll have tea and scones,' said George.

'Are you joking me? It's three o'clock there's no scones left.' The waitress flicked her hair again. 'You can have currant buns.'

'Then that's what we'll have,' said George, and the waitress walked away.

'She's rude and not very clean,' Alice whispered across the table.

At the next table, an eight-year-old girl picked up the salt cellar, held it over the sugar bowl and watched the salt cascade into the sugar. Alice giggled and touched George's hand to get his attention.

Suddenly the grey-haired waitress descended and snatched the salt cellar from the child's hand. 'You little brat, who's going to pay for the sugar and salt?' she barked.

'Don't you talk to my child like that, you auld whore!' snarled the child's father.

'The bloody cheek of you, who are you calling auld? I'm not serving you, get out.'

'What?' exclaimed the man.

Alice went bright red and George bowed his head, trying to stifle his laughter. The waitress glared at him. 'If I thought yous was laughing at me I'd throw yous out too.'

George laughed even harder.

'Right.' The waitress drew herself to her full height, flicking her hair again. 'Get out and take Miss Fancy Pants with you.'

'No, no...' spluttered George. 'I wasn't laughing at you, I was just thinking about a funny dream I had last night...'

'Get out or I'll call the police!'

Alice could take no more. Scarlet-faced, she leapt to her feet and rushed out of the tea rooms.

'Don't talk to me. That was so embarrassing,' she snapped, when George joined her. 'I didn't even want to go into that awful tearooms.'

'I'm sorry you were embarrassed, but you've got to admit it was funny.'

Alice stormed off down the street tying her scarf around her head. Still laughing George ran after her and took her hand. She stopped walking, her eyes softened and she burst into laughter. As if in response, the rain stopped, and they walked to the train station.

The excited din of the children changing out of their dancing clothes was ear-splitting. Ann was picking up the discarded costumes and putting them on hangers, while Alice helped the younger girls with their shoes. Tired of it all, Tess slipped out of the changing room and into the quiet of the studio.

'That's a catchy tune,' she said as she sat beside George on the piano stool.

'You like it? It's one of my own compositions. Alice said she wants to use it in the display.'

'Can I ask you a personal question?'

'Go ahead.'

'You like Alice?'

'I do.'

'You could do better,' said Tess and placed her hand on his arm.

George stopped playing. 'Tess you're a great girl, but its Alice I'm interested in.'

'Good, because I'm not interested in you.' Tess jumped to her feet, grabbed her coat and flounced out of the studio.

At the dinner table, Thomas informed his children that he wanted to talk to them after they had eaten. When Alice asked why, Thomas said it was a family matter and when Jarlath explained that it was prize-giving night at the polo club and that he'd have to miss the talk, his father glared at him with such ferocity that Jarlath whispered, 'I'll be there.'

After dinner, Thomas stood at the fireplace in the drawing room and cleared his throat.

'What I'm about to tell you is not to be repeated outside this room. Because of the depression, our financial circumstances have changed and we have to greatly reduce the household outgoings and overheads. Your mother and I have decided that with the exception of Mrs Foley all the servants must go.'

'Seriously?' Jarlath and Tess looked at each other in shock and disbelief.

'Mother will run the house and you girls will divide the housekeeping responsibilities between you. Jarlath, I want you to find gainful employment but until then I want you to look after the day-to-day household accounts.'

'Household work is for women!' complained Jarlath indignantly.

'Tess, Ann and I will be happy to help in any way we can,' said Alice. 'Won't we, girls?'

'Yes,' agreed Ann.

'I suppose so,' said Tess, reluctantly.

'One other thing,' Thomas said. 'Your personal allowances will be reduced by fifty per cent.'

'What?' Jarlath was disgusted. 'That's outrageous! I need every penny of my allowance. I couldn't live on less.'

'Jarlath this is not a discussion. These are decisions I have made and I must warn you further cuts may be necessary.'

CHAPTER FOURTEEN

I t was ten thirty in the evening, and Dublin city's theatres and picture houses had emptied their audiences onto the streets. The night was warm and a cool breeze shimmered through the leaves of the trees as George and Alice exited the Carlton Cinema. Alice slipped her hand under George's arm.

'Greta Garbo is really beautiful,' she sighed.

'Not my type,' replied George. 'She's a bit mannish looking.'

'That's a dreadful thing to say!'

'Would you say my namesake was good looking?' asked George, as they stood waiting to cross to Nelson's Pillar.

'Oh, John Gilbert's only in the half-penny place, you're a lot more handsome than he is,' answered Alice, smiling up at him from under her eyelashes.

'You are an observant woman of great intelligence, Alice Dalton.'

A large woman in front of Alice tightened her shawl across the broad of her back and, without disturbing the ash on the cigarette that dangled from her lips, billowed smoke through her nostrils.

'They should never have erected a statue to that Protestant adulterer Charles Stewart Parnell,' she said loudly to her companion. 'Every time I see it, it makes my blood boil.'

'Who the hell do you think you are?' demanded a bowler-hatted older man standing nearby. 'How dare you cast aspersions on one of the finest men Ireland every produced?'

'Ah shut your face,' retorted the large woman. 'You're probably a Protestant galutte, just like him.'

'Who are you calling a Protestant?' the man said and lunged at the woman but the crowd moved and the man, the woman and their argument was lost in the shifting, lumbering throng.

'Doesn't it annoy you to hear people say things like that?' whispered Alice as they waited for the double-decker tram to approach.

'Yes it does, even though my family is only half Protestant,' said George lightly.

'Half Protestant? How can you be "half" Protestant?'

'My mother is Catholic and my father was Protestant. The Catholic Church would only allow them to marry if any girls they had were brought up Catholic. Their sons were allowed to be Protestant though.'

'That's very strange.' Alice realised she knew very little about these inter-religious matters. The only Protestants she'd known up to now were the Brimcombe family. 'And do you have sisters?'

'Three – Dorothy, Freda and Alice.'

'Alice?'

'Yes and before you ask, having a girlfriend with the same name as my sister takes some getting used to.'

Alice laughed and thought happily: *He considers me his girlfriend!*

The tram clanked to a halt and she and George climbed aboard.

Alice was mounting the kitchen stairs with a pile of freshly ironed sheets, when her father appeared in the drawing room doorway and asked her if he could have a word. Worried by how solemn he sounded, Alice placed the folded sheets on a hall chair and followed him into the room.

He closed the door and asked Alice to sit. 'What I have to say is a little delicate. '

Alice's stomach clenched; someone must have told him about George.

'You know I have been asked to represent Ireland in the Earl's Court Hairdressing Exhibition, Alice?'

'Yes Father?' Alice relaxed a little.

'In the past, your mother has always been my hair model. However due to her many health problems, her hair is not what it used to be.'

'That's sad, Father.' Alice wondered where this conversation was going.

'I am contemplating using another model. No, I should say I have *decided* to use a new model.'

'Mother will be hurt,' said Alice quietly – although she thought "furious" would be a better word.

'Yes she will be hurt. But if I am to have any chance of winning this competition – and it is very important for all of us that I win – I will need a new model.'

'I see.'

'There's nothing to see. What do you say?'

'About what, Father?'

'Alice, I'm asking you to be my new hair model!'

Alice's head spun; she felt dizzy, excited and afraid. Her heart pounded with exhilaration and her thoughts raced: What will Mother say? What will Mother do? Can I really be an international hair model in London? What will I wear? When will we leave? Question after question presented itself to her excited mind, yet all she could do was sit and stare.

'Well, what do you say Alice?'

At Thomas's prompting, she found her voice: 'I say "yes"! But I don't know the first thing about being a hair model!'

'That we can deal with,' said Thomas, visibly pleased.

'When are you going to tell Mother?'

Thomas became solemn again. 'Soon,' he said, rubbing his chin. 'Soon, it has to be soon.'

Ann and Alice were lying on Ann's bed engrossed in conversation about Alice's forthcoming London trip when the door clattered open and Tess flounced into the room.

'I'm not washing any more sheets. It's demeaning. Look at my poor hands! They're as red as a servant girl's.' She flopped down on the bed beside her sisters. 'I don't care how bad the economy is, I refuse to be Mother's slave any longer.'

'I bet you won't dare say that to Father,' said Ann priggishly.

'Maybe I will, right to his face.' Tess grabbed a small blue jar from Ann's bedside table and rubbed the cream into her rough, red skin.

'Don't use my hand cream!' protested Ann, snatching the jar away from her.

'Oh stop annoying me,' snapped Tess.

'Tess, you can be very rude and quite insufferable!'

'I don't care. This stupid lack of money is driving me crazy.'

'Well, it won't last much longer. When Father and Alice win the hairdressing competition...'

Tess sat bolt upright. 'What?"

'Ann, you promised you wouldn't tell!' gasped Alice.

'You're going to win what?' demanded Tess.

'It's supposed to be a secret...'

'You told Ann!'

Alice sighed. 'You're right, it's not fair to tell Ann and not you. Father has asked me to be his hair model at the Earl's Court exhibition.'

155

Tess's eyes flashed. 'Why you? This is so unfair, I'm older than you and I have much better hair! I should be going to London, not you! And instead I'm going to be stuck in this stupid house, slaving away for nothing!' And she stormed out of the room.

Alice ran after her and caught up with her halfway down the kitchen stairs. 'Tess, Tess, listen... I didn't ask for it to be me. But what does it matter which of us goes? The important thing is for Father to win. The salons will make money again, life will get back to normal, and then you won't have to wash clothes anymore.'

Tess said nothing for a moment, gazing out of the little window into the garden. But then she said, 'You were very chummy with the piano player at rehearsal the other day.'

Alice was taken aback. 'I wasn't being "chummy". I was being friendly.'

'There's a difference between that and throwing yourself at a man?'

'I don't throw myself at men! I leave that to you!'

'Hit a nerve have I?' Tess turned to her on the stairs, eyes narrowed. 'Let me tell you something, little sister, your precious George asked me out but I told him: No thanks, I don't go out with Prods. What do you think of that, Miss High and Mighty?'

'I don't believe you,' replied Alice, trembling.

'That's your business, but don't say I didn't tell you,' smirked Tess and glided on down the stairs to the kitchen.

Left alone on the stairs, Alice bit her lip to suppress a sob.

A glum, self-pitying Jarlath Dalton sat at the counter in Neary's Pub in Chatham Street studying his reflection in the mirror above the bar and wondering what had happened to his once comfortable, predictable life. Where had all the money gone? Thomas Dalton had always claimed to be a brilliant businessman, but he was making an awful mess of the salons while pretending it was all the economy's fault.

He had just called another drink, when he heard a familiar voice emanating from the back of the pub. In a state of shock, Jarlath rose from his stool and headed towards the voice. Could that be who he thought it was? After ten long years?

Sure enough, it was Terrance, laughing and joking with four of his old Republican friends. He seemed delighted to see his older brother. 'Jarlath, how are you? Good to see you. Fellas, this is my brother Jarlath.'

Jarlath hastily shook hands with each of the four men and then took Terrance aside. 'When did you get back to Ireland?'

'Yesterday, but don't tell the folks, I want to surprise them.'

'Surprise them? You'll probably kill them with the shock. In Father's eyes and the eyes of the law you're still a criminal.'

'No I'm not, so you can stop looking around the bar as if at any minute it might be raided by the police!'

'But you were out on parole when you skipped off to Australia! That makes you a criminal!'

'Jarlath, you worry too much. Things have changed. Ireland is now a Free State and the government will give me a pardon.'

'Not this present government.'

'When Dev gets in I'll be pardoned. In the meantime, as long as I keep my head low, I'll be all right.'

When Alice arrived for the Saturday afternoon rehearsal, she had no idea how to behave or what to say to George. She kept thinking about what Tess had said and every time George looked at her, she looked away. Half way through the rehearsal she gathered her courage and approached him.

'There you are! I was beginning to think you were avoiding me,' George said breezily.

'I'm not avoiding you. I'm here aren't I?'

'Good. Can we talk to you about the cue sheet for the dress rehearsal?'

'I have it all written down.'

'That's wonderful. Listen, I'm really sorry about this and I hate to let you down but…'

'What do you mean, let me down?' She tried to stop her voice from shaking. So it was true about Tess.

George was sorting through his sheet music seemingly embarrassed to meet her eye. 'I've just found out I can't be here for the rehearsal.'

'Oh…'

'Don't worry. I've asked my friend John Olive to sit in for me. I'll stack the music in the order and I'll leave him the cue sheet.'

'George…'

'Please don't worry. He's very professional, he has lots of experience and will do a great job.'

'But George…'

'You'll like him, he's a gent.'

'George, there's something I have to say to you!'

'I promise I'll be back for the concert itself.'

'This isn't about the concert!'

At last, he looked up at her – clearly puzzled by the severity in her voice. 'Then what is the matter?'

Tears welled in Alice's eyes. 'Did you ask Tess to go out with you?'

He stared at her. 'Why would you even ask me that question?'

'Tess said you asked her out. Why would she say it, if it wasn't true?'

'You'll have to ask her that.' Shaking his head, he went back to organising the pile of music.

Alice felt hurt. 'Are you laughing at me?'

'No, I'm not laughing at you.'

'You're grinning like an idiot.'

'I am not grinning and you're being silly.'

'Oh, I'm silly now, am I?'

'Alice, I didn't mean it like that.'

'Why won't you tell me if you didn't ask her out?'

'Because it's a stupid question and you know it.'

'I don't know anything! I thought I knew you but clearly I don't!' And fighting back her tears, she stalked off to the changing room.

Days later, an odd-looking bowler-hatted man opened the door of the dancing school and stared around the studio. When Alice approached him, he removed his hat and revealed a head of thinning hair.

'Hello, can I help you?' she asked.

The little man took a moment and composed himself. 'Good morning, my name is John Olive. I'm a pianist and my friend George Gilbert asked me to come here to play for a childrens' dance display rehearsal. George said I should ask for Alice.'

'I'm Alice and I'm pleased to meet you Mr Olive.'

'And I'm pleased to meet you,' John held out his tiny hand and Alice shook it. 'Please call me John.'

'The piano is over there John,' Alice said

'What a beautiful instrument. Alice, I'd like to thank you ever so much, it's not everyone that would give me this opportunity. You must be one of our own,' the little man added conspiratorially.

Alice was about to tell John that she wasn't a Protestant, but he was such a nice man that she decided against it. 'George recommended you and we're delighted to have you.'

She hadn't spoken to George since their fight, and saying his name out loud made her heart hurt. Plastering a bright smile on her face, she opened the piano stool and the little man removed the orderly stack of sheet music and carefully placed it on the top of the piano.

'This is always the most exciting part, discovering what music I will bring to life. George said you have a cue sheet?'

'Yes, I'll go and fetch it. It will only take a moment.'

When she returned, John Olive was sitting at the piano lost in his piano playing. She stood and listened. The little man had pale, almost translucent skin and dark, sunken mournful eyes.

'How do you and George know each other?' she asked, when he stopped playing. Even though it pained her, she couldn't help wanting to find out more about George.

'We met in hospital.'

'Hospital?' She was surprised. 'What was George doing in hospital?'

John looked quizzically at her. 'Don't you… You are Alice, aren't you?'

'Yes, I am!'

'Ah, it was all such a long time ago I don't really remember.' He took the cue sheet from her. 'Now, time is short, so let's talk about the running order.'

'Yes, of course.' But she wondered why the strange little man had deliberately changed the conversation.

On the day of the display, the changing room and the dance studio were abuzz with excitement. Ann and Tess were helping the children change into their costumes while Alice greeted arriving parents and family members. A temporary stage had been erected at one end of the studio and rows of wooden benches were placed in front of it. When George entered the studio, Alice froze. He nodded at her but she turned away and chatted as brightly as she could to some newly-arrived parents.

George was already at the piano reading the notes John Olive had left for him, when Alice approached.

'Your friend John said he'd marked the new cues for you,' she said coolly.

'I see that.'

Her heart twisted. She wanted to tell George that she knew Tess was always lying and could be cruel and spiteful – but she didn't say any of that. 'Why couldn't you be here for the dress rehearsal?'

'Oh, just a family matter,' George replied after a moment's hesitation. 'I'm sure John's playing was more than satisfactory.'

'Yes, indeed. He was very good.' And then, for some unknown reason even she didn't understand, she found herself saying, 'I should tell you, we intend to make John our regular accompanist.'

'Oh.' George's face barely moved a muscle. 'Then you won't need me anymore?'

'That's right, we won't be needing you anymore,' White-faced, she walked away.

Ann's fiancé Braiden Doyle arrived in the studio minutes before the display was to start. A little over six foot tall, with thick black wavy hair and blazing bright blue eyes, Braiden strolled along the rows of wooden benches and stopped when he got to the piano.

'George Gilbert, I know we've had our differences in the past, but I hope there'll be no unpleasantness between us today.' Braiden removed his overcoat and loosened the silk scarf around his neck. 'Ann is very important to me and as I was instrumental, if you'll pardon the pun, in getting you this job, I hope there will be no unpleasantness between us.'

George glanced briefly at Braiden and returned to checking the sheet music. 'There will be no unpleasantness and there will be no pleasantness between us. There will be nothing between us. I don't like you and I don't approve of the way you treat people.'

'I ask nothing of you but civility,' snapped Braiden.

'There you are Braiden darling,' Ann said as she approached the studio stage, pushing her spectacles up the bridge of her nose.

Turning from George to his smiling fiancé, Braiden said in a louder voice, 'Ann, how lovely you look today!'

George watched cynically as the couple embraced.

The children took their final bow and the audience of family and friends burst into applause. Fifteen minutes later, the studio was almost empty. Tess had left early, announcing that she felt too tired to be of any further help. From the changing room door, Alice watched Ann hand George a brown envelope of money. Without saying a word, George put the envelope in his pocket; he glanced at Alice but she looked away and retreated into the changing room.

She was keeping herself busy packing the children's dancing costumes into a large wooden chest, when Ann joined her. 'Braiden had to leave to go to a meeting. He looked wonderful, don't you think?'

When Alice didn't comment, Ann closed the wooden chest and sat on the lid. 'You broke up with George?'

Alice shrugged. 'Yes.'

'Why? I thought you really liked each other.'

'What do you care? He is a Protestant, after all. I thought you'd be pleased.'

'Oh Alice, don't be so silly.'

'I'm not being silly! Why does everyone say I'm being silly about this?'

'Why, who else said you were being silly?'

'George...'

'So he didn't want you to break up with him?'

'No!'

'Then...'

Alice burst into tears. 'Tess says he asked her to go out with him, so obviously I'm just the consolation prize.'

'Oh for goodness sake, Alice. For the smartest person in this family, you can indeed be very silly. George didn't ask Tess out, she asked him out.'

Alice stared. 'You don't know that?'

'I overheard their conversation. Tess asked George out and he rejected her.'

'Why didn't you tell me about that before?' asked a shocked Alice.

'Because George dealt with her very kindly and quietly. I had no idea she was still causing trouble over it. Why on earth did you believe her?'

'I didn't think she'd tell me a such an awful lie…'

'Oh come on, you know what she's like. She's jealous. Do you really believe that a good-looking man asked her out and she said no? Try pulling the other leg.'

'Oh Ann, I've done something terribly stupid,' said Alice very softly.

CHAPTER FIFTEEN

Most Wednesday evenings during the football season, George and Dessie Gilbert met in Mooney's of Phibsboro and had a pint or two before attending the soccer match in Dalymount Park. Dessie was a fanatical supporter of Bohemians Soccer Club and never missed a match. George enjoyed going to the game, but what he really enjoyed was watching his older brother watching the game. He chuckled every time Dessie roared an expletive at an opposing team player; he laughed to himself every time Dessie cursed the referee; and when a Bohemians player scored a goal and Dessie danced his crazy victory dance, George could not contain his mirth.

The two brothers were having their usual pre-match beers in Mooney's Pub when Braiden Doyle and a female companion brushed past their table and took seats in a nearby booth. In full view of George, Braiden slid his hand across the table, took the young woman's hand and placed a kiss on it.

'What's the matter?' asked Dessie, catching the glum expression on his brother's face.

George flicked his eyes towards the neighbouring booth, saying nothing.

Dessie's face darkened. 'That's Braiden Doyle isn't it? The strutting peacock. I'd like to smash his fucking face.'

'We'd better leave or we'll be late,' said George, hastily reaching for his coat.

'I need some cigarettes,' Dessie said, and left the table.

George was pulling on his overcoat when the commotion erupted behind him. He turned and saw Dessie reach into the booth, grab Braiden Doyle by the tie and pull him across the table.

'You fucking bastard,' shouted Dessie, and slammed his forehead into Braiden's face.

Braiden's nose exploded in blood. Drinkers scattered, Braiden's companion screamed and a waitress dropped a tray of drinks. Braiden crashed backwards, hit his head against the wall and slid ingloriously to the floor.

George raced across the pub and pulled his brother away from the booth. 'What do you think this will achieve?' he demanded.

'You won't get away with this, you thug!' howled Braiden, as he staggered to his feet, his hand to his nose.

'This is a respectable establishment!' cried the red-faced manager, arriving at the scene. 'Take your dispute elsewhere or I will call the police! Now both of you get out – and Dessie Gilbert, you're barred.'

Dessie raised his open hands in the air and as he passed the blood-soaked Braiden, he faked throwing a punch at him.

Thomas spent several sleepless nights planning how to break it to his wife that he was not going to use her for the London Exhibition. The thought of her rage unnerved him. Yet one evening as he and Mariah sat over their after-dinner brandy in the drawing room, he summoned up his courage, got to his feet, pulled himself to his full height and coughed loudly.

'What is it, Thomas? Are you unwell?' asked Mariah, not even bothering to look up at her husband.

'I am well, thank you. However, it has occurred to me that although it is much to be regretted, you yourself might not feel well enough to act as my hair model in London next month. So perhaps we should give some thought to a replacement.'

Thomas waited for the inevitable outburst from his wife. But there was no outburst. Instead, Mariah said gently, 'Give some thought to it? I understand that you have already decided to replace me with Alice.'

Thomas flinched. 'Who told you that?'

'Tess. Is it true?'

Thomas took a deep breath. 'Yes, it is true.'

Mariah frowned. 'I wasn't sure. Tess can... exaggerate a little. Thomas, you are making a mistake. Your precious Alice's hair is far too wild for a professional model and she is too young to be running off to London without a female chaperone.'

'You were younger than Alice when you first became a model,' countered Thomas. 'And her hair is not wild, it's interesting. It will give my design an edge.'

'Tess has better hair. She is prettier and is much more sociable. Use her.'

'Tess's hair is good but she is too much of a flipperty-gibbert.'

'Do as you wish.' Mariah's voice turned cold and aloof. 'But first, I want you to speak to Alice about becoming my companion.'

Thomas fortified himself with a mouthful of brandy. 'I told you, I don't agree with your thinking on the matter. Perhaps you and Alice could use the trip to London to get to know each other a little better.'

'London? I have no intention of accompanying you and Alice to London and I don't care to get to know Alice a little better. It is Alice's duty to become my companion and it is your duty to make sure that it happens.'

An anxious Alice paced the drawing room. It was only three weeks before the Earl's Court Hairdressing Exhibition and she still hadn't found a dress to wear. She and Ann had visited Brown Thomas's, Switzer's and Pim's; they had even travelled to Belfast to the new House of Fraser store, all without success. When Wendy Brimcombe told Alice that Arnotts of Henry Street had put their new-season fashions on display the two sisters rushed off to find the elusive dress.

The tram came to a juddering halt at Nelson's Pillar, and the sisters disembarked; as they crossed O'Connell Street, a speeding cyclist crashed into Alice and sent her lurching forward. Alice collided with an oncoming couple, the young man staggered backwards and the young woman dropped her handbag. Alice steadied herself, picked up the handbag and held it out to the young woman.

'Still drinking in the afternoon, are we Alice?' asked the young man.

Alice froze. It was George Gilbert and he was smiling warmly at her. A jolt of excitement surged through her. She couldn't take her eyes off him – his dark hair, his deep brown eyes and the calmness he exuded made her feel alive and happy. Then she looked at the young woman accompanying him and her excitement dimmed. The woman was in her twenties, slim and pretty with silky long brunette hair.

'Oh, pay no attention to George,' smiled the young woman as she took the handbag from Alice. 'I've learnt that it's best to ignore him when he teases me.'

'I'm not going to ignore him? That man's brother assaulted my fiancé Braiden Doyle! His nose is broken and he will have a black eye for our wedding! Would you ignore that?' demanded Ann.

'I'm really sorry about your fiancé,' George said humbly. 'Alice, could I have a word?'

'No you could not, and I'm glad that she broke up with you!' Ann added still trembling with rage.

'But the fight wasn't George's fault,' said George's lady friend, trying to calm the situation. 'George, we have to go, we're already late.' And she took the young man's arm and led him away. He glanced back at Alice as he went, a ghost of a smile dancing briefly on his lips. But then he was gone, lost in the crowd.

'Ann, you're upset, let's go and get a cup of tea,' said Alice, putting her arm around her sister.

'I'm sorry if I embarrassed you in public, shouting like that. But Braiden looks so awful and I feel so sorry for him.'

'You didn't embarrass me. You had every right to say what you said. George's brother's behaviour was unforgivable.'

'George didn't waste much time getting a new girlfriend, did he?' said Ann, cheering up.

'Let's go and get that cup of tea and say no more about any of this,' said Alice firmly.

A cold wind whipped up the choppy waters of the River Liffey, as George and his lady companion crossed O'Connell Bridge. He flipped up the collar of his heavy overcoat and the young woman plunged her hands deep into her coat pockets.

'She still likes you,' she said, sternly.

'I don't think she does.'

'She likes you and you know it. What I don't understand is why you were flirting with her just now.'

'I wasn't flirting with her.'

'You assured me it was over between the two of you.'

'It is.'

'And you promised it would stay that way.'

'And it will stay that way.'

'Good.'

Alice spent most of the next two weeks sitting in a hairdressing chair being fussed over by her father and his chief stylist, Larry White. The first couple of days were spent with the two men lifting and holding her hair in all sorts of different styles. Then Larry would sketch Alice's hair and he and Thomas would sit and talk. On the third day, after much thought and consideration, Thomas decided that the basis for his design would be a classical Grecian cut. Every morning, Larry washed, shampooed and oiled Alice's hair. Then with great skill, efficiency and grace, Thomas's scissors delicately snipped at Alice's hair as he reinterpreted and modified the traditional Grecian hairstyle to something that was uniquely Thomas Dalton. As his design evolved, his hands moved with increasing speed, accuracy and efficiency and after much experimentation and adaptation, his design was complete. The basic Grecian style now featured a decorative Marcel wave with hanging curls that draped boldly onto Alice's neck. When Thomas showed Larry his finished work, the hairstylist beamed and fluttered his hands in the air.

'That's a world-class hairstyle, full of life, elegance and beauty! The cut is sharp and the style exciting. It is an exceptional design and Alice looks fabulous. Congratulations Thomas, you have outdone yourself.'

'What do you think Alice?' asked Thomas as he swung the chair around so she could see herself in the mirror.

'It looks wonderful, Father,' cried Alice, delighted. She thought happily: *I look like a glamorous film actress.* 'I'll be back in a minute!'

Upstairs, with Ann's admiring help, she changed into the new dress they had bought in Arnotts – a slender green silk that showed off her colouring – and descended again to the salon.

The two men applauded politely, but it was clear they were more interested in her hair and their own genius. Thomas spent the next half hour writing up the details of the processes and techniques he had employed to achieve his design. Larry made an almost life-size sketch of the result and when they had finished their work, the two happy hairdressers went out for a well-earned lunch without even thinking of inviting their model.

Alice remained in the chair, turning her head from side to side, indulging in a happy moment of personal admiration. For the first time in a while, she was almost able to banish George from her thoughts. Almost. She'd spent the last two weeks racking her brains over how to let the young man know she'd made a terrible mistake…

And then she saw Terrance's reflection in the mirror.

At first she thought she was seeing things, and blinked hard. But when she looked again, he was still there, standing in the middle of the salon. Spinning around in the chair, she jumped down and ran to throw her arms around him.

'It's so wonderful to see you!' she cried, when she'd finally released him. 'I'm so glad you're home!'

'It's wonderful to see you too, Alice.' Terrance held his sister at arm's length. 'Let me look at you. You're all grown up and you're beautiful! What's the occasion?'

'I'm Father's new hair model and we're going to London next week!' Alice did a twirl in front of her brother. 'What do you think? Do I or don't I look gorgeous?'

'You look gorgeous. You will drive those English chaps mad.' Terrance touched her curls lovingly. 'How is the family?'

'Everyone's fine. Ann is getting married in a few weeks. Do you know her fiancé, Braiden Doyle?'

'Yea, I know him.' He was still smiling, but Alice noted the coolness in his voice. 'Is his father still in the liquor business?'

'Yes, they have a warehouse in Lord Edward Street. Will you be here for the wedding?'

'Naturally, I will. I'm home for good.'

'For good?' Alice's eyes opened wide with pleasure. 'Does Father know you're home yet?'

'Not yet.'

'You just missed him! He and Larry went to lunch. I should tell you, Father's businesses are not doing well. It's something to do with a recession or a depression.'

'I know, Jarlath told me. Alice, I was hoping you could help smooth the way for me with Father? I want to make things right between him and me but if I simply turn up at the house unannounced, I'm worried he might refuse to see me.'

'So you want me to arrange a meeting?'

'I do.'

'What do I get out of it?' Alice asked coyly.

'My undying love.'

'I have that already.'

'You haven't changed, you're still a cheeky monkey.' Terrance placed his cap on his head. 'I've got to go. Arrange the meeting.'

A cold wind howled as a nervous Alice and a very unenthusiastic Ann walked up Rathmines Road to the Church of Mary Immaculate parish hall. It was the opening night of the Rathmines and Rathgar musical society's Gilbert and Sullivan spring concert and the footpaths were choked with last-minute concert goers rushing to the hall. Alice and Ann bought their tickets and while Ann went looking for two seats, Alice made her way to the piano where George and the master-of-ceremonies were talking.

'I came to wish you good luck,' Alice said to George when the master-of-ceremonies finally left.

He looked up at her. 'Thank you. I didn't know you were interested in Gilbert and Sullivan music?'

'Oh, I'm interested in lots of things.' She rested her elbow on the piano. She was wearing her beautiful green dress, and her hair was still perfectly styled.

George looked closely at her. 'You seem different?'

'Do I? You look much the same yourself. How are you?'

'Very well, thank you, Alice. The show's about to start. Perhaps you should take your seat.'

But Alice still hesitated, fidgeting, nervously plucking at the skirt of her dress. 'Can we talk after the show?'

'What happened?' asked Ann, when Alice sat down beside her.

'He said we can talk after the concert. He wasn't very friendly.'

'Oh dear… Oh, the curtain's going up!' Ann enjoyed the show, singing along under her breath and laughing at the antics of the comic actors. Alice, who was feeling desperately unhappy, thought that all the songs sounded the same and that it was all a bit silly. When the show was over and the hall was nearly empty, she approached the stage.

George had spent the show thinking about her. He desperately wanted to make up with her; he longed to hold her hand and see her smile. He wanted to kiss her and spend every minute with her. Yet he had promised not to pursue her, and he knew it was the right thing to do.

'Hello again,' said Alice. 'I just wanted to apologise for doubting you and accusing you of doing something you didn't do.'

He nodded, formally. 'You didn't have to come all the way here to say that, but thank you, it's nice of you.'

Alice placed her hand on his arm.'George, I mean it – I'm really sorry. I know there was nothing between you and Tess.'

George's face darkened as he looked down at Alice's hand. 'Alice, I may have given you the wrong impression. You're a lovely person but…' He hesitated. 'What I mean to say is, I'm not really interested in having a girlfriend right now.'

Alice stared at him, praying he was joking; when he didn't smile and his face remained serious, she wished the ground would open up and swallow her. She had never been so forward with a boy before and now she felt humiliated, rejected and more than a little stupid. 'I'm so sorry. I must have misunderstood you. I thought… Sorry, this is awkward… I'd better go. Goodnight.'

She walked away as quickly as she could and George looked down at the piano keys and hoped he had done the right thing.

'What did he say?' asked Ann eagerly, once they were out of the hall.

'He said he's not interested in me.'

'I don't believe that. I saw the way he looked at you.'

'I don't want to talk about it,' Alice replied and tears filled her eyes.

An anxious Jarlath paced his father's office in the rear of the High Street salon, waiting for Thomas to arrive. It was such an unusual occurrence for his father to ask him to the office that the young man felt it had to be good news. Yet at the same time, he hoped it wouldn't be a long meeting; despite the economic downturn, he still had a busy social life.

At five minutes past the appointed hour, Thomas strolled into his office and sat down behind his desk.

'I'm in a bit of a hurry Father,' Jarlath said. 'I have an important card game to get to.'

Thomas gestured to the chair in front of the desk, Jarlath hesitated and then took it.

'There are a few things I want to discuss,' said Thomas, drumming his fingers on the desk. 'First, what have you done about finding employment?'

'I'm still thinking about that,' Jarlath reassured him. 'Still, it might not be necessary. A good friend told me that he heard the economy is about to improve.'

'Whoever told you that is an idiot,' said Thomas, as he rummaged in the top drawer of his desk. When he found the papers he was looking for, he placed them one at a time on the top of his desk. 'This invoice is from your horse's livery yard, for feed and other associated costs. I have also received several invoices for club memberships.'

Jarlath was surprised. 'You said you'd cover necessary expenses?'

'Your horse and club memberships are not necessary expenses, Jarlath.' Thomas rotated the invoices and slid them across the desk.

'And what am I supposed to do with them?' asked Jarlath indignantly.

'You're supposed to pay them,' Thomas replied calmly. 'If you can't do that, you need to sell your horse and resign from your clubs.'

'If this is your way of trying to get me to work for you,' retorted Jarlath heatedly, 'then you can stop. I refuse to work in one of your salons.'

'Good, because that option isn't available to you,' said Thomas sharply, but then decided to change tack before their meeting descended into an argument. 'Jarlath, what do you like to do?'

The young man looked confused. 'I like tennis, sailing, canoeing, swimming and horse riding.'

'I meant what are your ambitions?'

Again, Jarlath looked quizzically at his father.

'Jarlath, what do you want to do with your life?'

'Oh, I see… Frankly, I have no idea. I have thought about it, but nothing seems to present itself to me.'

'Don't you have a dream?' asked Thomas, exasperation rising in his voice.

Jarlath realised his father was getting annoyed, so he answered as honestly as he could. 'No, Father, I can't say that I have a dream.'

Thomas wiped his forehead with his handkerchief. 'Most men of your age, Jarlath, have some sort idea of what they'd like to do with their lives.'

'You mean like Terrance's Republican dream?'

Thomas flinched and dropped the handkerchief on his desk.

With a slight smile, Jarlath rose to his feet. 'Now that he's back in Dublin perhaps you'd like to congratulate your second son on his ambitious dream. I ran into him the other day drinking with his Republican friends.' And he stalked out of the office, leaving a flabbergasted Thomas staring blindly after him.

Two nights later, after the close of business, Alice asked her father if he would come up to her room to take another look at the dress she had selected for the exhibition in London. 'I've made a few alterations with buttons and things, and I want to know if you approve...'

'It looked fine to me the way it was, Alice. I'm not sure I'm the one to ask about lady's apparel. You should ask your sisters or mother,' said Thomas, but he followed her patiently out of his office into the house next door and up the stairs.

Once he was in Alice's bedroom, his second son stepped out from behind the curtains.

'Hello Father,' said Terrance.

Thomas's eyes darkened. 'So it is true, you have returned to Ireland.' He ignored his son's outstretched hand. 'It's just like you to use your sister to trick me into meeting you. Before you say another word, let me tell you you have broken your mother's heart and brought shame on this family.'

'Father, I am sorry...'

'I have not finished. In the eyes of the law you are still a convicted criminal. Please leave this house.'

'Father, the world moves on and we have to as well,' sighed Terrance.

'What kind of talk is that?'

Alice moved to Terrance's side.

'Father, please. We are family. If Terrance is passionate about his vision of this country then that is his passion. He believes in what he is doing as you believe in what you're doing. Like you, I don't agree with Terrance but a lot of Irish people do and the government is not pursuing those people for their views. So perhaps, just perhaps, Terrance might be right.'

Thomas stood erect, his eyes filled with sadness.

'Alice, your loyalty to your brother is admirable and does you credit. So for your sake and the sake of your other brother and sisters, if Terrance gives me an assurance that he will refrain from all Republican activities while he's here in this house, he can stay.'

'I will,' promised Terrance.

'Say the words, Terrance,' Thomas demanded.

'I will refrain from all Republican activities while I live in this house.'

'One other thing. If the police come to arrest you, I want you to hand yourself over to them without protest – is that understood?'

'Yes sir,' Terrance replied.

'Very well, you can stay and you can thank your sister for it,' Thomas said coldly and left the room.

CHAPTER SIXTEEN

To be in London, the largest and greatest city in the world, the city of kings and queens and the beating heart of the British Empire, was so exhilarating to Alice that she could hardly contain her excitement. She and her father stood under the statue of the winged Eros on Piccadilly Circus and watched the busy traffic spin around them in organised chaos. The endless stream of trams, red double decker buses, motorcycles, sidecars, hansom cabs, cyclists and motorcars all moving, all honking horns or ringing bells, astounded her. The footpaths too were places of wonder. Exotically dressed people speaking in strange languages rushed, walked or strolled around the circle and disappeared into shops and department stores or down the dark entrances to the city's underground.

'Pick three places you'd like to visit,' Thomas said, as he and his daughter ambled up Regents Street. 'Tomorrow and the following day we work, but today we play.'

'I'd like to see Buckingham Palace, the Tower of London and the Houses of Parliament,' Alice replied without hesitation.

Thirty minutes later, Thomas and Alice were peering through the railings of Buckingham Palace and Alice was wondering if King George V was in the palace, and if so what was he doing. Reading a book? Drinking tea? Later, as they toured the eerie Tower of London, Alice thought about Terrance and the time he'd spent in one of His Majesty's prisons. In the afternoon, she gazed on the magnificence of the Houses of Parliament and thought of the many laws that were enacted there that had caused so much pain and upheaval in her own country.

After their day of sightseeing, a tired Thomas and a very hungry Alice sat in Mario's of Leicester Square and enjoyed a beautiful Italian meal. Towards the end of their meal, they were joined by Larry White and while the two men talked Alice's mind wandered. She loved the straw-covered Chianti bottles which the retaurant used as candle holders. How lovely it would be to sit with George at a table in one of those small alcoves! The candle would throw a flickering golden light on his handsome face...

Oh, she had to stop thinking about him!

The main exhibition hall at Earl's Court was gigantic; Alice had never seen the likes. It was divided into seven lines, and each line had thirty contestant stands. Every stand was exactly the same size and contained two large free-standing mirrors, a hot and cold water supply, a table, three electrical outlets and a comfortable hairdresser's salon chair.

Above their heads, a balcony encircled the entire floor area, from which spectators could observe the competitors at work.

Upon presenting their credentials, Thomas and Alice were directed to Stand 35, Aisle 2. As they walked down their line, Alice marvelled at the beauty and elegance of the exotic-looking hair models. When she and her father arrived at the stand, they found Larry White in the final stages of unpacking their supplies.

Day one of the competition was all about skill and technique. Each hairdresser was assigned a model of the day and required to style their hair in a certain way, although the competitors were expected to add a unique personal twist to their work.

While Thomas waited for his model to arrive, a tall, clean-shaven young man in a striped suit approached him.

'Mr Dalton,' the man began, in a strong Cork accent, 'let me introduce myself. My name is Eamon Maloney and it is a privilege to be in the same competition as youself. I wonder if I might shake your hand, sir?'

'Certainly, Mr Maloney.' Thomas shook the young man's offered hand.

'I would be extremely honoured if when the day's activities are over, you would come and say hello to my mother?'

'Certainly,' said Thomas politely. 'But right now, it is time to concentrate on the competition. It is a big day for all of us. Good luck to you, sir.'

'And good luck to you,' said Eamon Maloney.

'That boy is an upstart,' grumbled Larry White, the moment the youth was out of earshot. 'He's the last-minute replacement for the Munster area. The first and second alternatives became unavailable and he was the only remotely eligible candidate.'

A bell peeled and all persons except the competitors and their models of the day had to leave the floor. Alice and Larry retired to the spectators' gallery, from where they watched Thomas and the other two hundred and nine competitors go about their work.

Thomas was only just getting started when he was distracted by the competitor on the next stand calling out frantically to a passing steward: 'My assistant has failed to pack a razor comb and a thinning scissors! Would you be good enough to ask my boy to bring the missing implements to me?'

'Sir, once the day's competition has commenced no additional equipment can be brought into the hall,' replied the bowler-hatted steward officiously. 'However, it is within the rules to borrow from a fellow competitor.'

'Borrow from a fellow competitor?' exclaimed the excited hairdresser. 'Who in their right mind would help a fellow competitor?'

'A fair-minded one,' said Thomas, as he passed over a razor comb and a thinning scissors. 'I have brought spares.'

'Bless you sir, you are a gentleman,' replied the stunned but relieved hairdresser. 'I shall return them at the end of the day.'

When the allotted time was up, the bell peeled twice and a team of adjudicators walked from stand to stand and marked each competitor's work. Four hours later the scores were posted on the bulletin board outside the main hall. Thomas received ninety eight points, putting him in second place. To Larry's surprise, Eamon Maloney received eighty points, putting him in fifteenth place. Not bad for an upstart!

On the second day of the competition the exhibition hall was much busier and louder. Hairdressers, stylists and assistants rushed up and down the aisles carrying equipment, odd-shaped bottles and huge heavy brown boxes; all were talking excitedly, all were gesturing wildly and all were intense. While Thomas and Larry attended to last-minute preparations, Alice took a walk around the great hall. As she passed along the competitors' stands, she winced at the array of odd and dangerous-looking pieces of hairdressing equipment on the tables; some of the equipment reminded her of the instruments of torture she had seen in the Tower of London. Halfway down Aisle 4, a pale-faced, dark-haired young man came striding towards her. Her heart leapt with delight.

'You're here!' she cried, rushing up to him and when she immediately realised that the young man wasn't George she stopped.

'Are you all right?' the man asked, politely.

'I'm sorry, I mistook you for someone else,' replied Alice, flushed with embarrassment.

'Well, I hope he knows what a lucky man he is,' replied the young man, as he tipped his hat to Alice and walked on down the line.

A warning bell sounded and the assistants and stylists rushed to complete their tasks. By the time Alice had returned to Stand 35, the hall was quiet. The bell peeled a second time and the competition commenced. Thomas washed Alice's hair, applied some lotion, rinsed the hair and gently towel-dried it. He combed her hair, placed the hairdryer bag on her head and turned on his machine. He was preparing his special liniment for the next stage of his creation when the hairdryer groaned, emitted a foul puff of smoke and shuddered to a halt.

'No!' exclaimed a horrified Thomas as he rushed to switch off the dryer.

'What's wrong?' exclaimed Alice.

'I don't know!' He examined his malfunctioning machine, waited a few minutes and turned it on again. The noxious smell of a burning heating element filled the stand. Groaning, he unplugged the dryer and disconnected the bag; he leant against the table in despair.

'Can you not fix it, Father?' asked Alice tentatively.

'No, I can't. The fan has failed and the element has burnt out.'

'Then what are you going to do?'

'The only thing I can do. I have to ask some fellow competitor for the use of their machine.'

Thomas spent the next fifteen minutes going from stand to stand enquiring if he could borrow a spare hairdryer. He was unsuccessful. Word of his plight quickly spread around the hall and he received a lot of sympathy, but no offer of a dryer. Dejected, he returned to his stand to find Eamon Maloney deep in conversation with Alice.

'I heard you're in need of a dryer, sir,' said the Cork man, holding out a wooden box. 'I'd like to offer you the use of mine.'

Thomas was taken aback. 'Doesn't your design require a hairdryer?'

'I can easily manage without. Besides, we both know I haven't a chance of winning the competition. It's enough for me to be part of this great event. Please, the machine is yours. Take it, Mr Dalton.'

'This is unbelievably generous of you.' Thomas was overwhelmed by the young man's kindness.

'It's no more than you did for a fellow competitor yesterday,' Eamon replied. Then, turning to Alice, he added, 'I look forward to seeing you again, Miss Dalton.'

'And I you,' smiled Alice.

Using Eamon Maloney's hairdryer, Thomas resumed his work, trying not to hurry because of lost time. When Alice's hair was dry he applied his special liniment and gently worked the shape of the coiffure. The clock was ticking, and it was hard to keep his hands from taking risks, but once the curls fell the way he intended them to fall, he knew his creation was going to be a resounding success.

Just as he stood back to admire his work, the bell peeled, signalling the end of the session. The stewards called for all the hairdressers to stop work and to stand away from their creations. Moments later, a huge oak door at the top of the hall opened and five separate groups of adjudicators entered the hall.

After what seemed an interminable wait, the examiners arrived at Thomas's stand. Alice sat as still as she could and the adjudicators walked around her and scrutinised every detail of the cut and style. They whispered to each other and made a point of scribbling notes on their large, lined, yellow notepads then – with a silent nod to Alice and her father – they moved on to the next stand. Two hours later, after reviewing every competitor's work, all the adjudicators left the main hall to confer and decide on the results in private.

'This is the worst part,' said Thomas, as he paced the aisle beside his stand.

'Why don't we go over to Eamon Maloney and say hello to his mother?' suggested Alice.

'Good idea. I think Larry might have been wrong about that young man. If he's an upstart, he's a bright and generous one.'

'Yes, Larry was always a bit of a snob about non-Dublin people,' said Alice as she took her father's arm.

When they arrived at Eamon Maloney's stand, Thomas was amazed by the young man's beautiful hair design. It was young and fresh and extremely well-executed. If it had a fault, it was that the coiffure was drooping very slightly to one side because it had been fixed before it was fully dry.

'Why in heaven's name did you lend me your dryer?' asked Thomas in amazement. 'You could have scored very highly, and instead you virtually eliminated yourself from the competition!'

'Thank you for your kind assessment, Mr Dalton, but I fear you are overstating the case,' smiled the young Corkman.

'Not at all. You are an excellent hairdresser. Please, you must come and see me the next time you're in Dublin. There is much we can talk about.'

'I will,' said Eamon. 'It will be my pleasure. Now, let me admire your exquisite creation.' And he made Alice turn around and around, while he studied the elegant fall of her curls.

By the time Alice and Thomas returned to their stand, Larry had already packed away most of their belongings into travelling boxes.

Three hours later, all the contestants, along with their models and assistants, gathered in the exhibition hall's long bar for the announcement of the results. The chief adjudicator stood on a specially erected podium and asked for quiet. When the almost panicky chatter fell silent, it was announced that Mark Allen from London was the second runner-up and Pol Ó h-Ailín from Manchester was first runner-up. The inhabitants of the long bar held their breaths as the President of the International Hairdressing Committee opened the last envelope and announced that the overall winner of the competition and the winner of this year's Earl's Court Coiffeur's Trophy was Thomas Dalton from Dublin.

Jumping up and down, Alice hugged her father and Larry White. An excited Thomas made his way to the podium and in his acceptance speech, he thanked Alice and Larry for their help and assistance and then he thanked Eamon Maloney for his self-less generosity. 'Without that fine young man's help, someone else would be standing here accepting the trophy and there is every likelihood that person would have been Eamon himself.'

That night, Thomas, Larry and Alice celebrated their success with dinner in the exclusive Trocadero restaurant on Shaftesbury Avenue. After their meal, they were sitting listening to the orchestra play a Viennese waltz when Eamon Maloney approached the table and asked Alice to dance. To Alice's delight, it turned out that he was a natural dancer and she thoroughly enjoyed being swept around the floor in his arms. After their third dance, Thomas invited Eamon and his party to join the Dalton table.

The Maloney and the Dalton families talked and laughed and toasted each other and Thomas's victory. During their happy conversation, Alice found herself telling the table how she had mistaken a complete stranger for a man she knew called George Gilbert and how embarrassed she was when she'd realised her mistake. Everyone smiled and laughed, except Thomas.

'Isn't Gilbert a Protestant name?' he asked suspiciously.

'Is it? I suppose it is.' Alice was annoyed at herself for even bringing it up. It wasn't like George meant anything to her anymore. It was just that he kept popping into her head, unbidden...

'How are you acquainted with a man called Gilbert?'

'Please don't worry about it, Father. I'm not acquainted with him anymore.'

The mood at the table changed and shortly after that everyone returned to their hotels.

It was Sunday morning and a nervous George Gilbert waited across the street from St Audoen's Church. With a clatter, the church's huge oak doors swung open and men, women and children flowed out onto the street. Alice and Ann were passing through the church's heavy iron gates when George saw them. His heart beat faster and the palms of his hands grew sweaty. Alice removed her head scarf, shook her head and her magnificent hair fluttered in the breeze. Then she glanced his way, and their eyes met. He started across the street but Ann noticed him before he could reach the other side and ushered Alice away; Alice glanced back over her shoulder, met his gaze, then broke eye contact.

Not knowing what else to do, he followed at a distance.

When the sisters arrived home, they stood talking on the steps while George hung back. At last, Alice walked over to George while Ann waited.

'Why are you here?' she demanded. 'What do you want?'

'I want to talk to you.'

'You have nothing to say that would interest me.'

'It's about Braiden Doyle.'

Alice blinked. Whatever she'd been expecting, it hadn't been this. 'My sister's fiancé? The man your brother assaulted?'

'It's important, Alice.'

She flushed. 'If it's so important put it in a letter and don't bother me again.'

The instant the words were out of her mouth, she regretted saying them. But there was nothing she could do to take them back, so she turned and walked away.

The stylishly dressed John Swords and a dapper, grey-suited Thomas Dalton strolled through Stephen's Green on their way to the Hibernian Club. It was Thomas's first visit since he cancelled his membership and he was looking forward to it.

Having won the prestigious Earl's Court competition, his star had risen. He was photographed widely, interviewed by the newspapers and had even been asked to give the keynote address at the Hairdressing Society of Ireland's annual dinner. Most importantly, despite the continuing depression, his salons were for the first time in years, beginning to show a small profit.

Before following John into the building, Thomas paused on the stone step to listen to the bird sounds of the park mingling with the hum of the city. It felt like a rare moment of peace in his increasingly busy life.

'Thomas?'

'Coming, John.' He stepped through the entrance of the club.

After an exquisite meal and a fine Chablis the two men relocated to the club's Amber lounge and sipped two Remy Martin brandies. Thomas hadn't realised how much he missed his club: its beautifully appointed rooms, the waiters in white dinner jackets and the hushed voices of the members in quiet conversation. Thomas leaned back in his chair, gave a quick twirl to the tips of his moustache and cleared his throat.

'I have a favour to ask you John.'

John smiled, polishing his silver-rimmed spectacles with a white linen handkerchief. 'When you use my name in that tone of voice Thomas, I get very apprehensive.'

Thomas grimaced, and said lightly, 'Probably with good reason in this case. I'm looking for your help with my oldest boy, Jarlath. He needs employment.'

'The lad who had the perfume idea?'

'The very one, and it nearly succeeded. It was a good idea, and could have been a profitable concern.'

'I'm assuming from your expression that it wasn't a profitable concern?'

'You're right, it wasn't. Jarlath, I fear, had little real interest in the perfume business.'

'Then what is he interested in?'

'That I do not know,' replied Thomas with a sigh. 'I have asked the question but I didn't get a satisfactory answer.'

'That's not so uncommon in young men today. One of my lads was the same, but he came around eventually and now he's one of my greatest assets. Are you sure there is no aspect of the business that Jarlath would enjoy?'

'I fear not.'

'But the salons are busy again?'

'They are indeed, although it will take time and hard work to get everything back to how it was before the recession. By the way, I've said nothing about the improvement to Jarlath. He would only use the good news as an excuse to remain idle, and I think it will do him good to work for his living.'

'I see...' John rubbed his chin thoughtfully. 'I do have a need for a warehouse manager. It's not an arduous job but it is a responsible one. Jarlath would have to be there every day from eight thirty in the morning until six in the evening. It's a position of trust and he'll have to keep a watchful eye on the delivery men and on the warehouse staff. Theft is a big problem in the warehouse business. Do you think that might suit him?'

'I know it would,' said Thomas gratefully.

'Then I'll take him on a trial basis. I'll make the necessary arrangements.'

'Thank you, John. It's very good of you to help.'

The morning was warm and a bright sun illuminated the city as Alice and Ann arrived at Gertrude Finnie's design studio on Aston Quay. The appointment was for the final fitting of Ann's wedding dress and she was very excited, especially as Miss Gertrude Finne herself was going to be there. To get a personal appointment with Miss Finnie was a very rare thing, but Father had talked to someone who had talked to someone else, and somehow it had been arranged.

Ann stood beaming in front of a full-length mirror while Miss Finnie's assistant, the attractive if somewhat severe Miss McDonagh, buttoned up the back of the beautiful white silk wedding dress. Moments later, Miss Finnie swept into the studio, held her lorgnette to her eyes and sighed.

'You're a very short person,' she complained. 'If you were taller, my beautfiul creation would hang so much better.'

'I am a very *neat* person,' replied Ann, somewhat hurt. 'Perhaps if I wore higher heels?'

'If your heels were any higher you'd topple over. But perhaps there are things I can do to salvage the situation,' murmured Miss Finne, lifting the dress from Ann's slight shoulders and letting it drop again.

'Perhaps you could add a small train?' suggested Alice.

With a flourish, Miss Finne turned and studied Alice through her hand-held spectacles. 'I don't like extraneous people in my studio. Isn't there somewhere else you could be?'

The day Jarlath commenced his employment with Liffey Imports as warehouse manager, John Swords asked his yard supervisor, Gerry Dwyer, to keep an eye out for Jarlath and help him learn the ropes. Gerry Dwyer, a tall, thin balding man in hismid-forties, had worked for John for more than twenty years; he was nicknamed "the Grey Man" because of his grey eyes, grey sideburns and uncared-for grey hair. He showed Jarlath into a small nondescript office and explained to him his duties and responsibilities. Jarlath listened grudgingly. He knew he wasn't going to enjoy working in the warehouse but it seemed he had no alternative.

Tess was no happier than her oldest brother. She had been sick of hearing about Earl's Court and now she was fed up with the endless details of Ann's imminent wedding. To have her younger sister getting married before her was embarrassing enough, but to not have a beau of her own to bring to the wedding made the situation unbearable.

Another family member who had been driven to despair by all the wedding talk was Thomas; to avoid it, he had taken to having breakfast before the girls got up.

One morning, he slipped back into the breakfast room while his daughters were still eating their toast. 'Alice, this letter was included in my morning post,' he said, placing an envelope next to her teacup.

Alice glanced at the envelope, recognised the return address and decided to ignore it.

'Who's the letter from?' asked Ann, from across the table.

'George Gilbert,' replied Alice, in a low voice.

'That Protestant man?' Her father was still hovering behind her. 'Why is he writing to you?'

Alice's shoulders tensed. 'It concerns the dancing school, Father. George played the piano for us for a while, but we have a different piano player now.'

'I'm glad to hear it,' said Thomas, leaving the room.

Tess picked up the letter and was about to open it when Alice snatched it from her hand and stuffed it into the pocket of her skirt. 'It's addressed to me.'

'But it "concerns the dancing school",' protested Tess, in mock innocence.

Alice glared at her.

'Are you going to read it or burn it?' asked Ann.

Alice glared at Ann as well. 'I'll decide later.'

Alice stood waiting at the Dublin United Tramway stop in High Street. Swaying from side to side, an aluminium and brown steel tram clanked to a halt. Alice boarded the vehicle, sat on the wooden seat near the front of the tram and paid the sickly-looking conductor the fare. Alone at last, she removed George's letter from her pocket and opened it.

Dear Alice,

I apologise again for my brother's behaviour. I do not approve of violence but I assure you Dessie had good reasons to do what he did. I know one should not speak ill of people but when one person's actions impact on the lives of people you care about, it is wrong to stay silent. Your sister's fiancé Braiden Doyle is not all he appears to be. He presents himself as an honourable man but I know him to be anything but. He uses people for his own ends and then discards them. He had an involvement with someone my family cared greatly about and he treated her in an abominable fashion. It is possible that he has changed but I do not believe so. If you'd like to discuss this situation further, meet me at Merchant's Arch across from the Halfpenny Bridge on Saturday at 4 o'clock.

Yours sincerely,
George.

Alice rested the letter on her knees. She had no idea what to do.

Back in the drawing room of the High Street house, Thomas was reading about himself in that morning's newspaper when Tess slipped into the room and sat opposite him.

'What is it Tess?' asked Thomas, annoyed at this invasion of his private time.

'Father, there is something you should know.'

'Tess, I'm reading my newspaper. I can't go into the dining room for all the talk of the wedding. I came in here for a little peace. Please leave me to myself.'

'Father, this is important.'

With a sigh, Thomas folded his newspaper and placed it on his lap.'What is it that is so important?'

'It's about that Protestant man who wrote to Alice, George Gilbert.'

'As you know, I asked Alice about that, and she assured me that she has now employed a different acompanist.'

'But I think she is still interested in him....'

'I've heard all I want to hear from you, Tess, so please leave.' He shook out his newspaper and buried himself behind it.

Tess remained sitting where she was for a few moments; then with a loud snort, she stood up and flounced out of the door.

On the north side of the Liffey, in the back garden of 5 Primrose Avenue, George and Dessie Gilbert were preparing to spend their morning cleaning out the shed at the end of the garden. The shed had been their father's annual chore, but since his passing two years ago, it had been left untouched, just gathering rubbish. After much urging from their mother, the brothers had finally decided to do the job. They removed wooden boxes, coal bags and an assortment of tattered curtains and other debris. In an old tea-chest George discovered a battered well worn biscuit box with his name scratched on its top. When he prized open the lid, he found a rusting cap pistol, a faded and dented metal toy car and a tiny book of childhood rhymes. On a shelf at the back of the shed Dessie discovered an old bicycle pump. The two brothers were standing in the near dark of the shed examining their finds when their mother arrived with two mugs of tea.

'That's your father's bicycle pump,' Mary Gilbert said, handing each of her boys their tea. She took the device from Dessie and pumped it twice. 'It still works. I wish everything old could last so well.' She fell quiet and George put his arm around his mother. Elbowing him away, she rubbed her eyes with the palm of her hand. 'Will you get away with yourself, you'll have me ballin' in no time. Drink the tea while it's hot. The coal will be arriving on Monday, make sure there's plenty of room for it.'

When they had finished their work, George propped himself against the window ledge, took out a packet of cigarettes, lit one and inhaled deeply.

'You're very quiet today,' said Dessie. 'Are you not feeling well?'

'I'm very well and stop asking me that,' George said sharply.

'I only asked,' replied Dessie, holding his hands in the air in mock surrender. 'Anyway, how are you and that Dalton girl getting along?'

'We're not.'

'I thought you liked her.'

'I do, but Freda thinks it's best to put an end to it.'

'Don't mind Freda, what does she know?'

George hesitated, seemed about to say something, but then took a deep drag of his cigarette instead.

'Do you want me to talk to her?' offered Dessie.

'Not a good idea.'

'Only trying to help.' Dessie plucked the packet of cigarettes out of George's shirt pocket and helped himself to one. 'Why don't you just go and talk to the girl?'

'I wrote to her and asked her to meet me on Saturday.'

'Good, take her somewhere nice. I wouldn't recommend Mooney's Pub, I heard a lot ruffians go there.'

George frowned, then smiled and playfully punched his brother in the arm.

CHAPTER SEVENTEEN

F ive days after starting his new employment, Jarlath instructed a warehouse worker to load twelve boxes of brandy onto the back of George Brust's horse and cart. When the Grey Man saw what was going on he rubbed his stubbled jaw and said out of the side of his mouth to Jarlath, 'We don't use Brust to deliver valuable goods. He's not to be trusted above a certain amount.'

'I fully understand that, but this is an emergency delivery and I have cleared it with Mr Sword's.'

'If those are Mr Sword's instructions, then Brust it is,' murmured the Grey Man, scratching his rough, grey head.

Alice decided to visit the pro-Cathedral for guidance. Kneeling in the pew beneath the huge stained glass window of the Blessed Virgin Mary, she bowed her head and prayed. She prayed that Ann would find happiness in her coming marriage; she prayed for her father and his businesses; she prayed that her brothers would find their places in the world and she prayed that God would give her mother peace. Then she prayed with special fervour about George and, that when it came to it, she would make the right decision.

A depressed, dishevelled and angry Jarlath sat at the counter of the Ferryman's Pub on Sir John Rogerson's Quay and downed a large Jameson whiskey in one. That morning, everything had been going swimmingly and he'd been fairly happy in his life. At three in the afternoon, disaster had struck in the shape of his employer, John Swords.

'Good afternoon Jarlath,' John began, strolling into the office and removing his hat.

'Good aft…'

'Perhaps you'd explain to me why you had twelve boxes of the finest brandy loaded onto George Brust's cart this morning?'

'Well, I…'

'And why you told Gerry Dwyer that I gave you permission to do so?'

Beads of cold sweat trickled down the back of Jarlath's neck and soaked into the collar of his shirt. 'I have no idea what you're talking about,' he quavered, praying that the tremble in his voice would go unnoticed.

John sighed and ran his hand over his bald head. 'Very well. Are you saying you never gave instructions to have twelve boxes of VSOP brandy loaded onto George Brust's horse and cart?'

'I don't think I know a George Brust,' said Jarlath evasively.

'Oh, Brust is a most distinctive fellow,' said John. 'He's a middle-aged, chubby-faced man with a red beard and rather beady little eyes. My warehouse superviser informed me you gave specific instructions to have the boxes loaded onto Brust's cart.'

'I don't think I remember that,' Jarlath did his best to look innocent, while conscious that his face was burning red.

'What a bad memory you have, Jarlath. Well, Gerry Dwyer followed Brust and the merchandise to Pascal Doyle's warehouse in Lord Edward Street. There, Brust unloaded the stock.'

Jarlath's mouth was dry and his heart pumped so hard that he feared he might have a heart attack. 'You mean, Brust was stealing from you? That's disgraceful…'

'Which is exactly what I thought. I immediately informed the police and they arrested the man. But you'll be pleased to hear he wasn't stealing the brandy after all.'

'Oh thank God...'

'No, apparently he was acting on your orders.' Here John Swords paused and watched as Jarlath squirmed and racked his brains for an excuse and at last subsided in despair.

'You won't tell my father, will you?' whimpered Jarlath.

'No, I won't tell your father.'

Jarlath nearly wept with relief. 'Thank you, thank you, I vow I'll make it up to you...'

'I won't tell your father because I'm leaving that task to you. I will be seeing Thomas tonight by which time I expect him to know the whole story. By the way, there's no need to come to work tomorrow; you should stay at home and await a visit from the police.'

A shattered Jarlath was still staring into the mirror behind the bar when his soon-to-be brother-in-law, Braiden Doyle, sat down beside him.

'You made a right pig's micky of our arrangement,' snarled Braiden in an angry whisper. 'Brust sang like a canary and the police have confiscated the merchandise. What are you going to do about it?'

'What can I do? I've lost my job and now the police are involved.'

'My name better not be dragged into this.' Doyle spat saliva through his teeth and jabbed his finger into Jarlath's shoulder. 'I gave you twenty quid up front and I want it back.'

'I don't have it.'

'Get it.'

Jarlath shuddered. 'You'll have to give me a few days.'

'When I call on your sister this evening, you'd better have my money – otherwise I'll have to ask your father to cover your debt.'

'There's no point in that. My father's salons are still losing money. Why do you think I had to take the warehouse job?'

'Your father's not well-heeled?' Braiden's face grew pale. 'Then... does your mother have an inheritance?'

'Not to my knowledge. Are you going to buy me a drink?'

'Buy your own bloody drink,' snapped Braiden and stalked out of the pub.

Jarlath loosened his tie, opened the top button of his shirt and ordered another whiskey.

When Alice arrived at Merchant's Arch, she was disappointed to find that George wasn't there to greet her – even though she was half an hour early. But it was only five minutes later that she saw his dark head bobbing up and down among the oncoming crowd on the Halfpenny Bridge. Her heart quickened. She loved how he held himself; his elegant stride.

'Hello Alice,' said George tentatively, when he arrived at her side.

She answered with equal caution, 'Where do you suggest we go to talk?'

'Nolan's Tea Rooms. It's only around the corner in Temple Lane.' He didn't offer her his arm, but as they walked their hands brushed together accidentally and Alice's skin prickled with pleasure. She couldn't help stealing a glance at his handsome face and his shiny black hair; the half-smile around his eyes made her feel warm.

A few minutes later they were sitting in the tea rooms, and George was speaking and Alice – her hands cupped around her untouched tea – was listening intently.

'A few years ago Braiden Doyle met our next door neighbour, Claire Dennis. Claire was a really nice girl and she and Dessie were close. My mother always hoped they might marry. But then Claire met Braiden and everything changed. Very soon after they met, to everyone's surprise they got engaged. Braiden borrowed money from Claire and when her money ran out he borrowed from her father. When Mr Dennis stopped loaning him money,

Braiden broke off the engagement. Claire was heartbroken and when she learned she was pregnant with Braiden's child she was devastated. He maintained that the child wasn't his and he spread dreadful rumours about Claire and her family. The poor girl was so ashamed and distraught she attempted to take her own life. She survived but the baby died. Braiden skipped off to England and Claire never really got over losing the child. I only learned that Braiden had returned to Dublin when I discovered from Dessie that your poor sister was engaged to the scoundrel.'

'That's a dreadful story!' Alice stared at him wide-eyed. 'It's the wickedest thing I've ever heard! I'm glad Dessie hit Braiden, I'd do it myself if I was a man. What should I do? I should tell Ann... Oh dear, but she's so in love with him... Could Braiden have changed for the better? Oh, I'm sure he hasn't, he's probably after our father's money now... What do you think I should say to her?'

'I wish I had the answers to your questions.' George reached across the table and touched Alice's hand, this time definitely on purpose. 'I'm sorry to be the bearer of such bad news but I thought you should know.'

'It's not your fault and you did the right thing telling me, especially after I was so rude to you when you tried to speak to me before...'

'Don't apologise for that!' George's hand tightened on hers. 'Alice, I'm sorry I spoke to you the way I did at the concert. I didn't mean those things I said. I meant the very opposite.'

'Then why did you say them?'

'There are things you don't know about me.'

Alice's eyes glazed over with tears. 'It's that woman, isn't it? The one you were walking with in O'Connell Street. She's your girlfriend now.'

'Woman...' A puzzled look appeared on George's face and then he smiled.

'Why are you laughing? It's not funny! I hate making a fool of myself like this!'

'You're not! Well, not in the way you think. That woman was my sister. '

'Your sister?'

'Yes! My older sister, Freda.'

'I thought… Oh…' Alice was mortified. 'Oh George…'

'Do you think we can start over, Alice?'

'Oh, can we? I'd really like that. I've missed you so much.' And she took his hand in hers.

For the next two hours, the two young people talked and talked. George told her more about Freda and the rest of his family. Alice told the story of Terrance's homecoming, and about Jarlath's new job and then worried some more about Ann's coming wedding and what to do about it. Only when the waitress refilled the teapot for the third time, did Alice glance at her watch. 'Look at the time! My family will be wondering where I've got to.'

'We'll meet soon?' asked George, as they stood outside the tearooms.

'Yes,' replied Alice. 'Yes. I'd like that.'

'Next Saturday, same time and place? We'll do something special.'

'Surprise me!'

As George watched Alice disappear into the crowd, his smiled faded. Despite all the talking, he hadn't told her the most important thing about himself. He knew it wasn't fair to keep the truth from Alice. Yet he hadn't the heart to destroy the moment.

A beaten Jarlath knocked on the door of the salon office. He had been praying to avoid this moment, hoping against hope that John Swords would relent and let the matter drop. But when he had received his father's summons, conveyed by a puzzled Mrs Dalton, he had known the game was up. All he could do now was throw himself on his father's mercy and hope against hope that Thomas would choose family over friendship.

Thomas Dalton was standing behind his desk, his expression stony. 'Sit down Jarlath' he ordered coldly.

'I'm sorry, Father,' muttered Jarlath, hovering near the door. 'I was going to tell you, to explain...'

'But instead you chose to avoid me, and left me to find out the dreadful, mortifying news from my best friend. The friend I begged to employ you. Sit down, I said! You're not going to run out of here before I've finished with you.'

Miserably, Jarlath slouched across the room and crumpled into the chair facing the desk.

Sitting down himself, Thomas slammed his fist on the desk-top. 'Whatever possessed you to steal from the only man who was willing to employ you? You have shamed this family, shamed your own flesh and blood!'

'Father, I...'

'Be quiet! I'll start with the good news. I've persuaded John Swords not to press charges against you.'

Every nerve and muscle in Jarlath's body relaxed. So his father had chosen to put family first...

'Jarlath, pay attention!'

'Sorry Father...'

'There is a condition.'

'A condition?' Jarlath tensed again. Would he have to go back to that dreadful warehouse, and maybe work for free? It would be just like that stuck-up, fussy little John Swords...

'John has suggested – and I fully agree with him – that you should join the army. He thinks it will be the making of you.'

Jarlath's mouth fell open. 'I don't identify with the Irish army,' he spluttered.

'I'm talking about the British Army, Jarlath. You have an education, and for a small emolument – generously provided by myself – they will give you a commission.'

'But I don't want to join the British Army either!' protested Jarlath vehemently.

'It's the army or prison. I had hopes of eventually getting you a job in a bank but due to your dishonesty, that is now clearly out of the question. The army is the only option that remains.'

'But no one knows of my... indiscretion!'

'Dublin is a very small place, Jarlath. Good friend that John is, he won't breathe a word about your criminal behaviour. However, the lowlife you have involved yourself with won't be as kind to you. If you stay in Dublin, they will talk and in a very short time even the British army will close its doors to you.'

'Father, please, I don't want to be a soldier!' begged Jarlath.

An evening mist clung to the surface of Stephens Green's lake as ducks, swans and other water fowl pursued their never-ending search for food. Alice and Terrance strolled arm in arm past the artificial waterfall that fed the lake.

'I don't know what to do, Terrance,' sighed Alice. 'I never liked Braiden but nothing prepared me for what George told me about him.'

'This George – is he your fella?' asked Terrance, grinning down at her.

'That's none of your business. Please concentrate on what I'm telling you. What do you think?'

Terrance grew more serious. 'I think that whoever this George might be, unfortunately he is right. Word on the streets is that Braiden is a right boyo. Did your fella tell you that he's been engaged twice?'

'*Twice?*'

'Yes, and each time when his fiancée's money ran out, so did Braiden. He and his father run a dubious import and export company. They're up to all sorts of shenanigans.'

'Oh, Terranc, I have to tell Father!'

'No, don't do that. Father has enough on his plate and besides, he doesn't know how to deal with people like Braiden. Leave that boyo to me.'

'What are you going to do?' shivered Alice.

'I'll look after Braiden. Now tell me about this fella of yours?'

'I told you, he's none of your business!'

'Perhaps I should meet him.'

'No, and stop teasing me about him!'

Terrance laughed and turned the conversation to lighter subjects. But as they sauntered on around the lake, Alice wondered if involving her older brother had been the wisest thing to do.

Wearing his long, heavy black coat, Terrance stood in the Ferryman and surveyed the pub's clientele with steely eyes. It was Friday night, and the raucous, crowded public bar was hazy with tobacco smoke. The loud voices of dockers, tradesmen and warehouse workers fought to be heard over the din of traditional Irish music pumping from the back, and the whole place stank of stale perspiration and spilt porter.

'What can I get you?' asked a slightly hunched bartender, pushing back the last few sweaty wisps of hair on his mostly bald head.

'A pint of ale. Is Braiden Doyle in tonight?'

'Over there with Mick O'Brien.'

Pint in hand, Terrance moved through the boisterous crowd and when he arrived at Braiden's table he slammed his drink on the table, causing the beer to slop over the edge of the glass.

'What the hell?' complained Braiden, annoyed at the spillage.

'I'd like a word,' said Terrance, taking a chair.

'Who told you, you could sit at my table?'

'I did,' replied Terrance.

'And who are you?' sneered Braiden.

'Good question.' Terrance opened the top buttons of his long heavy coat, reached into his waistcoat pocket, pulled out a Maguire and Patterson matchbox and placed it on the table.

Braiden glared at the matchbox suspiciously. 'What's that?'

'You could call it a gift.'

'That's nice,' murmured Mick O'Brien, cautiously.

'Is this some sort of a joke?' barked Braiden, with a glare at Mick.

'Not a bit of it, Braiden,' smiled Terrance. 'It's a very serious gift.' And then, when Braiden didn't move, he leaned forward and dropped his voice almost to a whisper. 'Open your fucking present.'

Braiden jolted back in his chair, then slowly picked up the matchbox and slid it open. 'Jesus!' He dropped the box like he'd been stung and watched aghast as its shiny contents rolled around on the table. 'That's a bullet!'

'Correct, Mr Doyle. And to be even more precise, that's a bullet for a Webley revolver.' Terrance picked up the shiny object and held it poised between finger and thumb. 'Have you ever wondered why the Webley revolver is called a man-stopper, Braiden?'

'No...' Beads of perspiration oozed from Braiden's forehead.

'Well, maybe you should give it some thought. And to answer your earlier question, my name is Terrance Dalton. My sister Ann may have told you about me, but what she probably didn't tell you is that I have been detained at the pleasure of His Majesty's government. And before you ask, the charge was murder.'

'I remember you now!' Mick reacted as if struck by lightning. 'You were involved in the Caple Street pub murder!'

'That's right, Mick – what a good memory you have,' said Terrance, his eyes still fixed on Braiden.

'If this is about the twenty pounds your brother Jarlath owes me,' groaned Braiden, swallowing hard. 'Tell him to forget about it.'

'That's very good of you, Braiden, and I'll make sure to tell him. But that's not why I'm here. I know all about Claire Dennis and the other ladies you cheated and fleeced and jilted.'

'Oh...' Braiden wiped beads of perspiration from his forehead.

'Yes. And I don't want the same to happen to my sister Ann. I don't want her cheated, and I don't want her fleesed. Do you understand what I'm saying to you?'

'Loud and clear…'

Terrance replaced the bullet in his waistcoat pocket. 'I'll keep this gift for you, just in case you forget about our little chat,' he said, then stood and walked slowly out of the pub.

Braiden exhaled deeply.

'Does this mean you won't be getting married to Ann Dalton ?' asked Mick.

'Shut up Mick.' Braiden said and downed the last of his pint.

CHAPTER EIGHTEEN

An annoyed Alice stood outside 5 Primrose Avenue, lifted the hall door knocker and let it fall. Moments later, the door opened and a tired-looking Freda stood facing her.

'Freda?' Alice tried to hide her shock at the woman's drawn appearance. 'I'm Alice Dalton.'

'Yes, I know who you are.'

'I'd like to have a word with your brother, if I may. He was supposed to meet me at…'

'George is not here,' said Freda flatly.

'Who is at the door?' cried a female voice from inside the house.

'It's Alice Dalton!' called Freda, over her shoulder.

'I'd like to talk to her! Put her in the parlour and I'll be right there!'

'Is something wrong?' asked Alice anxiously, following Freda into the small front room.

'I afraid so, yes,' answered the young woman, taking the seat opposite Alice. 'George has had a relapse.'

'A relapse?'

'His illness...'

'Illness?'

Freda sighed. 'George never told you, did he?'

Alice was confused. The last time she had seen him, he'd seemed so well. 'What illness are you talking about?'

'He promised me he'd tell you. He has TB.'

Alice's hand flew to her mouth and her heart thumped so hard she found it difficult to breathe. She remembered when poor Mrs O'Donnell had had to leave their house because she was ill. The housekeeper had died very soon after and only Mrs Foley had gone to the funeral. 'Is George going to...?' She could not bring herself to say the word.

'The doctors in the sanatorium say he'll probably recover...'

'Oh thank God.'

'...from this relapse. But he'll be in the sanatorium for at least a month.'

'A *month?*' Alice was horrified. 'It takes that long to cure TB?'

Freda's fingers plucked miserably at the neck of her blouse. 'Alice, the first time George contracted the disease, he spent a year in hospital.'

'And it still came back?'

'Don't you understand? There is no cure.'

Alice felt a cold wave of fear flow over her. 'No cure?'

At that moment, the parlour door opened and a slight, clean-featured woman entered the room. 'So, Alice, we finally meet.' The small woman took a seat beside Alice on the sofa. 'I'm George's mother, and I have an apology to make to you. George asked me to write to you and explain...'

Alice's mind was still reeling with shock. 'I never received your letter.'

'That's because I could not bring myself to send it.' Mrs Gilbert's voice was soft, gentle and filled with pain. 'Knowing what I know, it seemed wrong to encourage you to care for him...'

'Why shouldn't I care for him?'

Mrs Gilbert rested her veined hand on Alice's wrist. 'I love my son and want nothing more than his happiness. But not at your expense. You are a young woman with your whole life ahead of you. Alice, I watched my big strong husband die of TB. First he lost weight, a lot of weight. Then it became difficult for him to breathe. He was tired all the time – terribly tired. But nothing was as bad as that dreadful, painful, hacking cough...' The small woman's lips quivered. 'That's why they call it consumption, Alice. It consumes a person's body. My beautiful big man just faded away before my eyes. Alice, I didn't send that letter because you are under no obligation to love my son. It's not too late to walk away. No one will blame you, especially George.'

'I can't walk away,' said Alice, so softly it was as if she was speaking to herself. 'I love him.'

Thoughts about George, the sanatorium and what George's mother had said plagued Alice's thoughts. Day and night her mind was in constant turmoil; she couldn't rest or sleep.

Late one evening, she was at the writing desk in the drawing room composing a letter to George, when a strange ringing startled her. She rested her pen in the inkwell and listened. It must be that newly-installed telephone contraption which Father had installed in the hall. She had never operated a telephone and the thought of answering the call was a little daunting. Still, everyone else was out or in bed...

As she opened the drawing room door, the ringing stopped.

'Hello? Yes, this is he.' Terrance was speaking into the receiver. 'What? Don't be ridiculous. Tell him it's only a bloomin' statue.' He went quiet for a moment. Then said in a much lower voice, 'I know David Falls is a Protestant and when we planned the job he was a Protestant.' Another silence. 'Of course I know who King

William was, why does he think we're blowing up the bloomin' statue in the first place? Don't let him go anywhere, I'm on my way.' And Terrance hung up the receiver, seized his coat from the stand and left the house.

Standing at the salon office door, Alice took a deep, nervous breath. After yet another sleepless night, she had made her decision. She would tell her father about Terrance's telephone conversation. She felt guilty about betraying her brother, but Terrance had given his word not to get involved in any Republican activities and he had broken his promise. She had just raised her hand to knock on the door when it swung open and an overly-joyous Thomas smiled broadly at her.

'Alice! Just the person I wanted to see! I was about to come and get you.' He ushered her into the office. 'I have a surprise for you. You remember Eamon Maloney don't you?'

'Of course I remember!' said Alice, quite relieved to be prevented from saying her piece about Terrance. 'It's lovely to see you again Mr Maloney. How are you?'

The immaculately-dressed Eamon Maloney held out his hand. 'I'm well and it's lovely to see you too Miss Dalton,' he said in his soft Cork accent. 'And please call me Eamon.'

'And please call me Alice.'

'Alice and Eamon! Quite so!' beamed Thomas. 'No need for formalities here. Oh, excuse me a moment, I think I hear someone calling me. Alice, will you please entertain Mr Maloney until my return?' And Thomas rushed out of the room leaving Alice and Eamon standing awkwardly together.

Eamon's lips twitched with humour. 'Parents can be a bit forceful, can't they? Please don't feel you have to stay.'

Alice smiled slightly in return. 'But I have been explicitly instructed to entertain you.'

'Rest assured, you are under no obligation to do so.'

'I'm glad to hear it, because I'm really wouldn't know where to start.'

'Eamon, I know I promised to bring you for lunch in the Restaurant Jammet,' Thomas declared just a little too loudly as he burst back into the office. 'But I'm afraid there's a bit of an emergency and I am needed in the Salon.' Then, like an actor in a melodrama pretending to have an idea, he raised his hand in the air, crying, 'Alice, I know – why don't you take Eamon to lunch in my place?'

Alice sighed. 'Father, I don't think Eamon...'

'If Alice is busy, I don't mind catching an earlier train,' said Eamon helpfully.

'I wouldn't hear of it,' insisted Thomas. 'Alice will take you to lunch. It's the least we can do for you. Alice, why don't you go and change while Eamon and I finish our conversation?'

'I thought there was an emergency in the salon?' Alice said crossly.

'No, it's nothing that can't wait a moment or two.'

Alice flounced up the stairs to her room and changed into the plainest dress she had in her wardrobe. It was mortifying the way her father was pushing her on Eamon Maloney.

As she was buttoning her dress, Ann burst into the room and – without saying a word – dramatically threw herself face down on her bed.

'Ann, what's the matter?'Alice said briefly forgetting about her own problems.

'Nothing,' said Ann in a muffled voice. Then, after a pause, she raised her head and added, 'Braiden has changed towards me.'

'How do you mean?' asked Alice, drawing closer to the bed.

'He took me to the Queen's Theatre last night but he hardly spoke a word to me.'

'He ignored you?'

'Not exactly, but when he did speak, all he wanted to talk about was Terrance.'

'*Terrance?*'

'Yes, Terrance. Who his friends were, what he was up to. I told him I didn't know anything about Terrance's activities but he kept on coming back to the subject. And he was acting really oddly. He kept looking around as if he was afraid of something. Then he told me he had to go to London and wouldn't be back until the day before our wedding. What could be wrong with him? And why is he so interested in Terrance?'

'I expect it's just business,' said Alice guiltily, wondering what on earth her brother had done now.

Eamon ushered Alice politely ahead of him through the plum-coloured front door of Restaurant Jammet. They were greeted by the *maître d'* who escorted them to their table, beneath Bossini's painting of the Four Seasons. Taking her seat, Alice gazed with interest around the elegant restaurant. Every place was taken. White-aproned waiters moved from table to table taking orders, while the commis waiters hurried between kitchen and dining room carrying silver platters, large and small.

After an elaborate three-course lunch Alice sat back in her chair, dropped her serviette on the table and told Eamon she was not going to eat for the next week.

Smiling, he folded his own napkin tidily several times before asking, 'Tell me, Alice – are you here because you wanted to be here or because your father asked you to accompany me?'

'Both,' replied Alice politely.

'I see. Is there... Do you mind if I ask... Is there someone special in your life?'

Alice thought of George stuck in the sanatorium while she was eating with another young man in the best restaurant in Dublin.

'There is, but if you don't mind I'd rather you didn't mention it to Father.'

'Ah. Your father doesn't approve of him?'

'You could say that.'

'Well, you can tell him from me that he's a very lucky fellow.'

'He's not all that lucky.' A wave of sadness washed over her and she shivered. Eamon reached across the table and touched her hand. Gently, she drew it away. 'Thank you for being so nice, Eamon. I've had a lovely time. You are a gentleman.'

'That's my curse,' Eamon said, with a resigned smile.

It was one o'clock in the morning and the clattering of the horse's hooves and the grinding of the cart's steel-rimmed wheels on the cobblestones of Pearse Street sounded like thunder to the driver and his passenger. Robbie Nolan was a sandy-haired older man, who before the Troubles, was a gentle, peaceful carpenter. He jerked the horse's reins to the right and the animal dragged the cart into the centre of College Green and stopped. Above them, on a double pedestal twenty feet above the street, was the bronze figure of King William of Orange. The statue which had once represented the pride and glory of the British Empire now only served as a resting place for the pigeons and seagulls of Dublin. The three-sided city-centre plaza was empty except for two drunken students staggering alongside the railings of Trinity College and a courting couple locked in each others' arms in the doorway of the Bank of Ireland building.

Terrance pulled his cloth cap down over his forehead and watched the two singing students pound on the small portal door in the college's main entrance. The portal opened and the two students staggered into the college.

'Now, we'll just wait until Romeo and Juliet move on,' whispered Robbie. 'Did you know that this place was once a burial ground for Norse Kings?'

'No, I didn't know and right now I couldn't care less.'

'Take it easy. It's not like I asked to be here. I thought David Falls was to do this job?' Robbie pulled hard on his cigarette. 'How come I got the call?'

'David said as a Protestant it didn't feel right blowing up a statue of a King of England.'

'Who does he think we're fighting, the Norsemen? Hey, Romeo and Juliet are gone – time to get to work.'

Robbie jumped down and checked around the green to make sure it was devoid of people. Terrance climbed into the back of the cart, picked up a long thick rope and threw it high into the air. On his third attempt, the rope lassoed around the bronze neck of King William's horse.

Robbie climbed into the cart and helped Terrance tie one end of a long length of twine around his waist. With big rough hands, he pushed aside a burlap sack that was covering a wooden box. Carefully, he lifted the lid of the box and removed a layer of hay, revealing six sticks of dynamite. These he placed in a cotton bag, cautiously checking that the long, thin fuse attached to the dynamite was free and clear. Then he tied the bag to the other end of the length of twine.

Meanwhile, pulling on the thick rope, Terrance hauled himself up to the base of the statue. From there, standing twenty feet in the air, he jerked on the length of twine tied around his waist. Robbie raised his hand, and Terrance carefully hauled up the bag of dynamite. He was busy attaching the bag to the belly of the bronze beast when a lone policeman on his bicycle stopped by the cart and dismounted.

'What are you doing?' asked the policeman. 'What's going on here?'

A startled Robbie didn't know what to say, but Terrance shouted down from his perch, 'We're cleaning the statue, officer! We want to have it looking good for the parade tomorrow.'

'I didn't know there was a parade tomorrow?' The policeman scratched his chin. 'No one tells me anything. I better get back to the station and see if there's any overtime going. Thanks for the tip.' And he mounted his bicycle and cycled off.

'Is there a parade tomorrow?' Robbie asked Terrance, grinning.

'Is the Pope a Protestant! We better hurry, that copper will be back in a few minutes.'

'Get on with it, then!' Robbie jumped into the driver's seat and took hold of the horse's reins. Terrance struck a match and as the fuse fizzed into life he slid down the rope. The instant his feet thumped the floor of the cart, Robbie snapped the reins, clicked his tongue and the wheels rumbled away over the cobblestones.

They had just turned into William Street when a deafening explosion destroyed the quiet of the night. Telephone poles were decapitated, windows smashed and burst water pipes spewed great arcs of water as the exploded statue rained a million pieces of bronze and stone down on College Green. The horse panicked and broke into a gallop and the lone cart raced wildly up the street. Terrance clung to his seat, shouting gleefully to Joe, 'Jesus, I'd say that was loud enough to wake the Norse kings from their resting place!'

The day was cloudy and warm and the air in the tram was thick and suffocating. A nervous Alice lurched forward as the tram juddered to a clanking halt at Chapelizod. The whole tram fell eerily quiet and the passengers either bowed their heads or stared straight ahead. Alice walked down the aisle and not one person made eye contact with her. As she stepped out onto the narrow open-air platform at the back of the vehicle, three excited children clattered down the stairs to get passed her off the tram.

'Will yis watch where you're going?' shouted the children's overweight mother as she lumbered down the stairs after them. 'You nearly knocked that lady down. Sorry love,' she said, pausing to peer into Alice's face. 'The childer get so excited. They're going to see their da.'

'Oh, are you visiting your husband in the sanatorium?' asked Alice.

The large woman took a sharp step away from Alice and settled her shawl around her shoulders. 'It's none of your business where I'm going,' she said and quickly stepped off the tram onto the pavement.

Alice stood and wondered what had just happened.

'Miss, are you getting off or not?' asked the conductor.

Alice smiled meekly at the conductor, alighted from the platform and walked over to the plump woman, who was attending to her youngest child.

'I'm sorry if you thought I was prying. All I wanted was directions to the sanatorium.'

'It's up that way,' the woman said dismissively, jerking her double chin towards the Phoenix Park. 'Keep going up the path and you'll get to the hospital.'

Alice walked briskly along the path until she came to two huge metal gates with the words 'St Mary's Sanatorium' embedded in the iron arch overhead. She carried on up the white gravel path to the hospital entrance, knocked on the wooden doors and pulled on the bell. While she waited, Alice imagined what she would say to George. *How are you?* No, that was too formal. *Hello, love.* No. What about just 'hello'? Alice was still picturing their meeting when a small hatch in the door clattered open and the stern face of a young nun peered out through the barred opening.

'Yes?' said the face.

'I've come to visit Mr George Gilbert,' replied Alice.

'Visitors are not allowed,' snapped the face, and the hatch crashed shut.

Alice nearly fell off the step, she was so stunned by the coldness and terseness of the nun's dismissal. Lost and disorientated, she wandered back toward the park and stood miserably just outside the hospital gates. The three children from the tram raced past, taking the path that curved around the hospital railings. Their portly mother paused to speak to Alice.

'They wouldn't let you in, would they?' she asked knowingly.

Alice shook her head. She didn't want to talk to anyone right now – let alone this awful, coarse, unfriendly woman.

'Sorry if I was a little bit short with you earlier but people can be very cruel when they know you have someone in St Mary's. Is it your husband that has the TB?'

'No, a friend,' Alice replied and her eyes became moist.

'This friend must be very important to you?'

'He is but the nun said I couldn't see him.'

They won't let anyone in but there is a way to see your friend. We come every week, the children love to see their da. Come on and I'll show you. How long is your friend in the hospital?'

'Three weeks,' replied Alice.

'That's not long. Who's paying?'

'I don't know. I suppose his family.'

'My Johnny's been in there a year and if he didn't work in Guinness's, he'd be dead. It costs a fortune in there. You know we couldn't afford to pay them hospital bills.'

'I'm sorry…' Alice's regard for the rough-looking woman was changing rapidly.

'Ma, can I have me apple now?' asked the woman's youngest child.

'Yes, Daisy you can.' Without breaking her stride the woman rummaged in her handbag, found an apple but before handing it to the child she spat on it and rubbed it on the sleeve of her coat. 'There you are Daisy, a nice, shiny, clean apple.'

Alice looked away and was trying to get the image of the woman spitting on the apple out of her mind when she felt a tug on her coat.

'Would you like a bite of me apple, Miss?' the little girl said holding up the apple to Alice.

'No thank you,' Alice replied. 'But it was very nice of you to offer.'

'Isn't Daisy great?' the woman said and without waiting on a reply added, 'They feed them very well in the hospital, they feed them like kings. They give them the best of food and drink. Every day they get three pints of milk and every night they get two pints of porter.'

'Does that help?' Alice asked, wondering at the accuracy of the woman's information.

The woman's face darkened. 'They say it helps, they say the treatment is lots of drink and lots of fresh air.'

'Why don't they allow visitors?'

'That's because TB is contagious, it's spread through the air, you breathe it in. You get it from someone who has it. That's why they lock them in and shut us out, it's so we won't get the TB.'

Up ahead a large group of men, women and children were peering through the hospital railings.

'This is it,' said the woman to Alice.

Screaming excitedly, the children raced ahead. A gap in the bushes behind the railings allowed the crowd an unobstructed view of the sanatorium. It was a long white building with a huge open-air veranda filled with patients and beds. In front of each bed was a deckchair and a small cabinet. Some patients were sitting in the chairs taking the sun while other were lying on their bed. Most of the men were smoking.

'My husband didn't smoke until he went in there,' said Daisy's mother, gazing through the railings. 'They say tobacco clears the lungs, but I don't know, how could it?'

'Where's Daddy?' asked the woman's son, as he tried to stick his head through the bars.

'He's over there Declan, there's Daddy, see beside the nurse handing out the glasses of milk.'

'Ma, Daddy just waved to me,' Daisy shouted and pointed excitedly into the distance.

'God bless your eyesight, Daisy,' the mother said and, lowering her voice, added, 'I don't know if it's Johnny or not, the men are so far away you can't tell one from the other. But what's the harm letting the children think they saw their da?'

'Does this hospital only cater for men?' Alice asked as her eyes searched along the long veranda for George.

'No, the women are on the other side and there's just as many of them,' said Daisy's mother.

'How did your husband contract TB?' Alice asked.

'Oh, it spread through the tenement like wildfire. Half the families living there were wiped out. I sent Daisy, Declan and Molly down to my sister in Carlow, otherwise they would have got the TB just like me other four.'

The woman stopped talking, put her arms around Daisy and the look of sorrow, love, longing and loss that filled the woman's eyes frightened Alice.

Less than a fortnight later, George Gilbert sat on a bench on the banks of the Royal Canal. It was a warm day and three small children and their parents were playing pat-a-cake in the shade of a giant willow tree. Nearby, a young mother and her daughter were feeding the ducks. The little girl threw a handful of bread then screeched excitedly when a pigeon fluttered to the ground beside her. George laughed to see the child's reaction. It was his first day out of the hospital and he was so happy that he felt almost light headed. In the distance were the high fortress walls of Mountjoy Prison. George felt almost like an escaped prisoner himself.

To make everything even better, now he could see Alice coming towards him from the direction of the Cross Guns Bridge. He swallowed hard as she grew nearer – she looked so beautiful with her wild hair gently moving in the breeze, her small face and deep blue eyes shining in the sun. He smiled; she smiled; without exchanging a word they folded themselves into each others' arms.

'How are you, George?' Alice asked, when they had finally released each other. 'Are you better?'

'A lot better. And definitely not contagious.'

'That's wonderful...'

He took her hand. 'You do know, if I ever thought for a single moment I was putting you in danger I would not come within a mile of you?'

She sighed. 'Let's not talk about that today. I just want to be with you right now. Shall we walk? Are you strong enough?'

'I'm very strong, according to the doctors. They say that if I look after myself and get plenty of rest I should be fine. Every day they are developing new treatments and techniques, and survival rates are improving greatly.'

He held Alice's hand and the two happy young people strolled along the canal. They were delighted to be enjoying the day together – a day full of the ordinary moments of life; a simple meal in a café, some window shopping and in the evening, a trip to the cinema – *Night Nurse,* at the Carlton.

After the film, the young couple stood waiting in the chill of the night for a tram. Alice buttoned the top button of her coat as she heard the rumble of the approaching vehicle. Suddenly the sound was drowned by the frantic peeling of a fire engine. Hot on the trail of the engine, an ambulance sped past and Alice made the sign of the cross.

A hunched older woman with bulging eyes slapped George angrily on the arm. 'You ought to be ashamed of yourself,' she snapped, glaring into his face. 'Why don't you bless yourself? Are you a Protestant?'

'And what business is that of yours?' replied George, quietly.

The woman recoiled. 'You are, by God! Young lady, you ought to be ashamed of yourself, stepping out with a Protestant.'

Alice stared, speechless. The tram clanked to a stop and the woman scurried on board.

A few minutes later, sitting a long way away from the woman on the upper deck of the tram, Alice placed her hand reassuringly on George's. 'She was an ignorant bigot and I apologise for her. Most people don't think like her.'

George smiled to himself.

'Why are you smiling?' puzzled Alice. 'It's not funny. You should be more annoyed.'

'I am annoyed, but things like that happen to me nearly every day.'

'Are you serious?'

'Oh yes. People may not always be as blatant about it as that woman, but their thinking is the same. When I was a child we were the only Protestant family on the street. The children jeered and taunted us all the time. They called us "proddy-woddies" or "black Protestant" and all that sort of thing. Dessie and I were left out of their games and we were never invited into any of the neighbours' houses. Even though Dessie was a good little footballer he was always the last to be picked for a team. As you grow older the prejudice becomes more subtle but the truth is, Catholics are always suspicious of Protestants. They see us as an enemy, as part of Britain. And I'm not only talking about ordinary people – I'm talking about so-called educated people.'

'But that's terrible.'

'Terrible or not, that's the way it is – and there's very little I can do about it, so I just ignore it as best I can.'

CHAPTER NINETEEN

Leaning against the wall of Merchant's Arch, George Gilbert warmed his hand in the pockets of his new woollen overcoat and mentally reviewed his plan for the evening. He had booked a table for two in the Jury's Hotel restaurant and requested an alcove table. He had arranged with Cyril, the *maître d'*, to have a half bottle of champagne waiting. And after an expensive meal selected from the á la carte menu, he planned to walk Alice along the river and at the Halfpenny Bridge he would profess his love.

Where *was* Alice?

The normally unflappable George was starting to get anxious. But then there she was, hurrying towards him, and his face lit up at the sight of her beauty, and his heart nearly burst with pride.

'Why, George,' she greeted him, 'you're all dressed up! Are we going somewhere special?'

'We are,' he replied, walking her up Crown Alley.

'Where are you taking me?'

'It's a surprise.'

When they arrived at Jury's Hotel in Duke Street, he escorted her through the heavy brass-handled doors into the magnificent foyer. The hovering *maître d'* acknowledged George's nod and disappeared to organise the champagne. Meanwhile, George helped a delighted Alice off with her coat and brought it to the cloakroom. When he returned with the cloakroom ticket, a tall military-looking man with a narrow head and deep set eyes was in conversation with Alice.

'George, this is Uncle Aiden, my father's brother!' Alice smiled. 'Uncle Aiden, this is George Gilbert.'

'It's a pleasure to meet you, sir,' said George politely.

'This is a surprise,' enthused the older man, shaking George's outstretched hand. 'Why don't you two young people join me for a drink?'

'That would be lovely, wouldn't it, George?' said Alice, smiling at him beguilingly.

'Of course. That's very kind of you, sir,' said George stiffly, thinking of the champagne. 'Our retaurant table is booked for eight o'clock, but we have a few minutes.'

'Nonsense. I know the *maître d'* here of old, he won't mind if you're a little late. Besides, an aperitif will give you an appetite!' And the old soldier took Alice by the arm and drew her into the hotel lounge.

The wood-panelled, gas-lit lounge was a dull room, full of elderly gentlemen reading newspapers, talking politics or arguing sports. Uncle Aiden seemed to know many of the residents, he stopped at one table and introduced Alice and George to two 'extremely old friends of mine' – who were indeed, extremely old.

'Every Wednesday evening since I retired, we military chaps all meet up in here for a little chat,' he explained, leading them to a quieter corner and ordering a round of drinks.

George tried his best to be good company, but all he could think about was getting Alice on her own. When he decided enough time had passed, he downed the last of his gin and tonic and said, 'Thank you, Mr Dalton. We won't keep you from your friends any longer.'

'You're not keeping me from my friends – you're facilitating my absence! Between you and me, they're a bunch of old gasbags!' Aiden laughed uproariously at his own joke. 'Anyway, you have to stay a little longer I've ordered another round of drinks!'

Forty minutes later, the *maître d'* approached their table and announced that last orders were being taken in the dining room.

'Thank you so much for letting us know,' said George, who had tipped the *maître d'* heavily for this purpose on his last trip to the gentlemen's cloakroom. But George's smile faded when the *maître d'* showed them to a table right in the exposed centre of the dining room.

'I asked for the one in the alcove?' he objected.

'I know sir,' replied the *maître d'*, respectfully. 'But that particular table is a great favourite and you did stay a long time in the lounge, so I'm afraid I had to let it go.'

'George, this is a perfectly lovely table – and look! They have given us a complementary bottle of champagne to make up for moving us!' enthused Alice.

'Very well,' sighed George, thinking about how much the half bottle had cost him.

The restaurant was very busy with waiters and commis waiters whizzing past the table; twice the wine bucket was nearly knocked over, once by an elderly woman when she collided into the back of George's chair, and once by an overly eager commis waiter rushing into the kitchen. *This is going dreadfully,* George thought, *and it's costing me a month's wages.* At least the champagne was still waiting for the main course.

They had just finished their *hors d'oeuvre* when a male voice called to Alice from the foyer.

'Oh look, it's my brother Jarlath!' cried a delighted Alice and she waved to the young man to join them.

'Splendid to meet you George,' said Jarlath, after Alice had made the introductions. 'This is a surprise, Alice I didn't know you frequented this hotel. Is that bubbly? Marvelous, George why don't you pour me a glass?'

Twenty minutes later, Jarlath drained the last of the champagne into his glass – or rather, Alice's glass, which he had taken for his own – drank it quickly and left for his weekly card game in a suite on the first floor.

After the meal, with which they drank water, the waiter brought coffee and as George paid the bill, he thought what a disaster the night had been.

'You were very quiet tonight George,' observed Alice, as they walked along the quay.

'I wanted tonight to be special,' he replied down-heartedly.

'But it was special. You met Uncle Aiden and Jarlath – and besides, every time we go out is special.'

'I just wanted everything to be perfect tonight.'

'Everything was perfect,' said Alice, and she smiled a smile that was so overpoweringly beautiful, he had to return it.

'The reason I wanted tonight to be special,' he confessed, still smiling, 'is because I wanted to tell you that I love you.'

Her eyes beamed at him. 'And I love you too, George, and I have been waiting for you to say it to me for *such* a long time. This is the most special night ever! Now stop talking and kiss me!'

And George took his lady in his arms and kissed her again and again.

Terrance whistled as he trotted up the stairs. It was the first time he'd been home since blowing up the statue of King William; three days later, his ears were still ringing from the noise of the explosion.

Alice had to call his name twice before he heard her.

'Good morning, little sister,' he smiled, pausing. 'How are you today?'

She stood in the doorway of her bedroom, hands on hips. 'You broke your promise, Terrance.'

'Promise?" he asked innocently.

'Don't give me that look. I know you were behind what happened in College Green.'

Terrance paled and he checked over the banisters to make sure no other family members were listening. 'I have no idea what you're talking about…'

'Yes you do. Who is David Falls?'

A flash of panic flickered in his eyes. 'I don't think I know a David Falls.'

Alice glared at her brother.

Terrance sighed and gave up. 'All right. But let me say this in my defence. No one got hurt.'

'That was not of your making, that was pure luck. I came very close to telling Father. I still might.'

Terrance looked shocked. 'Why would you do that?'

'Because you broke your promise, what will happen when the authorities find out?'

'They won't find out.'

'They did the last time.' Alice's eyes filled with disappointment and sadness. 'Why do you keep on doing such dreadful things?'

He sighed. 'You wouldn't understand, little sister. You're an honest and honourable person and you think the world is an honest and honourable place, but it's not. I did what I thought was right.' He hesitated a moment, then said, 'I'm really sorry you overheard that conversation.'

'So am I. And what on earth did you say to Braiden? Ann says he's acting very oddly.'

Terrance acted innocent again. 'Nothing.'

'*Tell me.*'

'Alice, there are things you are better off not knowing.'

Alice had never been to a party like it. It was noisy, joyous and filled with music. It was George's mother's sixtieth birthday and the small house was heaving with relatives: Mrs Gilbert's aging aunts and uncles, her many brothers and sisters, and what seemed like hundreds of cousins.

The great aunts and great uncles sat in the kitchen, eating sandwiches and listening to George's cousin Jamie play feverishly on his accordion, while another cousin Chloé pounded rhythmically on her bodhran.

In the parlour, George sat between his mother and Alice on the red settee while Dessie and George's three sisters and several more aunts, uncles and cousins sat around on the other chairs or on the floor and listened to Mrs Gilbert reminisce about her late husband.

When the music in the kitchen ceased, George's sister Dorothy tapped George on the knee and said, 'Give us a few tunes.'

'Make way for the maestro,' George said, as he made his way to the upright piano.

As soon as his fingers touched the keys, the magical instrument flooded the room with music and life. After dashing off a few favourites, George asked his mother what she would like him to play.

'I'd like you to recite your father's favourite poem, *The Green Eye of the Little Yellow God*,' Mrs Gilbert replied unhesitatingly. 'And play the music you wrote for it.'

'Yes, tell us about Mad Carew,' a light-hearted Dessie called out from the floor.

Then everyone started to chant, 'Mad Carew! Mad Carew!'

George ceremoniously raised his hands above the piano keys and in a great flourish of movement his fingers danced along the keys and produced a rumble of rising notes. He followed the piano roll with a few ominous notes and when everyone was paying full attention, in a voice filled with mystery and suspense, he began his recitation.

'George is wonderful,' Mrs Gilbert said softly to Alice. 'I love listening to him and watching him play. He reminds me so much of his father.'

I love listening to him too, thought Alice, and she sat back on the settee and lost herself in the story of the poem and the soft voice of the young man telling it. She smiled when he smiled and frowned when he frowned, and when his hand pushed back the flop of hair that fell across his forehead, she thought how lovely he looked. When George finished reciting the poem, the room burst into applause. Then Dessie sat on the piano stool beside George and the two brothers played chopsticks.

Alice watched how easily George interacted with his brother and how he charmed everyone with his quick smile and wicked sense of humour. Every now and again, he would break into a laugh and his dark hair would again flop forward and he would brush it back again. When he smiled at Alice, she smiled back and when he beckoned her to join him at the piano, she did so and for the next hour they sang and played rollicking music-hall songs and sad sea shanties.

When it came time for Mrs Gilbert's birthday cake, Dorothy asked Alice if she would help. In the kitchen, Dorothy lifted a beautiful home-made iced fruit cake out of a biscuit tin and Alice pressed six small birthday candles into the top of the cake. Dessie gathered everyone in the living room, Alice lit the six candles and Dorothy placed the flaming cake in front of her mother.

'Oh, it's beautiful,' breathed Mrs Gilbert

Everyone sang *Happy Birthday.* Mrs Gilbert blew out the candles, George raised a hand in the air and the packed living room fell quiet.

'I'd like to say a few words on my mother's sixtieth birthday,' he declared.

'My mother is not sixty? I don't believe it, I demand a recount!' Dessie shouted and the living room erupted with laughter.

'I would like to remind everyone that my brother Dessie still believes that the world is flat,' said George and again the room filled with laughter.

'Are you trying to shatter all my illusions in one evening?' Dessie called out.

'Will you two behave yourself,' Mrs Gilbert said and jokingly buried her face in her hands.

'Today we have gathered to celebrate the thirty ninth anniversary of my mother's twenty first birthday!'

More cheers and laughter.

Then George's face grew serious. 'Ma, you are a wonderful mother. No one ever had a better ma. You loved every one of us and you were always there to help and guide us. All through the Troubles you always managed to put good food on the table. God knows where you got it, but you got it and we thank you for it.' He paused, and his voice filled with emotion. 'I thank you for that and if Da was here, he'd thank you too. You are a great lady and I am so proud to call you my mother.'

'Will you stop it, George, you're embarrassing me,' said Mrs Gilbert, fumbling in her bag for a handkerchief.

'I'm nearly finished, Ma.' George kissed his mother on the forehead. 'Everybody raise a glass. Happy sixtieth birthday, Ma.'

In the early hours of the morning, when most of the guests had gone, Freda, Dorothy, George's sister Alice and Alice Dalton gathered to wash the dishes.

'How long ago did your father pass away?' Alice asked, rinsing a soapy plate under the cold tap.

'Two years ago,' replied Freda. 'We wondered what Ma would do without him. Would she survive, would she be able to keep going? Well she did, I suppose that's all you can do. She had a wonderful life with Dad and she still misses him terribly. Sometimes I see her sitting by the fire and I know she's thinking of him. George was great when Dad was sick. He looked after him, dressed him and put him to bed. He did everything for Dad. I suppose that's how he got TB.'

'Oh...' Alice caught her breath and tried unsuccessfully to stop the tears from forming in her eyes. 'What kind of man was your father?' she asked, wiping them away.

'He was a quiet man,' said George's sister, Alice. 'Very like George is now.'

'And he never complained.' said the third sister, Dorothy. 'But we knew he was in great pain – we could see it in his eyes. Sometimes in the dead of night, we heard him cry from the pain. He was in hospital for a long time. We sold our home in Killester to pay the hospital bills and we rented this house. When money from the sale of the house ran out we had to take him out of the hospital. We made the parlour into his bedroom. He lived for eight months but every day of those we lived in dread of his passing and then one day he just died.' Dorothy's voice caught; she stopped talking and resumed drying the dishes.

'How is George?' Alice asked, after a while.

'As well as can be expected,' sighed Freda.

'What about all the new treatments he talks about?'

'They're mostly talk, we fear. Little has changed in the last five years. He's a long way off being as ill as our father was but...' Freda stopped mid-sentence and all three of the sisters looked intensely at Alice.

The other Alice finished Freda's unspoken thought: 'Alice, it's really not too late for you to walk away.'

'It's far too late,' said Alice, and the four young women continued washing the dishes in silence.

Late morning sunlight flashed through the trees outside the drawing room window and flickered dappled sunlight onto Thomas Dalton's troubled face. Dressed completely in black, Mariah dropped into an armchair and sliced into one of Mrs Foley's cream sponges. Thomas left the window and repositioned himself at the mantelpiece. He fingered his moustache and cleared his throat.

'What is it, Thomas?' asked Mariah.

'Do you really think this is the right time to talk to Alice? Perhaps we should wait until after Ann's wedding?'

'The time will never be right, but now is as good as any,' said Mariah as she lifted a large slice of cake onto her plate. 'So please stop putting it off with one silly excuse or another.'

'It was you who insisted Mrs O'Donnell leave me.'

'I did that for your safety!'

'Still, it was your decision, which means it is your responsibilty to ensure I am properly looked after.'

At noon on the dot, Alice knocked on the drawing room door and entered the room. When she saw her mother, she froze in surprise.

'Hello, Mother. You wanted to see me, Father?'

'I did. Take a seat,' he said.

'We both wanted to talk to you.' Mariah swallowed the last of her slice of cake and carefully replaced the pastry fork and the plate on the tea trolley. 'Your father and I have come to a decision regarding your future.'

'My future?' Alice felt a knot tighten in her stomach.

'Yes,' said Thomas. 'Your mother has had some thoughts about your future.'

'I have had more than thoughts,' corrected Mariah. ' Starting next month you will become my permanent companion.'

Alice felt as if the room was suddenly devoid of oxygen; she could hardly breathe and thought she was going to faint.

'Your father and I are fully in agreement on this matter, aren't we, Thomas?'

'*Father?*' Alice turned to Thomas, but he had left the mantelpiece and was pretending to have noticed something very interesting outside in the street.

When her husband failed to respond, Mariah continued, 'Ever since Mrs O'Donnell left everything has fallen into disorder, everything is out of kilter.'

'Mrs O'Donnell was an employee – she was a paid housekeeper!' Alice's mind grasped for some semblance of logic and order.

'Yes and that's another matter that needs to be addressed. This arrangement of you and your sisters doing a little of the housekeeping whenever it takes your fancy is not working. I need you to take charge of the situation Alice. Of course, you won't have to wear a uniform but you will have full responsibility for the upkeep and order of the house.'

'But I don't want to be a housekeeper!'

'It doesn't matter what you want. It is your Christian duty to look after me. You will become my companion and my housekeeper, and that is that. In life we all have to make sacrifices.'

'Father, what do you say?' pleaded Alice.

Thomas continued to gaze out the window. 'Your mother needs you and as she says, it is your Christian duty to look after her.'

Alice wanted to scream. She wanted to tell her father how cruel and how cowardly he was being, siding with her wife against his beloved daughter. But she also knew that when her father made a decision, he clung to it stubbornly. It was how he had survived the recession – his sheer determination never to back down once he'd come to a decision.

'Are we finished here?' Alice asked bitterly.

Thomas nodded without looking around.

Summoning as much dignity as she could, Alice stood and left the room.

CHAPTER TWENTY

Alice sat silently on her bed, her face in her hands. She felt frozen inside. Numb.

How can my father treat me like this? How can he throw my life away as if it was nothing? How can he order me into servitude?

The lifelong consequences of her mother's decision struck her like a lightning-bolt:

I won't ever be able to get married. I'll have no home of my own. I will never have children. I'll grow into a bitter old spinster with no one to love me.

Raising her head, she stared into the space between herself and her tear-stained reflection in the mirror.

Why has Mother never loved me? Why does she never embrace me or hug me or kiss me? What did I ever do that was so wrong?

Trying not to cry, she prostrated herself on the bed, burying her face in her pillow. She knew there was nothing she could do to save herself. It was impossible and immoral to run away. This was her fate.

She is my mother and I have a Christian duty to look after her.

In her despair, the tears finally came and her body convulsed and she wept until a breathtaking wave of anger transformed her despair into helpless, pointless rage.

It's not fair! I have a life and I want to live it! How can they take it away from me like this? What did I do to deserve this dreadful fate?

Ann was seated in the summerhouse sketching out the seating plan for her wedding reception when Tess rushed in and placed her hands over Ann's design.

'What do you think you're doing?' asked Ann, through her teeth.

'You'll never guess what I heard!'

'I'm not interested in what you heard.' She plucked Tess's hand from the sheet of paper.

'I'm going to tell you anyway.' Tess sat down beside her. 'Mother and father have told Alice she has to become mother's companion.'

Ann stared at her sister. 'I don't believe you.'

'It's true,' replied Tess with a smirk.

'Alice won't do it.'

'She has no choice.'

'There's always choice,' said Ann, in an unusual display of independent thinking. 'The choices may not be pleasant or good, but there's always choice.'

Alice didn't feel like going out that evening. How could she face the world after what had happened to her? But George had tickets for the Gaiety Theatre and she didn't want to disappoint him – expecially as this was probably one of the last times she would be allowed out of the house to see him. At her dressing table, she patted extra powder under her eyes to hide the puffiness and applied mascara to her eyelashes and eyebrows to draw attention away from the redness. She donned her brightest dress and coat and set off to meet George.

The moment George saw her pale face and sad eyes he knew something was very wrong.

'What's the matter, Alice?'

'Nothing's the matter. Can we go into the theatre now?' she asked sharply.

'Yes, let's take our seats.' He ushered her into the auditorium, guessing she needed time to think before she could admit to what was upsetting her.

The play was an Irish comedy and while George laughed at the antics of the actors, Alice did not smile once. In silence, she replayed and replayed her mother's words: *You will become my companion.* She shrunk in her seat and many times she had to press her handkerchief to her eyes to dry her tears. At the intermission, George guided her through the chattering crowd to a secluded corner of the foyer.

'What's wrong, Alice? And don't snap at me.'

She shivered and when she spoke her voice was barely above a whisper: 'The worst possible thing has happened, George. My mother has made me her permanent companion.'

He stared at her in puzzlement, running his hand through his thick black hair. 'Companion? I don't understand?'

'My mother is frail, and she has lost her personal maid and housekeeper. She wants me to take over.'

'For a few weeks?'

'For ever, George. For my whole life. She wants me to spend my whole life looking after her. It means that I can never have a home of my own.'

'Alice, she can't do this to you… What about your father? What does he say?'

Hot tears spilled out of her eyes and down her cheeks. 'Father says it is my Christian duty to look after my mother. So there's no way out.' She wept into her hands. 'Oh George, I'm so unhappy!'

The interval bell tolled and around them people began to drift back into the auditorium, but the young couple remained where they were – Alice sobbing her heart out, and George standing beside her, in silent thought.

When the foyer was empty, he finally spoke. 'Alice you don't have to become your mother's companion.'

'I've thought about it and thought about it, and there's no way out.'

'Yes there is. We can get married.'

Alice's world suddenly went silent. She could see George's mouth moving but she couldn't hear what he was saying. She swallowed hard and focused, and finally she could hear his voice, although it was still as if he was speaking in the distance:

'... but when you think about it, it's obvious. I know we haven't known each other all that long – but how long is the right amount of time? I love you and you love me, so I think that's the right amount of time. Then there is the religious situation but I am happy to manage with you being a Catholic and me being a Protestant. There is the big question of my health and my continuing battle with TB. I am well now but I don't know what will happen tomorrow. I may have a relapse and then again I may not. I have no option but to live each day as it comes. So it suits me to marry you as soon as possible. What you have to decide is, would it suit you to marry me?'

For a long time she stared at him. And then she said in a puzzled voice, 'Somewhere in all those questions, ruminations and considerations, George Gilbert, did I hear you ask me to marry you?'

He thought about it. 'Yes, I think I did. But do you want me to ask you again, just to be sure?'

'Maybe you should. Just to be sure.'

With quick a glance around the empty foyer, he dropped to one knee. 'Alice will you marry me? Take as much time as you like to think about it.'

'No, I don't need time to think about it. I love you, George, and I think it suits me to marry you very much.'

Alice and Mrs Gilbert sat a little stiffly in the small front parlour of 5 Primrose Avenue; both women were nervous and wished that the conversation they were about to have was over. The table was set with Mrs Gilbert's best china but the tea had not been poured and the food had not been touched.

'George has told me that he has asked you to marry him and that you have accepted.' Mrs Gilbert entwined her fingers in her lap. 'Do you think that is a sensible thing to do?'

'We love each other,' said Alice.

'That is not what I asked. In life you have to be practical. George has TB.'

'He had TB,' corrected Alice.

'Has TB,' Mrs Gilbert said gently but firmly. 'Don't blind yourself to the truth. Another thing: George is vulnerable. If you hurt him, it could aggravate his condition.'

'I won't hurt him.'

'You mean, you wouldn't mean to hurt him.'

'I mean I won't hurt him. I love him.'

Mrs Gilbert placed her hand on Alice's hand.

'Alice, I am not your enemy. You're a nice girl and I like you, but you are young and I am experienced. If you and George marry, you could be a young widow in a very short time. Have you thought about that?'

Alice bowed her head and said nothing.

'Life can be cruel,' said Mrs Gilbert. 'People can be cruel. When my husband was ill, neighbours and more than a few friends refused to come near the house for fear of being infected.'

Alice looked shaken. 'Oh...'

The older woman nodded sadly at her. 'Did you not notice how few neighbours attended my birthday party?'

'George is going to be well, the doctors said so,' said Alice firmly.

'No, they didn't say that. They said he's well *now*. There is a difference. What have you told your family about George?'

'I haven't told them anything.'

'They don't know that he has TB?'

Alice shook her head.

'Do they even know that he is Protestant?'

Alice looked at the floor.

Mrs Gilbert sighed. 'How do you think they would feel about you marrying a Protestant?'

'I'm not sure.' But she knew exactly how appalled her father would be if he knew she was even seeing a Protestant, let alone wanted to marry one.

'What do you think your parents will say about you marrying a humble tradesman – George might be a good piano play but it doesn't bring in much money. George is a coach builder by trade.'

'My parents aren't snobs.'

'But they are wealthy. You don't work and you live in a big house on High Street.'

'Our house is not that big.'

'It's a Georgian mansion, for heaven's sake. I daresay George has never even seen the inside of such a house.'

'I don't care about money, and nor does George...'

Mrs Gilibert sighed. 'George is like his father was – a dreamer and an eternal optimist who believes that God will make everything all right. But God doesn't work that way, at least not in the world in which I live. Alice, do you realise that if you marry my son, you are likely to be shunned by many people?'

'No,' Alice said defiantly.

'Yes, and for many different reasons. You will be shunned because your husband has TB and that frightens people, shunned as a Catholic marrying a Protestant and shunned by your own class for marrying beneath your status. Alice, marrying George is not a wise thing to do. Everything, common sense, logic and reason dictate that you should think of a future without him.'

'You made it work for you and your husband,' said Alice gently.

'Yes we did,' Mrs Gilbert answered softly. 'But my husband didn't have TB when we married and our families were reasonably happy with our interdenominational marriage.'

'Are you going to ask George to abandon me?'

'No, Alice. Whatever you and my son decide, I will support. But make no mistake, it won't be easy. Now will you pour the tea or shall I?'

Two beautifully plumed white horses pulled the bridal carriage into the courtyard of St Audoen's Church and the clattering of the horses' hooves on the cobblestones broke the silence and sent pigeons and doves scattering into the sky. Wearing her handmade, full length, ivory satin and lace wedding dress, Ann looked at her father across from her and could not think of a single thing to say to him.

Her father stared uncomfortably back at her, his mind racing, also trying to think of something to say. And then for the first time in years, he paid her a compliment: 'Ann, you are a beautiful bride.'

'Thank you, Father.' Ann smiled slightly, and gently fingered the lace on the sleeve of her dress.

He added, 'And I wish you all the happiness life can bring.'

That is what he said. But it was not what he was really wishing. He was wishing his daughter was not marrying Braiden Doyle. He had heard rumours about Braiden's unorthodox business practices. Even John, a man who seldom spoke ill of anyone, had negative things to say about Braiden and his business dealings. Suddenly, he was unable to help himself. He placed his hands on his knees and leaned forward.

'Are you sure that Braiden Dolye is the man for you, Ann?'

Ann looked up at her father. 'What a funny question to ask me on my wedding day! But yes Father, I'm sure he is. Should we go into the church?'

'No, Alice will come to the carriage when it's time for your entrance.' Thomas leaned back against the dimpled soft leather of the carriage and thought how poorly that conversation had gone.

The church was crowded. Everyone was there – except for the groom, and his best man.

At ten minutes past the hour, the side door of the church squeaked open and the best man – tie askew and the top button of his shirt open –slunk in and tiptoed over to the Dalton bridal group, who were sitting all together in the front pew of the church. The congregation fell silent, nudging each other and watching. The best man muttered hurriedly to Jarlath and handed him a white envelope. Then, without making eye-contact with anyone else, he opened the altar rail and – to the sound of the congregation taking a collective breath – walked into the sacristy.

Jarlath looked at the envelope, then passed it to Terrance. After Terrance had read the name on the envelope, he stepped out of the pew and strode grim-faced down the centre aisle of the church.

In the porch, he spoke to the bridesmaids, Alice and Tess. 'It looks like Braiden isn't coming.'

'Oh Jesus, poor Ann,' said Tess, leaning weakly against the stone wall.

Alice crushed her hands to her cheeks, wide-eyed. 'You said something awful to him, didn't you?'

'I only did what any loving brother would do...'

'What are you talking about?' interrupted Tess.

'Nothing. Alice, this letter is for Ann,' said Terrance, holding out the envelope.

'No. No, this is you're doing. For once in your life you're going to face the consequences of your own actions.' She pushed the envelope back at her brother.

Grim-faced, Terrance marched out of the church and knocked on the window of the bridal carriage.

'Where's Alice?' Ann demanded, opening the window. 'What are you doing here?'

Terrance braced himself. 'There is no way to sugar coat this, Ann. Braiden hasn't arrived and according to his best man he won't be arriving. He left this letter for you...'

Ann went as white as her dress. 'What do you mean, he won't be arriving? Is he ill? What's...'

'The blackguard, I should have listened to John Swords!' blurted Thomas from inside the carriage. 'He told me Braiden was a deceitful person! Terrance, send Alice out immediately to her sister.'

'Yes, ask Alice to come,' whispered the ashen-faced Ann.

'I'm sorry, Ann,' Terrance said. 'I swear, I tried...'

'Just get Alice.'

When Alice saw Ann's deathly pale face and tear-filled eyes, her heart broke. 'Father, would you leave us for a few minutes?'

'Certainly,' said Thomas, delighted to vacate the emotionally-charged carriage.

'Read it to me,' demanded Ann, handing the letter to Alice.

'It's your letter. I'm sure it's private.'

'Read it,' Ann insisted, in a steely voice.

Alice ripped open the envelope and removed a single sheet of folded white writing paper. She read aloud:

Dear Ann,

I can only hope that in time you will forgive me but I will not be attending today's ceremony and I do not intend to return to Ireland. In the past I have not always been truthful with you nor have I always done the right thing. As Terrance has undoubtedly told you I have been engaged on two other occasions but there is no truth in the rumour that I extorted money from the ladies or their families. Your brother Terrance has threatened me and has made it very clear that he does not consider me good enough for you or your family. I want you to know that I care greatly for you and count the time we spent together the happiest time of my life.

With great regret,
Braiden Doyle.

Ann's broken-hearted wail of pain ripped through Alice's heart. Throwing the letter aide, she clasped her sister in her arms and held her tightly, while the poor young bride shuddered with grief and shame.

When Terrance returned to the carriage to tell the driver to take Ann home, the jilted bride lunged at him, clawed at him and screamed, 'How could you do this to me? I hate you and I will never forgive you!'

In the church, Thomas walked his oldest daughter, Tess, down the aisle through the whispering, staring crowd. When they reached the front pew, Thomas said to Jarlath, 'Take your mother and sister back to the house,'

Then he stood with his back to the altar rails, facing the congregation and without offering any excuse or explanation, he told the people to go home.

The bridal carriage stopped abruptly outside 8 High Street. The driver's heavily-nicotined fingers opened the door and in full view of the watching neighbours, Ann descended from the carriage in her wedding dress and – supported by Alice – walked to the front door, where Alice pushed the key into the lock and let them in.

Once inside, Ann leaned against the wall with her handkerchief to her eyes and burst into tears. 'What a mess. What a mess. Did you see everyone snooping from their windows? I don't know what to feel. I can't think… Am I going mad?'

'No, but the world is,' Alice replied. She put her arm around her sister and encouraged her up the stairs to her bedroom.

Ann carefully removed her wedding dress and Alice placed it in the Gertrude Finnie white box in which it came.

'Why did Braiden humiliate me so?' asked Ann, sitting on the bed.

'I don't know.' Alice sat beside her sister.

'What is going to happen to me? Am I going to be an old maid?'

There was a gentle knock on the door. Alice opened it and her father was standing sheepishly on the landing. 'How is she?'

'I'm fine, come in Father,' said Ann.

Thomas looked to Alice for help but she turned away from him and sat on her own bed.

'Ann, is there anything I can do?' he asked awkwardly.

'No, Father, there is nothing you can do. How is Mother?'

'Very upset. She has taken to her bed.'

'How caring of her,' murmured Alice.

'That's unfair!' snapped Thomas, bristling at his youngest daughter. 'Your mother cares for you all very much.'

'Yes, I suppose she does in her own uncaring way,' said Ann. 'Thank you for your concern, Father, you're very kind. But now I think I would like the company of my sister.'

'Of course,' said Thomas, and left the room.

CHAPTER TWENTY-ONE

Dark clouds slid across a grey sky and a troubled Thomas Dalton sat in the summer house smoking a Cuban cigar. Thunder rumbled and he thought of the turmoil in his family. Ann was still bursting into tears at the slightest provocation; Alice was still not speaking to him; none of the girls were speaking to Terrance; Jarlath had been largely absent since the wedding and most troubling of all, Mariah was slipping back into her old dark ways and spending far too much time alone in her bedroom.

Thomas quenched his cigar in the sand-filled ashtray and returned to his office. Ten minutes later, Jarlath pushed open the door without knocking.

'There you are Father, controlling your little empire from your throne,' he said, slouching against the office door frame.

'Sarcasm doesn't suit you,' snapped Thomas, without lifting his head.

Jarlath sauntered across the carpet, dropped into the chair in front of the desk and sat there sullenly, his eyes two pits of discontent.

With a sigh, Thomas ran his hands along the sides of his thinning hair. 'Dreadful state of affairs.'

'Yes, without a doubt the worst time of my life.'

'I'm talking about your sister and that Braiden person.'

'Oh, that,' Jarlath said contemptuously. 'Ann has had a lucky escape. That blackguard was always a crook and a thief. He belongs in prison.'

Thomas was taken aback. 'You knew the man was a thief and you said nothing?'

'Would you have believed me, Father?'

'Of course I would!'

'I doubt it.'

'You said it was vital that we meet this morning,' said Thomas, tiring of Jarlath's cynical self-pity. 'What's so urgent that it couldn't wait until tomorrow?'

'I've joined the British army.'

Thomas swallowed hard. Even though he had suggested that Jarlath should join the army, now the plan had become a reality, he felt a wave of grief.

'What regiment, Jarlath?'

'The Royal Corps of Signals.'

'Your Uncle Aiden's old regiment!'

'Yes, I met with Uncle Aiden and he suggested it. I am to report to the Royal Military Academy, Sandhurst, for training next Monday.'

'That soon?' Thomas fumbled in his top drawer, removed a brown envelope and handed it to Jarlath. 'I know I haven't always been the best father to you,' he said, sincerely. 'But for what it's worth I think you're doing the right thing. It will be good for you.'

'That's what you said when you packed me off to boarding school.'

'The boarding school was your mother's idea. I was not in favour of it.'

Jarlath shrugged, flipped open the envelope, glanced at its contents and – without saying thank you or goodbye – rose from his chair and walked out of his father's office.

Ann had lost all interest in day-to-day life. She refused to leave the house, cancelled her piano classes and didn't attend choir practice or the dance school. She completely neglected her household chores and spent most of her time sitting in her bed staring blindly out the window. When Alice gently suggested that they needed to start returning her wedding presents, Ann looked at her sister blankly.

Yet the following morning when Alice awoke, Ann was already downstairs at the writing table, re-addressing a gift. Alice joined her sister and the two young women spent the morning re-wrapping presents for return.

'You're feeling better,' Alice said.

'Well, better than yesterday. How are you?'

'I'm good.' Alice flushed and she could not suppress a slight smile.

'What is it, Alice?'

Alice put aside the brown wrapping paper and twine and placed her hands on her lap.

'All right. I have to tell someone or I'll burst. I know it's dreadful timing, but George has asked me to marry him.' After blurting out her news, she waited nervously on Ann's reply.

'Did you accept?' Ann seemed stunned.

'I did, Ann. I know he's a Protestant and I know you don't approve, but I truly love him.'

After a long pause, her older sister smiled gently and said, 'Then that's wonderful Alice. I'm really happy for you, congratulations.'

'Oh thank you Ann, that's very mportant to me...' breathed Alice, and the sisters embraced.

'I hope everything works out for you Alice, you deserve to be happy.' Ann's eyes darkened. 'But have you thought how you're going to persuade Father to let you marry a Protestant? And a tradesman, for that matter?'

'You think he'll mind about George being a coach builder as much as he'll mind about him being a Protestant?'

'You know how much Father values his social standing. What will you do if he opposes your wedding altogether?'

'If he had been against your wedding to Braiden, what would you have done?'

'I'd have married him anyway. If you love George, marry him. There is too little love in this family.'

On the landing outside the bedroom, Tess rested her head against the deep-green embossed wallpaper and released a long, shuddering breath. She had heard most of Alice and Ann's conversation and she felt humiliated, excluded and hurt. Any slight, real or imagined, usually caused Tess to be sarcastic and hurtful – but feeling deliberately excluded made her vindictive and cruel.

It was just another day in the lives of the inhabitants of 8 High Street. Terrance was in his room writing a letter. Mariah as usual was resting, Tess was reading in her bedroom and Mrs Foley was baking bread in the kitchen. Thomas was studying some legal papers in his office and Alice and Ann were sitting in the summerhouse having a conversation. The quiet of the house was suddenly shattered by a barrage of banging on the front door. Mariah's eyes jerked opened, Thomas looked up from his papers. Terrance went to his bedroom door and cracked it open a little.

Alice ran into the house. 'I'll get it!' she shouted down the kitchen stairs to Mrs Foley.

When she pulled open the front door, she was confronted by two stern-faced uniformed policemen. One of the policemen was unusually tall and the other looked like a boxer who had never won a fight.

'Hello,' gasped Alice, after she'd found her breath.

'I am Sergeant Gallagher of the Dublin Metropolitan Police and I have an arrest warrant for Mr Dalton,' the tall policeman said formally. 'Stand aside please.'

'Which Mr Dalton would that be?' asked Alice very loudly, without stepping aside.

Upstairs, Terrance slid open his bedroom window.

Thomas emerged from the dining room. 'What is this about?' he asked indignantly.

'We are looking for Terrance Dalton,' announced Sergeant Gallagher, regarding Thomas with open hostility. 'Are you Terrance Dalton?'

'No, I'm his father. What's this in connection with?'

Sergeant Gallagher brushed past Alice into the house. 'Your son was involved in the blowing up of the statue of King William of Orange in College Green. Constable Keogh, check this floor and basement, and I'll check above.'

'Good God, this is ridiculous,' cried Thomas as Constable Keogh plodded down the hall into the drawing room.

Meanwhile, Sergeant Gallagher climbed to the first floor, pushing past Tess who had appeared on the stairs. Tess followed him back up the stairs and when he threw open the girls' bedroom door, she followed him into the room.

'Where is he?' demanded Sergeant Gallagher, looking around the empty room.

'I doubt he's in here,' said Tess with mock politeness. 'This is a girl's bedroom, you see.'

Ignoring her, Sergeant Gallagher stomped across the room and pushed up the bedroom window; he stuck his small head out into the open, gasped and thundered back to the landing.

'He's in the garden!' he bellowed down the stairs.

Constable Keogh ran to the back door and found it locked; with a swift kick of his size twelves, he smashed it open. Terrance was already halfway up the oak tree. The constable gave chase,

Terrance jumped from the tree to the top of the wall and by the time the policeman reached the base of the tree, he had disappeared from view.

'If any of you were complicit in helping that man escape, you will be charged with aiding and abetting a criminal!' roared Sergeant Gallagher, furious at the unsuccessful raid. 'Rest assured we will catch this young man and he will go to prison!'

Tess knocked on her mother's door. It was over a year since she had last visited her mother's bedroom but the same sweet pungent odour of medicinal potions mixed with Yardley's English Lavender Water and stale air wafted into her face. The room was in near darkness, clothes were strewn on the floor and a half-eaten meal sat on a tray on the dressing table. Tess picked some clothes off the floor and placed them on a chair.

'Don't do that. I don't like people touching my things.' Mariah said sharply. 'What do you want?'

'I have something important to tell you, Mother,' said Tess, standing at the side of the large bed.

'If it's anything to do with those awful policemen that invaded our house I don't want to know.'

'No, it's not about that. I thought you should know that Alice is keeping company with a young man.'

Mariah blinked. 'Who gave her permission to do that?'

'Mother, the young man has proposed to her and she has accepted.'

Mariah's eyes grew large. 'She wants to marry him?'

'The man is a common tradesman.'

'Outrageous!'

'And a Protestant.'

'*A Protestant?*' Mariah had to take several deep breaths before she could speak again. 'Does your father know about this?'

'I don't think so,' Tess replied, and her eyes glowed with spite.

A mist hung in the air as George and Alice walked hand in hand along the wet cobblestones of Crow Street. It was dusk and an aura of fog hugged the street lights and created an eerie ghost-like atmosphere. The city's working day was over and workers were scurrying home through the mist. A glass-sided, horse-drawn hearse trundled passed and Alice made the sign of the cross. The clattering of horses' hooves faded. George shifted the suitcase he was carrying to his left hand and pulled open the door of Slattery's Public House. Alice stepped into the warm, smokey, ale-smelling lounge bar and George let the door clatter behind them. The pub's four inhabitants looked to the door. The wire-thin bartender nodded to George and the old toothless man he was serving looked questioningly at Alice. Two round-shouldered, bald-headed old men sitting at a table near the fire grunted and continued their whispered conversation. George walked Alice to a booth in the rear of the pub, placed the suitcase under the table and went to the bar and fetched a pint of ale and an orange drink.

'This is the first time I've been in a public house,' Alice said, looking around the pub. 'I don't think I like it here.'

'I only bring you to the best of places,' said George, and they clinked glasses. In the back, a céilí band started to play a set of jigs and reels. The band had moved on to playing patriotic ballads when Terrance pushed open the pub door.

'Sorry to ask you to meet me in a place like this, Alice,' he said, taking the seat beside his sister. 'But it's the only safe place I could think of.'

'How are you, Terrance?' Alice asked.

'As well as can be expected. Is this your boyfriend?'

'Yes, this is George – George Gilbert.'

'Pleased to meet you, George.' The two men shook hands. 'This sister of mine is a handful but she's all right. Alice, did you bring my things?'

'Yes, your suitcase is under the table. Are you planning on going to England?'

'No, that would be too dangerous a place for me right now. My name is on a steamer ticket going from Cobh to New York next Friday. But there are a few hitches. The man who has my steamer ticket money has been arrested and I need a safe place to stay for a few nights.'

'You can stay in my house,' George said. 'No one in my family is political so it's safe. I have some money I can lend you.'

'Why would you do that? You don't even know me.'

'I don't know you and I don't know if I want to know you but you're Alice's brother, so I'll help you.'

Alice squeezed George's hand.

Terrance smiled at her. 'You've got a good one here, Alice. Thank you, George – I'll take you up on your offer of a bed. We shouldn't hang about here. Why don't you take Alice home and I'll meet you in thirty minutes on this side of the Halfpenny Bridge.'

Moonlight glowed through the slight parting in the curtains of Alice's bedroom. Ann was asleep and Tess had not returned home from wherever she was. Alice got up and pulled the curtains tight together, plunging the room into near darkness. She got back into bed and pulled the covers up to her chin and listened to the creaking of the sleeping house.

What will Terrance do in America? she wondered. *He doesn't know anyone there and it's such a big place. And what about Jarlath – Father says he's joining the army – will he be happy in England? I hope he'll find a horse to gallop across some English countryside.* Her thoughts drifted further. *Oh, poor Ann when will she stop grieving for that cad Braiden?* She shook her head. *How long will I grieve if something happens to George?* That thought terrified her…

The bedroom door clicked open and Alice closed her eyes and pretended to be asleep as Tess crept in.

'Alice! Alice!' A very annoyed Mariah stood on the first floor landing calling her daughter's name.

It was the second day this week that Mariah had had reason to rise before noon. She had requested, through Mrs Foley, that Alice come and help her, but when Alice hadn't arrived Mariah had been forced to don her black silk dressing gown and go looking for her daughter.

The overworked Mrs Foley hurried up from the kitchen to the hall. 'Alice has gone on an errand, she'll be back in an hour!' she shouted up to Mariah.

'Don't shout at me, Mrs Foley. Come upstairs, I need assistance in dressing.'

'I'm the cook not the lady's maid!'

Mariah snorted angrily. 'Very well, Mrs Foley when Alice returns please send her to me in my room.'

An hour later, Alice appeared at her mother's door. 'Hello Mother,' Alice said gently. 'I'm glad to see you're feeling well enough to be out of bed.'

'Sit! I have something to say to you,' snapped Mariah, from the wing chair by the window.

Alice sat at the dressing table.

Mariah glared at her. 'I hear you have been walking out with a young man. You are in no position to form a relationship with any man, Alice. You are to be my companion, so put an end to this nonsense immediately. Now, be off with you.'

Alice remained seated, in shock. 'Mother, who told you…'

'It's none of your business! I told you to leave! And never speak to this young man again!'

'Don't you want to hear what I have to say, Mother?' Alice fought hard not to be intimidated by her mother's severe expression. 'Don't you want to meet George?'

'No, I don't want to hear what you have to say and I certainly don't want to meet this… your… "friend".'

'Mother, he's not a "friend". He is my intended husband. I love him.'

Mariah snorted cynically. 'You "love" him? What do you know about love? I'll tell you what love is. Love is heartbreak and disappointment, that's what love is. You love someone and they'll let you down…'

'Oh, Mother,' said Alice sadly. 'Did you always think like that?'

'Think like what?' Mariah clearly didn't believe she had said anything controversial. 'It's just the way it is. The world is a cruel place and you have to be hard to survive. Look at what love did to me. Look at what it's doing to you.'

'Mother, please, can't you just support me for once…'

'That's exactly what I'm doing. I'm looking after you. Someday you'll thank me for this. I'm trying to stop you making a fool of yourself.'

'Why do you say such awful things?' asked Alice and a tear formed in her eye.

'For God's sake, Alice, think about what you're doing. Where is your sense of shame? Your young man is a poor tradesman and a Protestant. It is socially unacceptable.'

'I don't feel shame walking out with George. I feel happy and I'm going to marry him!'

'Don't be absurd! He's a Protestant!' barked Mariah. 'It's against the teachings of the church. I forbid it!'

'I don't care what you forbid. I love him.'

Thomas was in the drawing room smoking when Mariah swept into the room. Astonished that his wife was up, Thomas's mouth fell open; the cigar fell from his lips and – in a burst of sparks – bounced off the leg of his trousers and onto the armchair. He jumped from his seat, wildly brushing the glowing ash from his trousers.

'You're up, Mariah,' he cried, flustered. 'You must be feeling better!'

'I'm feeling dreadful. Sit down we need to talk.'

Thomas sat down and continued to brush the very last of the ash from his trousers.

'Will you stop doing that?'

He stopped.

'Did you know that Alice is walking out with a Protestant tradesman?'

He recoiled. 'What! Who told you that?'

'Tess, and thank God she did,' Mariah said. 'And it's worse than that. The blackguard has proposed to her and the silly girl has accepted.'

'Good God, a Protestant? It's ridiculous! It's against God's law and everything we believe in! What would Canon Mulcahy think? I'll have a word with Alice and put a stop to this.'

'See that you do.'

'Are you sure Tess is not just saying this to cause trouble?' asked Thomas hopefully.

'No, the girl hasn't got that much imagination,' replied Mariah. 'Besides, Alice has admitted to it. That girl is without shame. This is clearly a blatant attempt to get out of being my companion. You have to speak to her, Thomas, and tell her it won't work.'

Alice knelt at a side altar in St Audoen's Church and prayed to God that Terrance would get safely to America. When she'd finished her prayers she headed up Thomas Street on her errand for Mrs Foley. The footpaths were busy with shoppers and children playing and street traders selling second-hand clothes and bric-a brac. Alice was manoeuvring past a young girl skipping, when Jarlath came up beside her.

'What are you doing in this part of the city? You're more a Grafton Street person,' he said, as they walked along the stalls of the street traders.

'I'm on my way to the shoemakers for Mrs Foley.'

'Have you heard I've joined the British army? I'm off to England in a few days,' he said, stepping over some litter.

'I heard. I'm sorry you're going.'

'It won't be forever.' He glanced around. 'How is Terrance? I'd like to see him before I go. Will you arrange a meeting?' When Alice hesitated, he added, 'I know Terrance and I haven't always been the best of friends, but he is my brother.'

Alice softened. 'I'll see what I can do. But you both have to be careful – there are so many informers about.' She moved closer to Jarlath. 'He needs money.'

'Don't look at me.'

'Do you think Father would help?'

'No. He'll tell you it's against his principles.'

'What about Mother – would she give you money if you asked her?'

Jarlath shrugged. 'I don't think so. Mother has all the maternal instincts of a slab of granite.'

The following morning after breakfast, Alice tracked down her father in the drawing room.

'Father, I want to talk to you.'

'And I want to talk to you,' said Thomas, unpleasantly.

But Alice was too intent on her mission to notice the anger in her father's voice. She positioned herself in front of the fireplace, her hands clasped behind her back. 'You're not going to like what I have to say, Father. Terrance is in trouble.'

Thomas glared sternly at Alice.

'He needs money for a steamer ticket to America. Will you help?'

'After all he has done, after all his lies and deceit, you ask me to help him – again?' Thomas's voice was measured and cold. 'Every time I have helped that young man he has thrown my kindness back in my face. He stood there, right where you're standing and promised me if I'd let him stay in the house he would refrain from his Republican activities. He lied to me and he lied to you. He cares for no one but himself.'

'He needs your help, Father. He's your son.'

Thomas shifted his weight from one foot to the other. 'Terrance is not the only one who has lied to me and deceived me, is he, Alice?' His eyes were icy and he never took them from Alice's face. 'I hear you are stepping out with a Protestant?'

Alice froze and took two deep, silent breaths. Then she said, 'That's not what I came here to discuss. But yes, I am seeing a young man who happens to be Protestant.'

'How could you do this to me?' Thomas made no effort to hide his contempt. 'Why would you bring such shame on the family? Is it true that you are contemplating marriage to this person?'

Alice remained erect and defiant. 'His name is George Gilbert and yes he has asked me to marry him.'

Thomas's eyes darted from side to side, as if seeking a way out. 'I suppose this is because your mother wants you to become her companion?'

'No, it's not. It has nothing to do with that.' Her voice shook. 'It's what I want to do. It's because I love George.'

With a groan, Thomas pulled a monogrammed handkerchief from his pocket, pressed it to his forehead and wondered why his life was tearing itself apart. 'Then it is truly beyond my comprehension why you would do this...'

'We don't choose who we fall in love with, Father. I thought you, above all people, would understand that.'

'Don't you talk to me about what I understand,' snapped Thomas.

'Will you help Terrance?'

'Don't change the subject, Alice. You must realise that it distresses me beyond measure that you are seeing a Protestant, let alone contemplating marrying one.'

'And it distresses me beyond measure that you will not help your son.'

As she stalked out of the room, Alice felt as if something had fundamentally shifted between herself and her father and her world had changed irreparably.

CHAPTER TWENTY-TWO

J arlath and Alice sat in the quiet of Slattery's Pub. Jarlath had a brandy in front of him and Alice had an orange drink. Both drinks were untouched. Alice looked idly around the almost empty pub and as the pub's antique clock chimed eight times, she thought how slowly yet quickly time passes.

'What are Terrance's plans?' asked Jarlath, lifting his drink to his lips.

'I'll let him tell you himself,' she replied and the clock's heavy brass pendulum swung through the air.

When the clock chimed fifteen minutes past the hour, the pub's door opened and George entered. He smiled at Alice, checked around the pub and held the door for Terrance.

'Didn't know you were one of our freedom fighters, George,' said Jarlath, as he rose to his feet and held out his hand.

'I'm not,' replied George and shook Jarlath's hand.

'A man of few words, good policy.' Jarlath turned to his brother. 'How's the blowing-up-statues business?'

'Satisfying but not lucrative,' said Terrance and sat beside his brother. 'And speaking of filthy lucre, I need some.'

'Don't we all,' said Jarlath.

'I asked Father to help but he refused,' Alice interjected.

The bartender approached and Terrance ordered two pints of Guinness.

'How much money do you need?' Jarlath asked.

'Forty pounds would do it.'

'I have that much, I can let you have it,' said George, as Alice gratefully pressed his hand.

'Save your money, George.' Jarlath reached into his pocket and pulled out a brown paper packet. He slid it across the table to Terrance. 'You'll need more than forty quid. There's a hundred in there.'

'You don't need it?' Terrance was amazed.

'One always needs money. But do you really think I'd leave myself short? Blood may be thicker than water but hunger beats blood anytime. Father gave me money for England, but I had already tapped Uncle Aiden for a few quid. And Mother had some money hidden away for emergencies.'

'But you said Mother...' Alice began, but stopped when Jarlath flashed her a childlike smile.

'Thank you, big brother,' said Terrance and stuffed the packet into the pocket of his jacket.

For nearly two hours, the foursome talked intensely about their different futures. Then, when the clock struck the hour of ten, Jarlath reached for his hat and coat. 'I'd better be off, I've got to pack for tomorrow.' He leaned over to his brother and whispered, 'Not good for us military types to be seen with Republicans!'

Terrance laughed and the brothers shook hands warmly. Then Jarlath and Alice hugged.

'Good luck, Jarlath. Write to me,' she said.

'I will and good luck to you, Alice. From what I hear you'll need it. My crime was that I stole a few things but your crime is greater. You're walking out with a Protestant. Good luck, George, look after my sister. See you, Terrance!'

Pulling on his coat, Jarlath walked to the door; glancing over his shoulder at his brother and sister he wondered if he would ever see them again.

In the morning, as Alice opened the bedroom drapes, Ann stirred sleepily in her bed.

'You were talking in your sleep,' Alice said, sitting on the bed beside her sister.

Ann struggled up and lifted her blue cashmere cardigan off her bedside table; she pulled it around her shoulders. 'I had that awful dream again. I was in the bridal carriage wearing my wedding dress and everyone rushed out of the church, gathered around the carriage and laughed and pointed at me. It was all so real. When will I ever stop dreaming and thinking about that day?'

'Give yourself time, Ann. It's only been a short while.'

Ann shuddered. 'It seems like a lifetime already. What am I going to do?'

Alice made an effort to sound cheerful. 'You're going to get up. We have to prepare the dancing school for the new term. I have to buy pencils and ribbons. Will you come?'

Ann shook her head and lay down again. 'Not today, Alice. Not today.'

Alice stood under Merchant's Arch on Wellington Quay and watched a fog drift up the river and envelope the city in a grey damp mist. She pulled up the collar of her coat and as she waited she shifted her weight from foot to foot. Snorting and neighing loudly, two huge grey horses suddenly emerged from the fog. The window of the elaborate, highly-polished carriage dropped open and a black gloved hand beckoned to Alice.

Alice flinched and took a step backwards.

The hand beckoned again.

Alice's heart pounded and she was about to rush away when George leaned out of the window. 'Come on, we're in a hurry!'

She ran laughing to the carriage. 'You put the heart across me! Where's Terrance?'

'Who do you think is driving?'

As soon as she had climbed aboard, George knocked on the roof and called out, 'Driver, take us to the Phoenix Park!'

'Where did you get the carriage?' asked Alice as they journeyed down the quays.

'It's owned by a Mr Paul O'Sullivan from Cork. It's new and I've been working on it for months. My boss asked me if I'd like to deliver it to its new owner in Cork. It works out really well. First I take Terrance to Cobh where he will catch his steamer to America. Then I'll go on to Cork city, hand over the carriage and I'll take a train back to Dublin.'

'I'd love to go with you.'

'That wouldn't be wise. In a few minutes, we'll be in the Phoenix Park. You can say a proper goodbye to your brother there.'

When the carriage halted in the park, Terrance jumped down from the driver's seat and opened the carriage door.

'I'll give you two ten minutes and then we have to be on our way,' said George, climbing out. 'We can't miss the steamer – there won't be another one for a week.' He stood outside the door of the carriage smoking a cigarette, acting as lookout while the brother and sister said their final farewells.

After ten minutes, he climbed back into the carriage. Alice was crying and Terrance was silent.

Fifteen minutes later, when the carriage stopped outside 8 High Street, Alice slipped out and stood waving forlornly at both passenger and driver as the carriage disappeared into the thick fog.

It was Ann's first day back teaching at the dancing school. She didn't really want to be there, but Alice had finally persuaded her to go. Tess was lighting a fire in the changing room. When the children arrived, Alice took their wet coats and hats, and helped the girls dry their hair.

Ann was helping young Laura Fitzmorris put on her dancing shoes, when the child asked, 'Are you still awfully sad about your wedding day?'

Ann's eyes welled up and she rushed out of the changing room into the dance studio.

'Did I say something wrong?' asked the child, seeing the shocked look on Alice's face.

'No, you didn't. Why don't you finish putting on your shoes?' said Alice and followed Ann into the studio. 'The child didn't mean anything,' she said.

'I know.' Ann was leaning against the piano, her face in her hands. 'Just give me a minute and I'll be fine. You go back to the children.'

In the changing room Tess was helping young Laura finish tying her shoes. She said to Alice, 'Is Ann going to get all weepy every time anyone mentions her should-have-been wedding day?'

'She's still very raw. It only happened a few short weeks ago. I think she is being very brave.'

'That's not being brave,' smirked Tess. 'Being brave is visiting Mother in her bedroom and telling her a few home truths.'

'What home truths did you tell Mother?'

'Oh, I'm sure nothing that you would consider important' replied Tess, but Alice caught the glint of guilt that flashed in her sister's eyes.

Alice pounced angrily: 'It was you who told Mother about George! I should have guessed.'

Tess tossed her head. 'You may not believe me but I did it to stop you ruining your life.'

'No you didn't. You did it because you can't stand seeing other people happy. You did it because you're jealous and nasty.'

'I did it to stop you doing something very stupid. If you continue seeing George, Father will write you out of his will.'

'That's nonsense. He'll come round when he realises George is important to me.'

'He wrote Terrance out of his will,' snapped Tess. 'I heard him tell Uncle John.'

'Why are you fighting with your sister?' asked young Laura plaintively. 'Grown ups aren't supposed to fight!'

'Oh shut up you stupid girl,' snapped Tess and stormed off into the studio.

When Alice turned to reassure Laura she saw sixteen little girls staring at her.

A flat-backed Henshaw's cart slowly made its way up Winetavern Street and two pasty-faced, shaven-headed boys took the opportunity to scut on the back of the cart.

'Get off the feckin' cart,' the driver shouted and cracked his whip at the boys.

The whip lashed against the floor of the cart and caught one of the boys on the arm. The boy screamed, let go of the cart, stumbled along the footpath and crashed into George Gilbert. The boy cursed and George watched him run after the cart, catch it and scut on it again.

George was on his way to Alice's house to meet her parents.

It had taken Alice a week of constant badgering before Thomas and Mariah had finally agreed to the meeting and Alice was full of hope. The appointment was for noon, and George had given a lot of thought to what he was going to say. Wearing his best Sunday tweed jacket and his brother's new tie, he stopped and studied his reflection in a shop window. He was settling his cap when he read the lettering on the shop window: *Dalton Hairdressers of Distinction*. A piercingly cold shiver raced down his spine; without noticing, he had already arrived at his destination. Now he wished he was with his brother in Dalymount Park. He felt like going home, turning on his heels and running down the street like the boy running after the cart. But he didn't, because he knew how important this meeting was to Alice.

He lifted the knocker on the green front door and let it fall. The third time the door knocker fell against its brass base a smiling but anxious Alice opened the door. George pulled off his cap and plunged it into the pocket of his jacket. He stepped into the house and was amazed by the size of the hall – it was as big as the living room in his home and the quality of the painting and decorating and the excellence of the carpentry and plaster work impressed him.

'Mother won't be joining us today,' Alice said, tugging George's hat out of his jacket pocket and hanging it on the coat stand. 'She said she was too ill to meet you.'

'I'm sorry to hear that,' said George, gravely.

'Father is waiting for us.' She knocked on the drawing room door.

'Come in!' called Thomas.

When the young couple entered, Thomas was standing in the centre of the hearth rug, his hands clasped behind his back.

'Father, I'd like you to meet George Gilbert,' smiled Alice eagerly.

'Pleased to meet you, Mr Dalton,' said George, holding out his hand.

Thomas kept his behind his back. 'Please sit.'

George dropped his hand, and he and a slighty crestfallen Alice perched side by side on one of the couches in the centre of the room.

After a long, intimidating silence, George ventured, 'You have a very beautiful home, sir. Such excellent craftsmanship and such beautifully-made furniture.'

'I'm sure as a tradesman you'd appreciate things like that.'

Alice cringed. 'Father...'

'I'm simply stating a fact,' said Thomas sharply. 'You don't mind my being factual about your being a tradesman, do you George?'

'I don't at all mind being a tradesman.'

Thomas looked smug. 'Then may I ask, why are you even here?'

'Because Alice wishes it. I have asked her to marry me, and she has accepted, but she very much values your opinion and support. So, sir, I am here to ask for your blessing on our union.'

Alice slipped her fingers into George's hand.

Thomas glared and spoke with cold contempt. 'You have a nerve, I'll say that for you, young man. But I will never agree to you marrying my daughter.'

Alice shrank in her seat, praying for the ground to open up and swallow her. But George squeezed her fingers and said softly, 'May I ask why not, sir?'

'Because you are completely unsuitable. Now if there's nothing else, you can leave.'

'Mr Dalton, why did you ask me into your house if you didn't intend to talk to me?' asked George, without moving. 'As a gentleman, I can't imagine you agreed to this meeting merely to insult me?'

Thomas's expression darkened and the veins on his forehead bulged. 'The fact is, I allowed you to come into my house to tell you to your face that I am resolved and determined that my daughter will never marry a bloody Protestant!'

With a gasp, Alice bowed her head in humiliation. It was one thing for her father to be prejudiced in private against Protestants, but to openly insult George's religion to his face... How could her father be so offensive? Why was he being deliberately hurtful?

George rose steadily to his feet. 'I admire your determination and resolve, Mr Dalton, but let me tell you, sir, this bloody Protestant has just as much determination and resolve as you have ever had, and Alice and I will marry.' He turned to Alice, 'Alice, will you walk with me to the door?'

Alice was never as proud of George as she was of him that moment. As they crossed the room together, she took his hand.

CHAPTER TWENTY-THREE

Thomas Dalton circumnavigated Blessington Basin, missed the exit to Primrose Avenue and found himself in a long open park with which he was unfamiliar. He approached a mother and child sitting on a bench and asked for directions. A few minutes later, mildly flustered, he stood outside 5 Primrose Avenue, lifted the brass knocker on the recently varnished hall door and let it fall. He was about to lift the knocker for a third time when the door swung open and a young woman greeted him.

'Hello, what can I do for you?' asked the young woman, looking puzzled at the immaculately dressed gentleman standing at her door.

'I'd like to speak to Mr Gilbert,' said Thomas stiffly.

'My brothers are at a football match so you're out of luck,' the young woman replied with a smile.

'But it is your father I wish to speak to.'

'My father died nearly three years ago. If you want to talk to him, you'll have to go to Glasnevin cemetery.'

Thomas's lips tightened. *A little respect for the dead, please,* read his stony expression.

The young woman took a closer look at the man's humourless face and said, 'I expect you're Mr Dalton?'

'I am. Is your mother at home or do I have to go to Glasnevin cemetery to talk to her too?' asked Thomas sarcastically.

'No, I'm not dead yet, Mr Dalton,' said Mrs Gilbert, appearing at the living room door. 'Freda, show the gentleman into the parlour. I'll make a pot of tea.'

'I do beg your pardon, Mrs Gilbert,' blurted Thomas, hastily removing his hat. 'I thought perhaps you might be visiting your husband's grave.'

But Mrs Gilbert had retreated out of sight, and Thomas coughed awkwardly and followed Freda into the parlour.

'I'll let some fresh air in,' Freda said and opened the top half of the window. Your Alice is great fun at parties, she has a lovely singing voice. Do you sing, Mr Dalton?'

'I do, I sing in my church choir.' Realising he was making idle conversation, he stopped abruptly. 'But I'm not here to discuss my voice. I wish to speak to your mother.'

'Then I'll go help her with the tea,' said Freda, the corners of her lips curling upwards.

A few minutes later, Thomas, Freda and Mrs Gilbert sat uncomfortably in front of a pot of tea and plate of home-made scones.

'I'll let the tea draw a minute or two,' said Mrs Gilbert. 'It's as well we have scones. We weren't expecting callers. Are you in the habit of making surprise visits, Mr Dalton?'

Thomas fidgeted and cleared his throat. 'I certainly am not, but there is an urgent matter I'd like to discuss.' He glanced at Freda Gilbert. 'If we could have a little privacy...'

'Mr Dalton,' said Mrs Gilbert, 'you are a stranger to me and I do not entertain strangers alone. Besides I believe in openness in families. Secrets are unhealthy.'

'Very well. I'll come straight to the point. I am here to object to the dreadful situation that has developed between your son and my daughter. I am a devout Catholic and my church frowns on interdenominational marriages...'

'I understand.' Mrs Gilbert raised a hand to stop him speaking further. 'I too am a Catholic, Mr Dalton, and I am more than aware of the implications of an interdenominational marriage.'

Thomas stiffened in surprise and gave an awkward little laugh. 'I understood you to be a member of the Protestant community, Mrs Gilbert?'

'Then your understanding is wrong, Mr Dalton. My daughters and I are Catholics. Freda, why don't you pour the tea?'

'I don't understand!' Thomas was getting flustered again. 'Your son George told me he is a Protestant.'

'That is correct, George was reared in the Church of Ireland faith. His father was Church of Ireland, as was his father's father before him. For someone objecting to my son, you are not very well informed about his family, Mr Dalton?'

'I may have got some details wrong,' replied an embarrassed Thomas.

'You certainly have.'

'Yet what you have just told me doesn't change the situation. Your son has asked for my daughter's hand in marriage.'

'I know,' replied Mrs Gilbert. 'He told me.'

'And you agree with his behaviour?'

'It does not matter whether I agree or disagree. My son is an adult and I support him in the decisions he makes. I did not object when George invited your son Terrance to stay here and I did not object to George accompanying him to Cork. I thought it was the Christian thing to do.'

'What?' Thomas shook his head in disbelief. 'Terrance stayed here? And is now in Cork?'

'No, your son is not in Cork. He's on a steamer on his way to America. You don't seem very aware of the whereabouts of your children.'

'That is not your concern!' A red stain was creeping up Thomas's neck into his cheeks. 'I came here to discuss your son and my daughter!'

'Well, your Alice seems like a very fine young woman. I like her, she's full of life. My son is a fine young man and he will be a good husband to her and I would be happy to have her as my daughter-in-law and beyond that I have nothing more to say.'

'Well, I have a lot more to say,' cried Thomas angrily.

'Mr Dalton, if you have something to say to George you must say it and you should say it to him before it's too late.'

'Would you like a scone?' Freda asked the dumb-struck Thomas. 'My mother made the gooseberry jam from fruit grown in our garden.'

Thomas did not reply.

'Who do you know in St Mary's hospital in the Phoenix Park?' Ann asked, pushing back her bedclothes as the dawn sun streamed in the window.

Alice was at the dressing table fixing her hair. Flushing, she kept her eyes on the mirror. 'Why on earth would you ask a question like that?'

'I borrowed your copy of Joyce's *Dubliners* from your bedside table, and there was a pamphlet about the hospital tucked inside. And you'd made pencil marks in the margins, about the latest treatments for TB.'

Alice rested her hands on her lap, staring intently at her pale, drawn reflection. She hadn't intended to tell anyone in her family about George having been ill, yet the knowledge was a heavy burden to carry alone. 'It's George. He had TB.'

Ann clasped her hand to her mouth. 'Isn't that what poor Mrs O'Donnell died of so soon after leaving us?'

Alice said quickly, 'No, George's TB was different from hers. He's completely recovered from it.'

'I heard that Mrs O'Donnell got better too, but it came back. Might that happen to George? It says in the pamphlet that often...'

'No, I told you. He is well now and he'll stay well.'

Alice and George sat in a booth in the rear of Bewley's oriental café and smiled at each other as the waitress set a large slice of apple tart and a glass of milk in front of George, and a cup of coffee and a slice of fruit cake in front of Alice.

'I love going to the films in the Savoy Cinema,' said Alice, cupping her hands around the hot coffee. 'It's like... I don't know... Travelling to a different, magical place for one night! It's like going to Venice for the night!'

'What would you know about Venice?' asked George, digging his fork into the warm apple pie.

'I know it's full of canals, lots of lovely little bridges and it's the most romantic city in the world.'

'You've got that all wrong.'

'Really?' Arching her eyebrows, Alice raised the coffee to her lips.

'Venice is not romantic at all, the canals smell, the place floods all the time and it's a very expensive place to visit.'

'Is it?'

'Oh, yes, it's a terrible place. Did you know that Casanova the great lover was imprisoned there?'

'Oh my, was he?' Alice rested her chin on her hand. 'That's terrible. Do tell me more.'

'I will. Casanova is the only person ever to have escaped from the prison in the Doges' Palace.'

'And where do you come by all this information?' Alice asked in mock amazement.

'You'd be surprised what I know, Miss Dalton,' laughed George, 'about reckless lovers.'

But then his face grew sober and Alice, guessing what he was thinking, slipped her hand over his. 'Father will come round. I'll work on him. I know he was rude and horrible to you, and I know he still thinks I should be Mother's companion but underneath he's always loved me and he's just very protective. He'll come round. And if he doesn't… But he will.'

They left the café and sauntered down Grafton Street. Alice took George's arm and every now and then they looked at each other and laughed just with the delight of being young and together.

Yet soon, Alice began thinking her own sober thoughts, and as they passed by Dublin Castle, she stopped walking and pulled him around to face her. 'I've an apology to make. I told Ann that you once had TB. Don't be angry with me.'

George stood gazing down at her, one eyebrow arched. 'I'm not angry, Alice. You were right to tell her, because it's the truth. Only, it's not the full truth. I *have* TB. I'm in remission now and everything is good but, I still have TB.'

'That's what I said, you *had* TB,' said Alice stubbornly, sticking out her lower lip like a stubborn child who refuses to acknowledge that everything isn't right. 'And she promised not to say anything to anyone.'

'But perhaps someone should say something. Alice, I know this is hard for you on top of what's already happened with your father, but perhaps it's best if your parents hear it from you rather than from someone else.'

Alice's eyes flashed. 'Stop telling me what to do! Everyone is always telling me what to do. I will talk to my parents when I'm ready and not before.'

George raised his hands, in mock self-defence. 'Alice, I'm not telling you what to do. I'm only telling you what I think. And it's not me you should be angry with.'

'Then who should I be angry with? God? The doctors? *Who?*' Then just as suddenly as it had arisen, her anger dissolved into the air and she dropped her head. 'I'm just so afraid, George.'

Placing one finger under her chin, he raised her face to his and kissed her gently on the lips.

'I'm well now.'

The last of the children bounded nosily out of the dance studio to their waiting parents. When Alice had finished tidying up, she sat on the piano stool beside Ann and listened for a while to Ann's playing, then placed her head on her sister's shoulder.

'What's new?' asked Ann, her fingers still running over the keys.

'George thinks I should tell Mother and Father about his illness.'

Ann stopped playing. 'That's not a good idea.'

'He said I should tell them before someone else does. In his family they talk about everything and he doesn't understand why our family doesn't do the same.'

'Families differ. We don't talk.'

'I'm going to tell Father. He might understand.'

Ann placed her hand on Alice's hand. 'He won't and you'll just be giving him another stick to beat you and George with.'

Thomas Dalton returned from Sunday Mass and went into the drawing room to think about what Canon Mulcahy had said to him.

Upstairs on the landing, Alice watched her father close the drawing room door behind him, then she walked slowly down the twenty-seven steps to the ground floor. Despite Ann's doubts, she had decided to take the risk and tell her father about George's illness. On her way down the stairs, she reviewed her words.

Father, George spent some time in hospital but you'll be happy to know that now he is cured...

She knocked on the drawing room door and entered.

'Father, I have something to tell you about George.'

Thomas's expression changed from pensive to tense. 'Not now, Alice. Why don't you talk to your mother about it?'

'No one can talk to Mother about anything except herself and her imaginary illnesses.'

'Don't speak of your mother like that. It's disrespectful and I don't expect it from a daughter of mine. The influence that boy has had on you is clearly not good, encouraging you to defy your parents and to reject your mother's need of you as a companion…'

'Father, not wanting to be Mother's companion has nothing to do with George.'

'Canon Mulcahy spoke to me this morning about your situation, Alice. He said I should take a firm hand with you and forbid you from seeing this boy.'

Alice squeezed her small hands into fists. 'Canon Mulcahy would say that. Priests say that God is love, yet they do everything in their power to get in love's way.'

'Don't denigrate priests!' Thomas was getting seriously annoyed. 'What has become of you, Alice? You were such a nice girl before you met this George person, and now look at you. I'm ashamed of you. You are a disgrace to your church and your family. The canon was right. I forbid you to see him again.'

'I'm not a child and you can't forbid me seeing anyone,' cried Alice angrily and tearfully.

Her father bristled. 'You are testing my patience, young lady.'

Alice took a step closer. 'How about my patience? I know you went to George's home behind my back and insulted his mother and sister. How could you do that to me?'

Thomas flushed. 'I insulted nobody! And I am not answerable to you for my actions!'

'And I am not answerable to you for mine!' She stopped herself, took a deep breath then said pleadingly, 'Father why are you acting so strangely? I thought you loved me. I've always loved you. But now you're like a different person. I wish I had my old father back.'

His lips tightened under his moustache. 'I haven't changed, Alice. Perhaps it is you who has changed.'

Alice's eyes flashed. 'Yes, Father, you're right. I have changed. I am no longer a child, I am a woman. But you are still treating me like a child!'

Dark clouds gathered over Stephen's Green as Alice passed through the gates of the Arch of the Royal Dublin Fusiliers. She walked blindly along the ornamental lake, crossed over the small bridge that led into the People's Gardens and sat on a bench in front of the water fountain. She was still gazing into the distance when George sat beside her.

'You don't look very happy, dearest. What happened?'

'I had another fight with Father. I tried to tell him about your illness, but he wouldn't listen. George, he said some awful things to me.'

'He probably didn't mean them. Like you said, he's protective of you. He'll come round.'

'No, he meant what he said. You should have seen the look on his face when he shouted at me. He said I was defying the church and that I was a disgrace to my family and he was ashamed of me.'

'Well, he's wrong. Nobody in their right mind could be ashamed of you. You are a good person, you're the best person I know.' George took Alice's hand and his expression turned serious. 'Alice, I love you and I want to marry you, but if it's all too much for you, if you want to change your mind, I won't like it but I'll try to understand.'

She sobbed and smiled. 'Don't ever say that again to me! I love you, George Gilbert. I want to marry you more than anything in the world and no matter what my parents say we will marry.'

The sky grew darker and when Alice looked up, a large raindrop fell on her cheek.

'We'd better shelter,' said George, drawing her to her feet and pointing to the Victorian summer house at the side of the lake. As they dashed hand-in-hand for cover, the rain grew heavier and by the time they had reached the shelter it was falling in great sheets.

Standing deep in thought, George barely appeared to notice the rain lashing the surface of the lake. Finally, he said, 'When would be the best time to call on your father tomorrow?'

'Call on my father?' asked Alice, astonished.

'He should not have spoken to you the way he did. He upset you and hurt you. I cannot allow that to continue. The time has come to show your father how determined we are to be together. It's time I fought for you.'

Fight? thought Alice anxiously. *No, I don't want you to fight for me. I just want to be with you.*

'Alice, please tell me when your father will be available.'

'Are you sure you want to do this? You know how he spoke to you before.'

'I don't care. I think maybe if he sees how serious I am about you, if he sees how much I care about protecting you, then maybe this time he will listen to me.'

After an unsatisfactory meal of boiled rabbit, parsnips and soapy potatoes followed by a dull trifle, Thomas remained at the dining room table; he struck a match and lit a cigar.

'Must you smoke that thing here?' complained Ann, as she piled the plates on top of each other.

'Yes I must smoke it in here and I'll thank you not to comment on how I choose to behave in my own house.' Thomas exhaled a long, taunting mouthful of grey smoke. 'Do you know that your younger sister came to see me yesterday?'

Ann clattered the plates. 'The way you were shouting at her, everyone in High Street knows about it.'

Thomas huffed and puffed on his cigar. 'I may have raised my voice, but could anyone blame me? She wanted me to agree to her liaison with that Protestant tradesman.'

'As usual, Father, you completely misunderstood the situation.'

He knocked ash into the ashtray, sending a glowing spark across the tablecloth. 'Really? Then why don't you enlighten me?'

'I'm not going to do that,' frowned Ann, dabbing out the spark with a napkin.

'Why not?'

'Why would I tell you the very thing I advised Alice not to tell you?'

'That's the kind of convoluted thinking one expects from someone like you,' he sneered.

'What do you mean "someone like me"?'

'An old maid,' said Thomas nastily, and took another long draw on his cigar.

'I am not an old maid!' gasped Ann. Enraged, she leaned over the table towards him, pushing her face into his. 'Alice was trying to tell you that George has been in St Mary's hospital in the Phoenix Park.'

Thomas flinched back and his luxuriant moustache quivered wildly. 'What? That's a TB hospital!'

'Exactly.' Ann stared defiantly into his eyes.

'Are you telling me that the boy has TB? Jesus Christ, has the girl gone completely mad? Good God, what on earth could she possibly see in that fellow?'

'She loves him.'

'That's nonsense.'

'It's not nonsense,' snapped Ann. 'Did you never love? Is that what's wrong with this family?'

'That's an outrageous thing to say!'

'It may be outrageous, but is it true?'

CHAPTER TWENTY-FOUR

On Monday morning, George marched up High Street. He stopped outside the Dalton's Ladies' Hairdressing Salon, pushed on the door and entered. There were two customers in the salon, Ireland's premier soprano, Mrs Nuala Flaherty and Ireland's foremost lady golfer, Mrs Liz Lillis.

George was so astonished at the elegance and extravagance of the hair salon, that for a moment he stood immobilised. The assistant stylist Ursula Carleton saw the look of wonder on the handsome young man's face and approached him with a smile. 'Can I help you?'

'I'd like to talk to Mr Dalton,' said George, coming to himself.

Larry White had entered the salon as they were talking; he took one look at George and said, 'Mr Dalton is not available.'And walked away.

The assistant stylist took George aside, out of ear shot. 'Mr Dalton's office is through there, but there is a gentleman with him so you might have to wait.'

'Thank you.'

George strode to the back of the salon, knocked once on the office door and flung it open. A startled Thomas and John Swords stopped talking.

'Mr Dalton, I'd like to talk to you, sir,' said George, hoping his nervousness wasn't too apparent.

Thomas's eyes flashed with terror as if George had threatened him; he got to his feet. 'Keep your distance, young man. Stay exactly where you are.'

'Who are you, young man?' asked John Swords in astonishment. 'Have you come to do violence against Mr Dalton?'

George stuck out his chin. 'I threaten violence to no-one. I am here to speak with Mr Dalton.'

'Then perhaps this would be a good time for me to leave,' said John Swords. 'Young man, would you be so kind as to give me one minute alone with Mr Dalton? And then, to use a bad pun, I'll be out of your hair.'

George stepped back from the office door, letting it close.

John leaned across the desk and said softly to his friend, 'That is Alice's young man, isn't it?'

'Yes,' answered Thomas sharply.

'I'll go. But for God's sake be very careful, Thomas. Your children are people in their own right.'

'You have no idea of what you're talking about.'

'You'd be surprised at what I know. Think of your family and forget your pride.'

Thomas glared at his friend.

John retrieved his hat from the coat rack. 'Join me in the club when you've finished. We can resume our conversation there.'

On the way out of the office, he stopped to speak to George. 'So you're Alice's young man.'

'I am, sir. George Gilbert is the name.'

'Nice to meet you, George.' John shook George's hand, placed his hat on his head, tapped it into place and left.

As George re-opened the office door, Thomas called sharply from behind the desk, 'Stop right there! Do not enter my office! Don't touch anything! I'll give you two minutes to say what you have to say before I call the police.'

George recognised the look on Thomas's face, and his heart sank. He knew Alice hadn't managed to tell her father about the TB, but someone else had clearly done so. George had seen that look a hundred times before – a toxic mixture of fear and disgust and hatred. And every time he saw it, it hurt. But he stood tall, ignoring his own feelings. 'Mr Dalton, I don't care how disrespectful you are to me. But the way you spoke to Alice was shameful and no way to treat anyone, particularly your own daughter. Don't ever speak to Alice like that again.'

Thomas glared in astonishment at the intruder. His mouth fell open, his face reddened and he spat out his reply. 'How dare you come here and tell me how I should treat my daughter!'

'I will not be intimidated by you, sir,' said George firmly. 'Alice was devastated by the way you spoke to her.'

'I will not be lectured by you. You have a nerve. But then, Protestants always have.'

'What you believe about Protestants is neither here nor there. You were cruel and unfair to Alice and I don't want it to happen again.'

'You "don't want it to happen again"? Who do you think you are? I was cruel? I was unfair? What about you?' Thomas's voice rose to a frightened shriek. 'What about you and your TB? It is you who is being cruel and unfair! Did you never think how you could infect my daughter and everyone else you come into contact with? If you truly cared for my Alice, you would never see her again.'

George looked Thomas in the eyes and said calmly and quietly. 'If I thought for one single moment that I was putting Alice or anyone – including you – at risk, I would not be here!'

'Get out of my office,' howled Thomas. 'Get out, leper!'

Alice had been in the garden dead-heading roses when she heard the commotion from her father's office next door; when she recognized George's voice, her heart leapt. She ran to the fence in time to hear him declaring that he would never, ever put her or anyone at risk. But when her father shouted 'Get out, leper!' Alice went into shock. Even though she knew how prejudiced Thomas Dalton was against Protestants, for the first time she realised the full extent of his intolerant and his irrational prejudice against anything he didn't understand.

In a daze, she retreated to the summerhouse and sat. She dropped her face into her hands; her body shook and she wept bitterly. *What must George think of me and my family? How will I ever face him again? Will he still love me?* When the initial shock of her father's words passed she felt a breathtaking burst of anger explode within her. *How dare Father speak to George the way he did? I will never forgive him.* Then anger slowly gave way to shame. *Am I such a dreadful daughter? What did I do that was so wrong?* And then guilt washed over her like a giant, cold wave. *Was it so wrong to fall in love? Did I bring this on myself and everybody?* For the next hour, she lived in a whirlwind of conflicting thoughts and emotions. One minute she was outraged, the next minute angry, the next guilty and then the cycle would start again and again.

Sitting in the Hibernian Club's private dining room, John Swords looked out onto Stephen's Green and glimpsed a flustered, red-faced Thomas Dalton exit a hansom cab and walk briskly into the club. Clarence, the club's elderly waiter had just placed a gin and tonic in front of John when Thomas took the seat opposite him.

'I though a private table would be best,' John said quietly.

'Very good,' said Thomas, looking over his menu. 'Clarence, while I'm choosing, would you be so kind as to bring me a gin and tonic and make it a large one.'

'Yes sir,' replied Clarence with a bow.

'Things didn't go all that well with Alice's young man, I gather,' John said, taking a sip of his drink.

'The arrogant young pup tried to tell me how I should treat my daughter.' Thomas glared around the private dining room, looking for the waiter.

'Relax Thomas, your drink will be here presently.'

'John, sometimes you can be quite insufferable.'

'I'll say no more until your drink arrives,' said John and pretended to read his menu.

'I'm sorry,' Thomas said after a moment. 'But that young man upset me greatly.'

'As you probably upset him. Children today are different than in our day.'

'They are still our children,' Thomas replied sharply.

'They *were* our children, and now they are adults and it would be wise to treat them as such,' said John, leaning forward for emphasis.

Thomas glared at his friend. 'Is that more of your modern thinking?'

'Thomas, we have to listen to our young people. If we don't, we run the risk of losing them. Take care. Is Alice to be the next to leave?'

Thomas's eyes softened and sadness momentarily flickered in them.

John Swords seized the moment, saying persuasively, 'The girl's in love. He may not be your choice but he is Alice's choice.'

'He's a most unsuitable fellow,' Thomas replied and the softness and sadness disappeared from his eyes. 'Besides it's not up to her to choose.'

'Have you made your choice, sir?' Clarence asked as he placed a gin and tonic in front of Thomas.

'Yes, sadly I think he has,' replied John, laying down his menu.

On Thursday afternoon, Dublin was visited by a late summer storm. Alice spent most of her time in her room thinking and listening to the howling winds pelting rain against the window. At four o'clock she went to the hall, put on a hat and a heavy raincoat, grabbed an umbrella from the stand and stepped out into the raging gale. Even though she held the umbrella low over her head the wind whipped freezing rain under the umbrella and lashed it into her face. When a tram juddered to a halt outside St Audoen's Church, Alice jumped onto the vehicle's semi-exposed platform; when she closed the umbrella there was a tearing sound as a broken metal rib ripped through the canopy. Holding the dripping umbrella point downwards, Alice entered the carriage and sat. In O'Connell Street, she changed trams and when the tram stopped at Dargan's Chemist on Berkley Road she disembarked into the still raging gale. She was attempting to open the damaged umbrella when a violent gush of wind caught the brolly and blew it inside-out. Frustrated and upset she stomped her feet and rainwater splashed onto her legs, stockings and shoes. Then, with the umbrella dangling from her arm and rain beating into her face, she walked through the Blessington Basin, exited the circular reservoir park at Primrose Street and, thoroughly soaked, knocked on the door of 5 Primrose Avenue.

'Come in girl, you're saturated,' cried Mrs Gilbert, when she saw Alice standing at the door. 'That umbrella's seen better days.' The older woman ushered Alice into the warm living room and sat her at the fire, then fetched a towel from the scullery.

As Alice towel dried her hair, she began to tell Mrs Gilbert about George's visit to her father.

'George told me all about it,' interjected Mrs Gilbert, shaking her head.

'Oh... Is he here?'

'He's out on an errand, he'll be back in a minute.'

'It must have been so horrible for him,' sighed Alice.

'Don't you worry. It's not the first time people have said things like that to him and it's not going to be the last. He's a big boy. Just because he's quiet, doesn't mean he isn't strong.'

Mrs Gilbert was folding the wet towel when a key turned in the hall door and footsteps hurried down the hall into the kitchen; a few seconds later George popped his head into the living room. His face was wet and lines of black hair were clinging to his forehead.

'Hi Ma, there you are – oh, hi Alice, nice to see you, terrible day out there!' He ran his fingers through his sodden fringe. 'Hey, I love your hair – what did you do to it? It's all frizzy and lovely.'

'That always happens when it gets wet,' Alice said and her eyes and lips broke into an enormous smile. 'You like it?'

'I like it.'

'Son, dry your hair,' Mrs Gilbert said handing George the towel she had just folded. 'I'll go make a nice cup of tea and give you two a bit of privacy.'

'I overheard your conversation with my father,' said Alice, as soon as Mrs Gilbert had closed the door behind her.

'How much did you hear?'

'The last part of it. It must have been awful for you. I'm so sorry about my father. He had no right to talk to you like that. I don't even know how he found out you had been ill.'

George shook his head. 'I get the impression that he thinks my having TB is worse than my being a tradesman and almost as bad as my being Protestant. Clearly, it was naïve of me to think anything I could say to him would make any difference.'

'You weren't being naïve, you were being lovely and brave and I love you for it.' Alice leant her head against his shoulder. 'I don't think my parents are ever going to agree to us getting married.'

George put his arm around her. 'I know. I've been thinking about that. Alice, we may really have to get married without your parents' permission. How would you feel about that?'

'I'd hate it. I'd like to get married in St Audoen's and have my whole family there. Would you mind very much if I tried to talk to my father one more time?'

'Alice, all I want is for you to be happy. You can talk to your father as many times as you like, but I want to be there.'

'There's no need for that.'

'There's every need. Things could get very ugly. Your father will fight this all the way. He could do anything, say anything. He might even ask you to leave home.'

'He wouldn't do that.'

'He might. He really believes he's right and he's very angry about us.'

'But he can't ask me to leave. Where would I go?'

'I have an Aunt Nora who lives alone in Drumcondra. You met her at my mother's birthday party, remember? I'm sure you could stay with her until we're married. '

'George, my father wouldn't let things go that far.'

He looked at her for a moment, then said, 'I'm sure you're right. Now let's change the conversation and talk about happy things. I have something for you.' He reached into the inside pocket of his jacket, took out a small brown envelope and placed it in her hand.

'Is this what I think it is?' asked Alice, her eyes beaming with delight.

'Open it.'

Alice carefully opened the envelope and shook it. A key fell out with a tag attached. Written on the tag was the address: *23 Furry Park, Killester.* 'Oh, it is what I think it is!'

'I've just borrowed it, in case we want to have a look around,' said George and kissed Alice on the cheek.

'Have you seen it yourself?'

George winked.

'Have you? Is it nice?'

He did not reply.

'Don't keep me in suspense! Tell me!'

He kissed her again. 'I've seen it and it's perfect.'

'Oh George! When can I see it?'

'Whenever you like. And I have enough money for the deposit, so if you like it as much as I do, then it's ours.'

'Oh George!' And Alice smothered him in kisses.

The late summer storm passed and the following day was warm and sunny and the garden smelt of lilac, roses and lavender. Ann and Tess were sitting on a blanket. Tess was rubbing a lotion into the white skin of her forearms and Ann was reading a book.

In the house, Alice and her father had just concluded another heated conversation and moments later a downcast Alice strolled into the garden.

'The course of true love not running smoothly?' said Tess.

'Try to be nice for once in your life.' Alice sat down beside Ann.

'Are you coping?' asked Ann gently.

'Just about,' replied Alice.

'What were you and Father arguing about this time?'

'I was trying to get Father to agree to meet with George and me tomorrow evening.'

'And did you succeed?' asked Tess, as she replaced the cork in the bottle of lotion.

'I did,' answered Alice quietly.

'How did you manage that? What did you have to promise?'

'I told him that if he agreed to this meeting I would never ask for another.'

Tess snorted and lay down on her back.

CHAPTER TWENTY-FIVE

Alice spent an anxious night thinking about George and her father and the upcoming meeting. The little sleep she had was fitful and filled with disturbing dreams of her fiancé and her father arguing and fighting. When the dawn finally arrived, she felt apprehensive, tired and unrested. The morning seemed endless and the afternoon even longer. By the time five o'clock came, she was already hanging over the bannisters outside her room waiting for George to arrive.

Half an hour later, he knocked on the hall door.

'So, is your father home?' he asked as Alice hung his coat and cap on the coat rack.

'Yes and he's been acting very oddly,' she confided in a whisper. 'He seems very agitated and he's been avoiding me all day and after lunch he and Mother had a long conversation. Then he left the house and I think he brought someone back with him. I heard voices in the hall, but I didn't look out of my room in time. It sounded like a man.'

'Was it Uncle John?'

'Maybe, I hope so. Anyway, nobody has left the house since so I suppose they're all three in the drawing room, waiting for us.'

'Good, let's go talk to them.' George took Alice's hand. 'Everything is going to be fine this time, I'm sure.'

All day George had thought about this upcoming meeting. He'd thought about what he might say and how he might say it. He knew that Alice wanted her parents to attend their wedding and he was going to try his hardest to have them there.

Alice's small hand knocked on the drawing room door and Thomas promptly opened it. Sitting on a couch in the centre of the room were her mother and the diminutive, barrel-shaped parish priest, Canon Mulcahy. So that was the man her father had brought back to the house, not John Swords. Alice tensed and glanced apologetically at George but he nodded reassuringly at her.

Alice led him to stand in front of her mother. 'George, you haven't met my mother,' she said with a slight tremor in her voice. 'Mother, I'd like you to meet George Gilbert.'

'Pleased to meet you, Mrs Dalton,' said George and held out his hand.

'And I am not pleased to meet you,' Mariah replied curtly and looked away.

'George, I'd like you to meet Canon Mulcahy,' said Alice and again George extended his hand.

The prelate took George's hand and shook it limply. 'How do you do?' the priest said, with a slight nod.

'I'm well, thank you,' replied George, before moving on to Thomas and once more politely offering his hand. 'Good evening, Mr Dalton.'

'Please take a seat,' Thomas said, ignoring the gesture. 'You don't mind if Canon Mulcahy joins us?'

'Don't be ridiculous, Thomas,' Mariah interjected and settled herself deeper into the couch. 'How could anyone possible object to Canon Mulcahy? He's God's peacemaker.'

The prelate gave a self-satisfied nod.

'Mr and Mrs Dalton, I don't mind Canon Mulcahy being here, but I have to ask why you feel the need to have a clergyman present at a family meeting.'

'I never said I *needed* Canon Mulcahy to be present,' Thomas replied, a little flushed in the face. 'Young man, you are implying something that is not so.'

Alice and George sat on the couch, facing the trio.

'Where shall we begin?' asked George with a smile.

'I'll begin,' Mariah snapped. 'Alice is not available for marriage, she is to be my companion and that is the end of this silly matter.'

'No Mother, it is not the end of the matter.' Alice's voice quivered as she spoke. 'If George and I were never to marry I would not become your companion.'

Mariah gasped and clutched her fist to her bosom.

'Alice, that is a very insulting thing to say to your mother, especially in front of a stranger,' snapped Thomas, his eyes glancing towards George. 'Apologise immediately.'

'Father, if you are insinuating that George is a stranger you couldn't be more wrong. And if anyone has to apologise, it is you and mother for not shaking George's hand. What I said was the truth. I don't want to be just a shadow in my mother's life. I want to have a life of my own.'

'Alice, this is all very disrespectful and most unseemly,' Canon Mulcahy said raising his hand in the air as if he was Moses parting the Red Sea. 'Remember, God is love.'

'I wonder why you didn't say that to mother when I was a child,' snapped Alice.

'Now young lady you are not only being rude you are being childish. You should think before you speak,' said Canon Mulcahy.

'I do think before I speak and I wish more people would do their own thinking rather than blindly accepting the thinking of others.'

Thomas decided to ignore Alice's last remark. In his own mind, he was a logical, practical man who never thought blindly. Which was why, when he next spoke, his words were frank to the point of insulting.

'Let's get down to brass tacks. Young man do you think it's fair of you to ask Alice to marry you, when you have TB and could be dead tomorrow?' And when Alice gave a little cry, he added pompously, 'I only speak the truth, Alice.'

She was about to answer, when George placed his hand on her arm. 'You are right, sir,' he said calmly. 'I don't know how much time I have. But then, no one does. And it is because my time may be shorter than most that I prize every moment I'm given. I am well now and with God's blessing I will be well tomorrow. I love your daughter and after we marry I intend to fill every moment of our time together with joy, happiness and love.'

'Poppycock,' Mariah scoffed and folded her arms.

'No, Mrs Dalton, it is not poppycock. My doctors have assured me I am in remission and my future looks bright. I would like to take this opportunity to ask for your daughter's hand and hope you will be present at our wedding.'

Mariah gasped and Thomas clenched his jaw.

'You are a Protestant and have no right to ask for my daughter's hand,' he said with undisguised contempt.

'Thomas, why don't you leave this to me?' the canon said. 'Young man, you may not be aware that the Catholic Church has an aversion to marriage between Catholics and Protestants. Mixed marriages are greatly discouraged by Mother Church and the Vatican. To be frank, they are actually frowned upon.' The canon leaned back on the couch and gave an ecclesiastical smile that said he had explained the situation fully and that no further exploration of the topic was necessary.

'Canon Mulcahy, I am well aware of the Roman Catholic position on what you referred to as mixed marriages. My mother is a Catholic and my late father was a Protestant. Your church may frown on interdominational marriages, yet it allows them. Besides I came here to talk to Alice's parents and not a representative of the Roman Catholic Church.'

'Canon Mulcahy is here because I asked him to be here,' interjected a furious Thomas.

'I came here in good faith to talk to you and your good wife, sir. I didn't mind Canon Mulcahy being present but I refuse to negotiate with him or any other Roman Catholic clergyman.'

'This is not a negotiation,' snarled Thomas and the veins in his forehead started to pulsate. 'Canon Mulcahy is here for your guidance and you will pay attention to what he has to say.'

'Mr Dalton, with all due respect, Canon Mulcahy and I are of different Christian dominations, so his guidance in matters of doctrine do not apply to me and as he is a bachelor with no personal knowledge of marriage or adult family life he has little expertise to offer me.'

Crimson-faced, Thomas jumped to his feet and as he spoke his fingers stabbed the air. 'You are a tradesman and a bloody Protestant who has TB! I will never give my permission for you to marry my daughter!'

Alice looked at the frantic expression on her father's face and the terror in his eyes and experienced a moment of absolute lucidity. In that moment she realised that the wall of hostility her father had built between them was so complete and impenetrable that further discussion was futile. She knew that the three people sitting across from her had no interest in considering the merits of George or her thoughts or arguments. All her parents and the clergyman wanted was for George and her to capitulate to their beliefs and to their view of marriage.

She rose and looked into her father's manic eyes. 'George and I came here to talk. We hoped you'd be fair and would talk honestly with us about our concerns and your concerns. I hoped to convince you that it would be a good thing for us to get married in St Audoen's and that both of you would be present at the wedding. I knew we probably wouldn't be allowed to marry on the high altar, but there are side altars. But I was wrong, it won't happen, will it? You never intended to listen and consider what we had to say. All you want is for us to do your bidding blindly without thinking about it. Father I am over twenty one now. I do not need your permission to marry.'

'You may not need your father's permission, but you do need God's permission,' Canon Mulcahy announced self-righteously.

'You mean, we need your permission,' said Alice, looking down on the rotund little man.

'As long as I am parish priest of St Audoen's you will never marry there,' the canon announced with absolute certainty.

'Then we will marry in a Protestant church if they will allow it or in a registry office,' replied Alice.

'What?' exclaimed the priest.

'If you do that I will write you out of my will,' cried Thomas, glaring at his daughter. 'You will inherit nothing!'

'And you will never be welcome in this house again!' added Mariah.

Alice looked at her mother and then at her father. 'Father, is Mother speaking for both of you?'

'Yes! If you persist with this madness you give me no other choice!' Thomas turned to George. 'You have brought nothing but sorrow and misery into my home. I ask you to leave.'

'Father, George did not bring sorrow and misery into this house. It was here long before I ever met him. Please withdraw your request for George to leave.'

'No Alice, I won't withdraw my request.'

'When you ask George to leave you ask me to leave.'

'Don't be absurd. Where would you go?' Thomas demanded.

'I will stay with George's Aunt Nora until we marry.' Alice took George's hand. 'Mother, do you have anything to say to me?'

Mariah's eyes fell to the floor. Alice looked to her father and he looked towards the window. Canon Mulcahy stared around as if he had no concept of what could be happening to the Dalton family.

'Then I have some packing to do,' said Alice softly, to no one in particular.

George thought Alice had never looked more beautiful than she did that moment. He took her hand and together they walked across the room. When they reached the door, Alice looked back at her parents.

'Goodbye Mother, goodbye Father,' she said.

Thomas continued to gaze blindly out the window and her mother continued to stare at the floor as George opened the door for Alice.

'Wait for me here in the hall. I'll go pack a few things for tonight,' Alice said to George, after he had closed the drawing room door behind them.

She rushed up the stairs and when she reached the landing she leaned on the banisters for a moment, then stood erect, wiped the tears from her eyes and entered her bedroom.

When Ann heard the door open, she jumped up from the dressing table and ran over to her sister. 'It didn't go well?'

'No it didn't. It was dreadful. It was worse than dreadful.'

'I'm so sorry I told father about George's TB…'

'Was it you? It doesn't matter. He had to know sooner or later. And it was better that he knew sooner.' Alice walked to the wardrobe, took out a suitcase and started to pack some clothes. 'And it didn't make any difference. It was enough that George was a Protestant. And a tradesman.'

'What are you doing?'

'I'm packing a bag Ann. I'm leaving home.'

'Oh God. Do Mother and Father know?'

'Yes they do.'

'Oh Alice, don't do this, don't go. What will I do without you?'

'They gave me no other option,' said Alice and tears rolled down her face. 'I have to go.'

The two sisters embraced and held each other, until a slight cough from the landing caused them to turn towards the doorway. Grey-faced, their father stood gazing forlornly into the room.

'Father, this is all wrong,' Ann pleaded. 'Tell Alice not to go!"

'Please give us a moment alone together, Ann,' said Thomas, looking past her at Alice.

Ann left the room and Thomas entered and sat on the bed and placed his hand on the suitcase.

'Alice,' he said. 'When I married your mother, I did love her and I thought love would be enough. It was never an easy marriage. I don't know when we stopped loving each other, it just happened. I don't think your mother or I have been happy for years. We exist or coexist in this house. Alice, you are doing exactly what I did. You are pursuing the illusion of love. When you're young, you do foolish things, you don't understand how the world works, and that is why the church and state and society have rules and laws. They guide us and protect us. One of those rules is that Catholics don't marry Protestants. How many people in mixed marriages do you know? One, and that's out of all the people you know – just one. This Protestant man can't make you happy. Even God advises against it.'

With a sad sigh, Alice sat on the bed beside him. 'No Father, God doesn't advise against it. You and Canon Mulcahy and the Catholic Church advise against it, but God never said anything about it. George is not you and I am not my mother. George and I are in love and our love will last. George is a good man and I am a good woman and we will look after each other. But this has nothing to do with George or me. This is all to do with you and what you believe. Are you so certain that what Canon Mulcahy tells is so right that you are willing to lose me over it? What kind of a God would ask you to do that?'

'It's what I know to be true,' said Thomas and bowed his head. Alice stood, closed the suitcase and lifted it off the bed.

'I am truly sorry this has happened between us. I love you, Father, and you will always be welcome in my home.'

'Alice, your Protestant is a tradesman. He earns little money. How can he keep you in the comforts to which you are accustomed?'

'George's grandmother left him some money. Not enough to buy a house but enough for a deposit on one. It won't be as fine a house as this, but it will be a happy home.'

Thomas swallowed hard and his face grew sadder. 'Please don't marry this man.'

'You can't even say his name, can you, Father?' said Alice, her eyes burning with tears. 'Goodbye Father, and say goodbye to Mother for me.'

Carrying her suitcase, Alice walked out of the room and down the stairs. George took the suitcase and opened the hall door. Alice looked back into the house and saw the motionless, bent figure of her father standing in shadow on the staircase. Alice gave a little wave and left her childhood home.

EPILOGUE

Two months after Alice had left home, she received a visit from Father Jim Reid, the new curate at St Audoen's Church. The ill-at-ease, newly-ordained young priest told Alice that he had been instructed to inform her that if she wished to be married in St Audoen's Church, it was possible.

Seven weeks later, Alice and George were married on the small side altar in St Audoen's Church in a non-nuptial-mass ceremony. The ceremony was performed by the new curate who was instructed not to attend the wedding breakfast. George's brother Dessie was best man and Ann was the bridesmaid. Apart from Ann, Mrs Foley was the only representative of the Dalton household to attend the wedding. Alice's mother refused to attend the ceremony, as did Tess. All of George's family were present.

Unknown to Alice, her father did visit the church during the wedding service. He stood at back of the church for a short time and left before the ceremony concluded. He never regretted the large financial contribution he had had to make to St Audoen's to have the ceremony performed there.

During the first four years of their marriage, Alice and George had three children. In the fifth year, George's TB returned and within six months he was dead. Alice never reconciled with her parents and the only member of the Dalton family that remained in constant contact with her was Ann.

In the spring of 1937, Jarlath was killed in a freak horse riding accident in Gloucestershire and in the spring of the following year Thomas died of a heart attack. Ann reluctantly became her mother's companion. Tess married an elderly shopkeeper, John Brown, and they both worked in his small grocery shop in Rathmines until they were killed in a car accident in 1951.

Terrance thrived in America but never returned to Ireland. Mariah died of cirrhosis of the liver and Ann died in 1971 of natural causes in a small flat in York Street.

Alice awoke and George was sitting by her bedside.

'Hello George,' Alice said with a smile.

'Hello yourself,' replied George.

'I want you to go to the garden and dig up a few nice spuds and then pick a handful of nice cooking apples from the tree nearest the house,' Alice said, her eyes alight with all the life and excitement of a young bride.

'I'll do that,' George replied.

Alice looked quizzically at the young man.

'You're not George, are you?'

'I am George.' The young man smiled. 'I'm not your George but I am George.'

'I know who you are. You're young George.' Alice looked around the room. 'Am I in the parlour, son?'

'You are, Ma, I put your bed in here so things would be easier for you.'

'I'm sick, aren't I?'

'Yes Ma, very sick. I'll get a glass of water so you can take your medicine.' George kissed his mother on the forehead and went to fetch the water.

Alice looked around the room and when her eyes fell upon the upright piano she smiled. In the distance she heard the faint sound of a piano playing and then she saw her George sitting at the piano and the music grew louder, George smiled at her and she drew her last breath.

Alice was fifty eight years old when she died. She had been suffering from cancer for four years.

ACKNOWLEDGMENTS

Most books have one named author but many people contribute to the creation of a book. I, like most authors have people who read, advise, edit, proof read, format and design my books. To each of my contributors I say thank you, I couldn't have done it without you. Now, take cover you are about to be named.

My first thanks goes to my mother and father for their inspirational story which is at the heart this novel. My mother, an unassuming woman, would have been mortified that I used part of her life as a basis for my book. I would like to point out that while Alice and George were real people most of the characters and events described in the book are completely fictional.

Next I'd like to thank my first readers Mary and Joe Brennan and Leslie Lawrence for their encouragement, observations and helpful criticism on earlier versions of the book. I am greatly indebted to Helen Falkner for her expert, insightful and clear editing of the book. Many thanks to Gerry O'Hara for his input on all things historical, if there are any historical inaccuracies in the book, the blame is mine, not his. I would like to thank my eagle eyed proof-reader Miriam O'Hara for her thorough and diligent work on the novel. My thanks to Roseanne Mooney for her oil painting of the Halfpenny Bridge used for the book's cover and my thanks to Brendan Beirne for designing the book's cover and for his great generosity in sharing his knowledge of Irish history.

A very special thanks to my family, Paul, Therese, Chloe, Jamie, Mark, and Maeve for their indulgence and endless interest in the developing book. Finally nobody deserves more thanks and credit than my wife Julie, her endless patience and ongoing support during the writing of this labour of love was vital and endless.

This book is available as a paperback and an e-book from
Amazon.com
My website can be found at www.cecilallen.ie
You can e-mail me at
cecilallen93seapark@gmail.com

**If you've enjoyed reading "Constructing Alice"
why not read another Cecil Allen novel.**

THE ACTOR

A story of love and passion set in a time of war and violence.
A story of one man's struggle to find his place in the world.
A story of theatre.
A story of life.

I n 1914 a young Jim Brevin runs away from his comfortable, middle-class Dublin home and joins a theatrical fit-up company travelling around Cork and Kerry. Two years later, on the day he becomes an apprentice with the famous *Ira Allen's Company of Irish Players* he reluctantly gets involved in The Rising.

Jim is mistaken for a spy, marries a rebel's sister, discovers fraud and theft in the family business and suffers a horrendous personal tragedy. In time he becomes a celebrated actor and at the moment of his greatest theatrical success he is faced with a stark choice.

The Actor is a page turner, full of colourful characters, wit, tragedy, humour, life and theatre. It illustrates how the emerging Irish state impacted on the lives of ordinary people, shaped one man's dream and closed the Queen's Theatre.

Drawing extensively on the life of my grandfather, the playwright and actor Ira Allen, the novel places readers at the centre of the organized chaos and theatrical magic that was melodrama, and at the core of a violent changing Ireland.

Available in paperback and e-book from Amazon.com

Printed in Poland
by Amazon Fulfillment
Poland Sp. z o.o., Wrocław

45704833R00183